Aly Monroe

Aly Monroe was born and educated in England. Trained in linguistics, she has lived abroad – mostly in Spain – and speaks several languages. She is married and has three children. *The Maze of Cadiz* is her first novel, and the first in a series of Peter Cotton novels.

Praise for *The Maze of Cadiz*

'*The Maze of Cadiz* is a splendid debut mystery . . . Monroe provides terrific and convincing historical atmosphere; I am delighted that she is writing more Peter Cotton novels' *The Times*

'Aly Monroe has created an impressive novel with an extraordinary, dream-like atmosphere . . . The next can't come too soon.' *Financial Times*

'Aly Monroe is a newcomer to crime writing, whose accomplished debut, *The Maze of Cadiz*, is set in 1944 . . . Monroe's portrait of Cadiz in the aftermath of the civil war is atmospheric, and in a surprising twist the mild-mannered Cotton turns out to be as devious as his adversaries' *Sunday Times*

'Cotton's investigating is clever and fascinating' *Guardian*

'Addictive' *Sunday Telegraph*

'Her writing is skilful and evocative . . . *The Maze of Cadiz* is a stylish and impressive debut' *The Economist*

'I have been quite captivated . . . The book had me totally convinced that Ms Monroe knows her Spain and, more to the point, knows the Spain of 1944 . . . wonderfully atmospheric, very well-written' *Shots*

Also by Aly Monroe

Washington Shadow

Aly Monroe

The Maze of Cadiz

JOHN MURRAY

First published in Great Britain in 2008 by John Murray (Publishers)
An Hachette UK Company

First published in paperback in 2009

3

© Aly Monroe 2008

Extract from 'Spain 1937' from *The English Auden* by W.H. Auden reproduced
by permission of Faber and Faber Ltd © The Estate of W.H. Auden

The right of Aly Monroe to be identified as the Author of the Work has been
asserted by her in accordance with the Copyright, Designs and Patents Act 1988.

A CIP catalogue record for this title is available from the British Library

ISBN 978-1-84854-032-3

Typeset in Monotype Sabon by Servis Filmsetting Ltd, Stockport, Cheshire

Printed and bound by Clays Ltd, St Ives plc

John Murray policy is to use papers that are natural, renewable and recyclable
products and made from wood grown in sustainable forests. The logging and
manufacturing processes are expected to conform to the environmental
regulations of the country of origin.

John Murray (Publishers)
338 Euston Road
London NW1 3BH

www.johnmurray.co.uk

To my children

I

PETER COTTON's plane touched down at an airfield on the outskirts of Madrid just after 3 p.m. on 5 September 1944. It was the hottest time of a very hot day. The air felt dry enough to cure meat, was far hotter outside his lungs than in. The glare made him wince, and the heat rising back off the concrete apron made his eyes smart. At the indication of the gloved driver, he kept his hands away from the metal of the car sent to fetch him. He sat back as far as he could out of the sun, and took off his hat.

Even when the car drove off and the air buffeted his face, he did not feel cooler. His scalp prickled as drops of sweat formed. Then the sweating stopped. Cotton had been this hot before as a child of about seven years old in Mexico, when he had felt his forehead and pronounced it 'spongy'. 'Oh, you're transpiring, dear,' his mother said. 'We'll get you something to drink. But do remember to sip. Gulping is bad for you.' She had also given him a definition of transpiring. 'When you're too hot to sweat, dear, the water sort of wafts out of you. It can be rather dangerous.'

Cotton looked out. Near the airfield some effort had been made to do the French thing and have shade trees along the roadside, but a couple had been struck by shells, several had died, and the bleached-hay colour of the drooping leaves on the survivors was due not to autumn but to drought. Past the trees, the front wheels of the car churned up dust. Cotton wound up the window, and found the glass had discoloured. It gave a rusty tinge to the dun, bare landscape round Madrid. They passed some abandoned farm buildings. One whole wall had been whitewashed and something between a shadow and a stencil applied to it: the huge, bespectacled face of a Nationalist war hero. When the car came to an old stone bridge, Cotton saw that there was no flow left in the river under it, only a straggle of disconnected pools surrounded by some prickly scrub and a few goats.

Rising from the river valley, the beginnings of Madrid itself added grey stone, cement and small red brick to the dun and rust. The Spanish Civil War had been over for five years, but there was still a lot of damage to see as they drove up the slope: some bombed-out buildings, but many more shored up and boarded up from the effects of close fighting. There were soot marks by some windows, many pits left by bullets round doors, and little sign of much repair or building except for a church being painted and the base of something new and monumental in white stone that they passed. This was the only site he saw that had workers on it, these all dressed in prisoner's grey, watched over by a couple of soldiers on foot and another on a gleaming chestnut horse with white sweat lines like a foaming contour map around the saddle.

Otherwise, even in the centre of the Spanish capital, there was little traffic and very few people about. Those who could kept to the shadows. The original Madrid, built on a hill or escarpment in a high plain, was full of narrow, shaded, cobbled streets, but later development had been prone to avenues and some eighteenth-century rectitude. Enlightenment and Spanish sun. About a mile north of the centre, in the street called Fernando el Santo, was the British Embassy. It had been the Marquis of Álava's palace forty years before, and Cotton surprised himself by thinking of 'lion's head and paws' – his mother's description of a showpiece building with a central block and two short, forward-projecting wings – as they came through the gate. The car drew up at the main entrance. Cotton got out and narrowed his eyes against the sunlight again.

'I'll fetch your bags, sir,' said the driver.

Cotton nodded. He had not in any way expected memories of his mother. She had died in 1938, when he had been at Cambridge. He had received a second telegram from his father with news of her death before the first arrived. 'Mother gravely ill. Expect the worst.' 'How very British,' someone had said – referring, it turned out, not to his father but to the cock-up.

Cotton squinted at the sandbags and defensive positions, and followed the driver up the steps. Initially relieved to get out of the glare, his first surprise, after the almost deserted streets outside, was to see how crowded the entrance hall was. For a moment the marble floor felt beautifully cool, but almost at once Cotton heard how it contributed to the echo and hubbub of all those warming the place up. Signing in at the desk, he had to lean forward to hear what he had to do. He could hear a lot of murmured English, slightly more voluble Spanish, a couple speaking French, and then something he thought might be Polish from a man wearing a beret and wagging his finger at a small girl dutching a doll with red spots on its cheeks.

His bags were checked in. A beefy military policeman took him down to the basement, where he had to provide identification and sign in again at another desk. He was then given an envelope and shown to a cubicle. It had a half curtain, rather like a voting booth. Inside there was a shelf, and above it a mirror.

He paused. Cotton had spent two months at Hanslope Park near Newport Pagnell studying the often dubious intelligence of various Nazi plans to smuggle the so-called Dutch gold, the gold reserves robbed when the Germans invaded Holland, to Spain. He had then been sent for a week to Camp 020 near Ham in Surrey to read the transcripts of the interrogation of Ernesto Hoppe, code name Herold, a captured German-born Argentinian, who claimed the Germans had a plan to ship the gold and 'other valuables' by submarine from Spain to Argentina. There was some doubt that Hoppe's submarine story was true, some acceptance that the Dutch gold was already in Spain. He opened the envelope and read.

P. J. B. Cotton. Code name Pedrillo. Proceed directly to Cadiz. Relieve R. A. May of his duties on arrival. Close office and return with R. A. May. Arrest if necessary.

Cotton blinked. He read his orders three times. He had flown the first part of the journey from Kent huddled by the empty bomb bay of a Lancaster. From Bordeaux he had been flown to Toulouse. From Toulouse he had been driven to an airfield near Perpignan. And now he was being ordered to be some sort of policeman? He had been told he was to do something 'of extraordinary importance to the war effort'. He wasn't even sure if 'R. A.' were the man's initials or some rank or post he had not heard of. He considered himself in the mirror. He looked pasty and irritated.

So he closed his eyes and reconsidered. He breathed in. He was not sure where Cadiz was, except that it was on the sea somewhere in the south. He shook his head. He had no idea who R. A. May might be, what he was doing in Cadiz, or why he had to be removed.

Cotton inclined his head towards his own reflection and stepped out. The military policeman showed him into a small office. A very bald person who identified himself briskly as Naysmith asked where he was going.

'Cadiz,' said Cotton.

Naysmith grimaced. 'Oh Christ,' he said and jerked a thumb at the map of Spain behind him. Cadiz was on the far south coast of Spain, about ninety miles south of Seville, about ninety miles west of Gibraltar.

'Have you been there?' asked Cotton.

'What? No. I have not.' Naysmith was a man with books attached to his desk by string, with a stickler's ruler and a propelling pencil. 'Train then.' He began flicking at a railway timetable. 'Code book,' he said, indicating a fat brown envelope. 'Check.'

Cotton looked in. He had been given Lord Byron's *Don Juan* in London. This was an identical copy sent in the diplomatic bag.

'Check,' said Cotton.

'...t we can do is noon tomorrow,' said Naysmith. 'Pick ...our tickets in the morning.' He dropped the railway ...netable and picked up another guide. 'Yes,' he said. He double-checked. 'Yes. Hotel Buenavista in Cadiz.'

'Right. Where do I stay tonight?'

'Not my department, old boy.' Naysmith looked up. 'Anything else?'

'The briefing?'

Naysmith looked only momentarily surprised. 'That's not my pigeon,' he said.

Cotton nodded. 'What about cash?'

'Cashiers' office, upstairs. There's a chitty with the book.'

'Thank you.'

'No call for that, old boy. Let's all get on, shall we?'

Outside, Cotton saw that the military policeman had gone, but he found the cashiers' office upstairs and handed over the flimsy note. The clerk counted out money.

'Money belt?'

'No.'

The clerk handed one over and took back a little of the money.

'Sign here,' he said.

Cotton did, and gathered up the money. One large silver coin caught his attention. He held it up. It was a five-peseta piece with the profile of a baby's head on it.

'That's Alfonso XIII,' said a voice behind him. 'Still legal tender, of course, but rather a sad story.'

Cotton turned. A short, wide-set man wearing a dark-grey shirt, rust-coloured tie and ink-blue braces was

6

smiling at him. With his round glasses, he looked like a schoolmaster in a modern-languages department. He had very short, very dark hair, but with a small area, about the circumference of a quail's egg, just above and behind his left ear, that was completely white.

The man held out a hand. 'Douglas Houghton,' he said. 'Feeling lost?'

'Peter Cotton,' said Cotton. 'Obviously looking it.'

Houghton smiled. 'How long have you been here?'

'About forty-five minutes.'

'Staying long?'

'I'm off tomorrow.'

Houghton pointed down a corridor. 'Come along. I'll show you around.'

Cotton put the money in the belt, picked up his copy code book, and followed. He noticed he could barely feel his feet on the marble. They went down to the basement again and called in on an office where Houghton picked up a buff file. There were a number of people fanning themselves with whitish heart-shaped things made of some kind of woven leaf.

'Those are pay-pay,' said Houghton, as he indicated they keep going down the corridor. 'Philippines, I think. It's marginally cooler down here, but the air doesn't circulate well except in winter, and electric ceiling fans are unreliable and far too low for comfort.'

'How long have you been here?' said Cotton.

'I arrived in time for the stoning of the embassy.'

Cotton looked over at him.

Houghton smiled. 'Nineteen forty-one,' he said. 'When Franco's government simply couldn't restrain the

7

indignation of people in fascist shirts and brought them along by lorry. Ah, this is me.'

They turned into a narrow room with a vaulted ceiling. At the far end was a solitary window, hardly bigger than a shot-hole and barred on the outside. There were three desks in close proximity along one wall. That left only enough room for a narrow aisle and a bench on the other side.

'Sit,' said Houghton. He went behind the desk nearest the door and flicked through some papers.

'All right,' he said. 'First time in Spain?'

'Yes.'

'Mm,' said Houghton, picking up a pencil and jotting something down. 'Where's your Spanish from?'

'South America. I lived there when I was a child. Recently I had a refresher course from a Catalan lady in Oxford.'

Houghton looked up. 'That wasn't Margarita Gil, was it?'

'Gil yes, but her name was Montserrat.'

'Of course. Sisters. I can never remember which one is the elder. I met them when I was teaching there. Rather distinguished father. He's a don now, I think, at my old college.'

'You're a Hispanist?'

'Mm. Calderón de la Barca, mostly. I've always loved theatre.'

'Right,' said Cotton. He thought Calderón de la Barca might have been seventeenth century. Plays and masques. Yes, *La Vida es Sueño. Life is a Dream.* It was not a play he knew.

The phone rang. Houghton picked it up and began speaking in French. Cotton watched Houghton's voice and body change. He became loud, his face contorted, his free hand agitated. Then he put the phone down and reverted to what he was in English.

Cotton's French was that of a schoolboy, but he had understood something – 'The border is officially closed and the Pyrenees are still there. He'll have to accept that. They are the Pyrenees. Forget Chateaubriand. He'd be far better heading for Switzerland.'

'Sorry about that,' said Houghton. 'I have to make a call.'

'Of course.'

Houghton dialled. While training, an instructor had told Cotton that he might meet 'those who put the opera in "operative"'.

Houghton had another, quieter, personality for Spanish, that was for sure, but Cotton heard that he was talking about a Lieutenant Barton, for whose name he was entirely English again.

'Sorry about that,' said Houghton again. 'This department has really been reassigned, but there are still a few poor bastards wandering about Occupied Europe.'

Cotton raised his eyebrows.

'Oh, we've been getting British servicemen in and then out of Spain. About two thousand so far.'

'I see.'

Houghton smiled. 'Marie, *mi mujer*, is on the Jewish run. She's been involved in rather more than two thousand getting out through Gibraltar or Portugal.'

Mujer means both 'woman' and 'wife' in Spanish. Cotton was mildly interested that Houghton had said this in Spanish rather than English, but rather more puzzled by 'the Jewish run'. Surely he meant 'route'. Or did he really mean 'run the gauntlet'? Didn't they 'run' bulls at Pamplona? He closed his eyes. 'Please remember not to run away with yourselves,' he had heard in one class with rain rattling on the Nissen-hut roof. 'Do remember you have to have a basis for your conjectures – and that's usually prosaic. Agitation or nervousness or adrenalin – whatever you want to call it – has two dire effects. One is sexual. But, let's not be prim, you all have hands. The other is mental tension. You *must* learn how to harness that. Why? To carry out whatever mission you are given *and* to save your own skins. Make the mental tension work for you. Or it will certainly work against you.' Opening his eyes but not yet focusing, Cotton decided they were not married and that Marie was at least half-Jewish.

Then Cotton realized he was sitting on the bench, with a money belt and the envelope containing a copy of his code book on his lap, and that Houghton was looking at him as he had looked at him upstairs when Cotton had been holding the coin with the baby's head on it. Cotton blinked. He thought he was about to black out. He put his hand to his chest and looked down. His shirt was soaked with sweat, but it felt cold.

'Would you like some water?' said Houghton.

'Yes, I would, thank you.'

Houghton bent down, picked up a bottle of water, and tossed it to him. Cotton's eyes opened wide, but he managed to catch it. He saw his hands were trembling when he opened the bottle. He drank. He had the impossible sensation that the water was spreading through the veins on his chest.

'So,' said Houghton, 'would you like to meet her?'

For a moment Cotton didn't know who he was talking about. Marie. 'Yes, of course.'

'Have you anywhere to stay tonight?'

'Not yet,' said Cotton.

Houghton smiled. 'I thought that,' he said. He picked up the telephone again and called. '*Hola, mi amor,*' he said, '*tenemos corderito para cenar. Ah, y pasará la noche.*'

Cotton blinked. Houghton had said they were having 'lamb for supper – and to stay the night'.

Houghton listened, laughed. '*Hasta las ocho, mi ángel.*' Until eight, my angel.

Cotton was not sure why, but being compared to a lamb somehow cheered him. He drank some more water. His head was thumping.

'She'll want all the news of home,' said Houghton chattily.

'Yes, of course,' said Cotton.

'How are you feeling?'

'Rehydrated.'

'Good. It takes a little time for the body to get into balance. Shall we get on then? Mm. What's your code book?'

'Byron's *Don Juan*.' Cotton was surprised to recognize only then that Houghton was the person briefing him. He drank some more water, as if his thoughts depended on it.

Houghton sighed. 'All very literary,' he said. 'What did you do before?'

'I was a soldier until fairly recently.'

'Really?' said Houghton. 'Unusual. Things must be changing. We're used to more . . . well, those of a certain louche brio. Like ex-journalists, a novelist or two, linguists, and of course the occasional wonderfully inventive operative.'

'Ah,' said Cotton.

Houghton smiled. 'We had an agent, a Spaniard, who had a large group of entirely invented people the Germans believed existed. An absolutely amazing feat.' He started getting up. 'But now it's less about creating confusion than clearing it up.'

'Yes.' Cotton got to his feet.

'How tall are you?'

'About six one.'

'And do you mind telling me how old you are?'

'No. I'm twenty-five.'

'Really?' said Houghton. He made a face. 'I'm thirty-nine. Come along and I'll let you get on. Do bring the water.'

Two doors down, they turned into a much larger room with a cross-vaulted ceiling. There were bookshelves on every wall except where there were three venerable-looking strongboxes. There were two long tables with chairs on either side. By the door were a couple of cubicles of the kind Cotton had already seen. At a desk sat a middle-aged woman.

'Hello, Agnes,' said Houghton. Houghton wrote some numbers on a slip of paper and gave it to her. Agnes went to one of the safes.

'Let's sit down,' said Houghton.

They sat opposite each other. Houghton spoke as quietly as if in a library.

'Geography and so on is over there,' said Houghton, pointing. 'Now I mustn't be au fait with what you are doing – that's for your chief in London – but you need to tell me your code name and any others given. You should give me my code name too.'

Cotton wrote. The code worked simply enough. Any code-breaker would need to know what book was being used. Real people were given characters' names – for example, the Spanish leader or *caudillo*, General Francisco Franco Bahamonde, was code-named Lambro, a pirate in *Don Juan*. Cotton's boss in London had chosen for himself the name of a girl in the Sultan's harem, Dudù. For more security, these names were transmitted using a similar-looking but separate code based on Byron's short poem 'There be none of Beauty's daughters'.

Houghton had been given the code name Baba, a eunuch. Houghton raised his eyebrows, but nodded. He took the piece of paper. 'We'll come for you,' he said, and left.

Agnes brought him a file. It contained just a few sheets of paper. Almost all related to May's job in Cadiz. As far as Cotton could tell, this involved checking all imports and exports passing through the port. The only variations in dull lists of ship names, consignment numbers, ports of origin, declared destinations and 'nature of cargo' were when a shipment of 'nitrates' or 'agricultural machinery' called for reaction from London. All consignment details were then sent on to agents elsewhere to cross-check.

The only other sheet of paper contained a list of messages sent to R. A. May since mid-July. 'Expenditure excessive. Justify.' This was followed by 'Send accounts forthwith' at the end of July. Then by 'Insist on full accounts immediately' at the beginning of August, and a week later by 'If clear accounts not sent by return all expenditure will be stopped.' There was then a ten-day gap before 'Accounts not clear.' The final, week-old, message was 'Stay at your post. Await instructions. Expect contact. Code name Pedrillo.'

Cotton sighed. It was like reading bank manager's letters in telegram form. He could vaguely remember the stir and subsequent hush at his father's bank when an employee in Guadalajara had 'gone off the rails' and misappropriated funds to enable the purchase of expensive presents for a young lady from a rich family. He also wondered why he had not been given May's replies. Was that deliberate or just incompetence? Or hadn't there been any? He drank some more water. What was clear to him was that his boss had known all this before sending Cotton to Spain. So what was this job? An initiation test? An apprenticeship?

He gave the file back to Agnes and went to the reference section. The item on Cadiz looked as if it had been lifted from an encyclopedia. 'Cadiz was founded by the Phoenicians some three thousand years ago as Gadir,' he read. The Romans had called the place Gades. He read on, sometimes coming across a familiar term like the Armada or an English name like the Earl of Essex or the Duke of Wellington, and little by little he finished the bottle of water.

At eight Houghton and Marie looked in. A tiny person, not five foot, and strikingly thin, she wore a dowdy brown dress but had an extraordinarily cheerful face and manner.

'Welcome to Madrid! Did they give you one of those huge baby coins?'

Marie's theory was that the embassy had a hoard of them left over from the First War and were now getting rid of them 'one by one, whenever the chance presents itself'. Some people took them as a good-luck charm or talisman, some as a 'perverse talisman' to soak up bad luck. 'They do have a certain weight to them.'

They signed out and left the embassy, Cotton with his suitcase and attaché case. Marie put on a brown hat and tied it in place with a chiffon scarf round her chin. Houghton took a beret out of his jacket pocket and put it on his head. He didn't wear it to the side like a soldier, but tugged it forward as if it had a peak.

'We're not far,' said Houghton. 'We're in Zurbarán.' He pointed at Cotton's suitcase. 'Heavy?'

'No,' lied Cotton. He saw that the pair of them were holding hands.

'We'll stop off and get some things,' said Houghton.

'Then I'll go on,' said Marie, 'and get cracking.'

'Right you are,' said Houghton.

Cotton was unsure about Marie's accent. It wasn't quite French, but it wasn't quite English. His puzzlement must have shown.

'Marie was brought up in Corsica and Nairn,' said Houghton. 'She was born in Corsica, but her father – he was a marine engineer originally – got religion when she was about ten and took the whole family to Nairn and became a reverend. Quite big in the temperance movement.'

Cotton looked at him to see how serious he was, but Houghton's face remained straight.

They stopped at a grocer's shop. The place was like a small cave, and smelled of cheese and mould and spilled wine. They stood by the counter. After a small wait, the grocer jerked his chin at them.

'But what is it you want?' he said.

It was really the first time Cotton had heard a Spaniard speaking Spanish in Spain. The words were clear enough, but the exasperated tone – as if the grocer felt they were pestering him unconscionably – struck him as novel.

Houghton quietly ordered some chorizo, ham, grapes, coffee and bread. 'The bread's rather . . . *thin* these days,' he said. 'It doesn't have much chew. It tastes of flour, but in a dusty sort of way. Do you want anything?'

'No, thank you. Is the grocer normally this friendly?'

'Oh, that's just Madrid. I understand the Castilians could be taken as quasi-hostile even before the war.' He looked up at Cotton and smiled. 'We'll talk,' he said.

Two flights of rickety wood stairs up, Marie and Houghton's flat had one largish room overlooking the street, and directly off it were a kitchen, a bathroom and the bedroom. Through a square arch from the main room was a small area arranged as a library. Along one wall was a couch. Cotton was to sleep on that. The place was not well furnished, and some of the paint was peeling. The exiguous electric light Houghton described as 'cloudy

16

night, some moon – and prone to flicker'. There were candles at the ready for power cuts.

They talked and drank and ate. They gave him a soup plate of *habas*, broad beans cooked in tomato, with bits of chorizo and ham laid out round the edge. Houghton had been right about the bread. There was crust and then something that tasted as bland as cotton wool but was not so substantial. It had an almost medicinal aftertaste that Cotton could not trace. Cotton saw that Houghton used the wine like some kind of mouthwash.

Houghton and Marie tried to fill him in on Spain. Marie giggled and insisted Houghton do his imitation of Franco. Every morning, she explained, Franco would sit for breakfast and review the executions for that day.

'There are about nine every day, and in theory he can give a pardon,' said Houghton.

'But he doesn't,' said Marie.

'Mm,' said Houghton. 'He shows no emotion, but has breakfast and signs each order.'

'Do it!' said Marie. 'Do it!'

Houghton assumed a face between sleepy and prim. Then in a quiet, high-pitched, bored little voice he said, '*Enterao.*' He paused, mimed signing something, then picked up a crumb of bread and ate it, chewing small. He swallowed. '*Enterao,*' he said again. '*Enterao.*'

Cotton's eyebrows rose, partly in enquiry. *Enterao* or *enterado* means 'seen' or 'understood'. Marie laughed delightedly. '*Y pasao por las armas.*' She performed a little mime to show that these cases were 'passed' in front of a firing squad.

17

'Douglas does him *igualito igualito*' – to a tee – said Marie. 'He really is a dull little man, but he has learned how to keep Spain in thrall. How? Would you say it was a variation of divide and rule?'

'Well . . . ' said Houghton.

'He plays both sides always,' said Marie. 'This is a man who believes in a Judaeo-Masonic conspiracy. Who has sent trains containing some Jews at least, along with other groups, to help the German war effort. But this is also the man who has allowed Jews to escape through Gibraltar and Portugal. What kind of man is he? A hero for helping? Or part of the persecution? He always hedges his bets. It's very simple. So far it always works. Oh, and he has handed out passports to some Jews in other countries. I think he thinks of them as his Jews.'

'What?'

'Sephardic Jews. The Jews expelled from Spain in 1492. Those are the only Jews he'll save!'

Houghton smiled, but not very comfortably. Cotton liked them. To him they were middle-aged and sincere and rather touchingly demonstrative.

'Oh,' said Marie, 'and nobody ever quite knows where he is. He lives in a palace removed from Madrid, has his own hospital there, and won't appear for weeks on end. People begin to panic. Franco is dead. Franco has resigned. And then he turns up in Valencia or somewhere until the next round of rumours.'

Houghton had begun stroking her forearm. She shook her head at him, good-naturedly, and concentrated on Cotton.

'I take it they've thrown you in at the deep end.'

'Perhaps.'

'No perhaps about it. It's part of the preparation. I think that's what they believe anyway. You're on your own. The British always prefer to give you string and, when it breaks, hope you're good at knots. The Spanish prefer intimacy to privacy. They can make you feel you're being suffocated. You must remember that. You're going to be quite alone, but always surrounded. You will remember that?'

'Yes,' said Cotton, 'yes, I will.' He looked up. 'Have either of you ever been to Cadiz?'

'No, I haven't,' said Houghton. 'But the people are supposed to be rather amusing, witty. That may have been quashed, of course.'

Cotton felt grateful but tired. He finally got to his makeshift bed about two.

Around four he woke. For ventilation, his part of the flat had an internal glass window that had been opened. It gave on to Houghton and Marie's bedroom.

He heard her say, '*Te necesito*,' I need you, and a rustle or two later the squeak of springs. He pulled his pillow round his ears. Alone but in company was about right.

Houghton woke him at six. They drank coffee and ate bread from the evening before. It was already very dry.

'I could toast it,' said Marie.

'Put more butter on,' said Houghton.

Cotton washed. As he was shaving, Houghton knocked at the door.

'Did you bring soap?'

'Yes,' said Cotton.

'What kind?'

'Pears.'

Cotton heard a sigh from Marie. Then a murmur.

'I say,' said Houghton, 'you couldn't leave it, could you?'

'My pleasure,' said Cotton.

He heard Marie clap her hands in delight, and smiled.

They arrived at the British Embassy a little before eight. The military policeman at the desk stood up and saluted.

'Captain Cotton?'

'Not any more.'

'You're needed urgently in Operations, sir.'

'Go,' said Houghton. 'We'll take your stuff down.'

Cotton followed the MP and saw Agnes again. She handed him an envelope and the code book.

'Security, please,' she said.

Cotton went into another cubicle and opened the envelope. It took him half an hour to decode:

May dead repeat dead. Likely date of death 1st September. Revised orders. Proceed to Cadiz. Secure position. Close office. D.

Cotton had not quite three and a quarter hours before his train. During this time he learned that the delay in hearing of May's death had been caused by 'consular channels'. In other words, the death had been belatedly reported to the embassy in Madrid by the vice-consul in Cadiz. He sent a message to D: 'Have two hours before departure. Cause or circumstances of death?'

Shortly before he had to leave, he received a reply: 'Neither cause nor circumstances known. Situation doesn't add up. D.'

Cotton picked up his railway ticket and went to say goodbye.

'Good luck,' said Houghton. 'That business Marie told you about always being on your own?'

'Yes. No man is an island in Spain because someone will always be looking over your shoulder?'

Houghton smiled. 'Mm. It's usually true.'

'Thanks,' said Cotton. 'You've been very kind.'

Houghton shook his head. '*Suerte*,' he said in Spanish. Luck.

Cotton smiled. 'And thank Marie for me.'

'Of course.'

They shook hands. A few minutes later he was being driven to Atocha station to get the express south.

2

COTTON HAD ample experience of wartime rail travel in Britain – packed compartments, crowded corridors, the blackout, dreary delays – but it had not quite prepared him for Atocha. An industrial sort of conservatory roof for the station was familiar enough, but there was little defensive about the place, no sand-bags or air-raid wardens. Atocha was crowded all right, but partly by squads of different police and military forces and a group of strutting, blue-shirted men involved in some touchy pecking order among them-selves that rebounded mostly on the travellers. The sounds around him were parade-ground sharp, but without any sense of order. Cotton had never before seen young conscripts cowed by a policeman. There was a group of women in headscarves squatting on the floor round cloth bundles being jeered at by the blue-shirts.

Cotton's driver, already tense, stiffened up further and moved fast. Whenever someone looked at them he blurted, '*Diplomático británico. Primera clase.*' British diplomat. First class.

Cotton made him stop, and bought two bottles of mineral water for the journey before moving through to the platform.

There he found a train that looked like an expedition-ary force into hostile territory. There were armed guards in a kind of turret on the roof at the rear. The carriages after that were entirely of wood, like varnished, shuttered coops, and looked as if they were just perching on the bogies and wheels. Then there was second class, with more metal and glass, a restaurant car in brown and white, and finally two carriages for first class at the front, painted a dull, gunmetal green, another turret, and an engine that looked like something left over from the era of stovepipe hats. Lofted up on either side of the tender were two large Nationalist Spanish flags.

The embassy driver brought Cotton's bags on board, wished him well, and asked him if he should stay. Cotton shook his head. He thanked him, and set about settling down. He had Byron's *Don Juan* to read on the journey – five hundred and twelve pages of narrative poem. According to Cotton's calculation, that was a little more than a page a mile.

On the flyleaf of his code book D had written a question. What did Cotton think of T. S. Eliot's criticism of Byron's English – that it was merely that of 'a schoolboy or an accomplished foreigner'? Cotton had wondered at the time if this was some kind of joke, but now, sitting on a hard train seat made for bodies on a much smaller scale than his, he thought first that it might serve as a diversion, and second that it might be D's way of reminding him what Doña Montserrat Gil had said. Despite her own tendency to be rather prissy in English – 'Oh, I'm glowing,' she had said, and patted at the sweat on her forehead with a very dainty handkerchief – she had been forthright.

23

'Your vocabulary is that of an educated man, but your syntax can lapse towards childish forms. You are missing the Spanish in the middle – street Spanish, normal Spanish. Spaniards swear a lot.' One of his first tasks was to revise a long list of Spanish swear words and euphemisms. 'There is also that Mexican touch to your accent. In Spain that can be regarded as charming but also rather innocent.' Cotton had been praised when he managed what sounded rather nasal and sibilant. 'It doesn't make you feel quite yourself? But that may be the point. It's not about yourself. It's about doing your job without getting lost in byways and bad habits.'

The train seats had very straight backs. Cotton arranged his legs as best he could and picked up the book. In Canto 1 Byron wavered between Seville and Cadiz as the handsomest city in Spain. In Canto 2 he called Cadiz 'a pretty town' with 'such sweet girls'.

Despite what Marie and Houghton had said about intimacy and privacy, almost all those who looked in on his compartment immediately shied back and moved on. But an hour on, just before the train pulled away, one person put his head round the door and came in – a man with centre-parted, plastered-back hair that had the look of an insect that had not quite settled its wings. Spanish has the word *escuálido*, 'squalid', but it means 'thin', not 'dirty', and can also refer to sharks. Cotton's thin travelling companion was a chain smoker and kept using his handkerchief to mop his face but not to blow his nose. He sniffed, hawked and swallowed, and then began over again. Each cigarette he simply dropped to the floor, sometimes stabbing at it with a shoe, but usually just leaving it to burn out.

Cotton shifted in his seat and tried to concentrate on his book. He laughed once or twice. The man sniffed and hawked again. Cotton put down the book. The air was stifling, and his eyes were stinging from the cigarette smoke. He tried to pull down the train window, but it was jammed tight. The hawker watched him struggle, then shrugged, took a piece of cloth out of his pocket, unwrapped a small, stale piece of bread, and ate it, masticating noisily, breathing through his mouth.

Around 2 p.m. Cotton walked along to the dining car. He found a much-used cardboard notice informing him that the service was unavailable. Inside the carriage, however, he could see four Spanish army officers at a table, smoking and drinking brandy. He knocked at the door, and a waiter opened it to say, 'We're closed.'

'Can I buy some food?'

'*No hay.*' There isn't any. The waiter jerked his head at the army officers behind him. 'They brought their own brandy.'

'Will you be taking on supplies further down the line?'

The waiter shook his head. 'I doubt it.'

Cotton turned back. Wearing the money belt had been a mistake. It dug in and made him sweat even more. He went to the bathroom and took it off. He took the Alfonso XIII coin out of the belt and put it in his trouser pocket. He didn't think of it as a talisman.

He went back to the compartment, put the money belt in his attaché case, drank some water, and picked up his book again. The train was crawling through La Mancha, a barren bleakness punctuated by windmills that were not turning and occasional flocks of sheep. The train wheels made a listless, looping click . . . click . . . click. *I travel badly*. Cotton could not get words and rhythm to match. *I trundle badly* did not match either. Between cantos, he tried to doze.

Two members of the Guardia Civil, in their green uniforms and strange black hats, carrying their rifles in front of them, walked up and down the train every two hours. Cotton was not sure whether their shiny headgear was leather or lacquered or both. He had seen and heard them four times and drunk both bottles of water before the train reached Valdepeñas at dusk. Lights came on in the station, but not in the compartment.

Cotton dozed for a while and woke, still in Valdepeñas, because of the sweat running down his nose. He jumped up to stretch his legs, tugged hard at the window again, and managed to open it halfway. The hawker's snores paused, then resumed with a loud grunt. Several other heads were leaning out along the train. A small boy was walking along the platform carrying a round clay pot with a spout. Cotton watched as a man in the next carriage lifted the pot and poured water into his mouth.

'*¿Agua señor?*' said the boy.

Cotton nodded and took the pot. He lifted and poured. The water was miraculously cool. As he drank, he let a little splash on to his face. He smiled and handed the pot back to the boy.

'*¿Y para comer?*' he asked. Anything to eat?

The boy shook his head.

'*Sólo agua, señor.*'

He pointed behind him. Several carriages along, a man with one leg shorter than the other was balancing a tray on one hand like a waiter. Cotton nodded and gave the boy a coin. By the time the tray-bearer reached Cotton's carriage all that was left was a couple of sticky-looking chocolate-covered buns. Not what he had in mind, but he bought one anyway. Thick, cloyingly sweet confectioners custard squelched from the centre as he bit. He chewed, swallowed, wrapped the remainder of the cake in the paper it had been wrapped in, and went back to his book.

Around midnight the train moved again. A wavering light came on in the compartment. Cotton's companion stretched out, and Byron's hero had travelled through the whole of Europe, including Turkey and Russia, before the cantos ended. Cotton had read them all before they reached Cordoba at dawn. There the train became noticeably lighter when many people got off, mostly women carrying cloth bundles.

'*Chusma,*' said his companion. Scum. And then '*Mierda,*' shit, as he crumpled up his last pack of cigarettes and threw it on the floor.

Cotton bought some weak coffee and an orange from a man who came down the platform with an almost empty trolley. The orange was small and juiceless, the segments pale and almost as dry as straw.

'Don't you know it's not the season for oranges?' said the hawker.

Wearily, Cotton nodded. He had merely remembered the refreshment in an orange. 'I was hungry,' he said.

The hawker shrugged. 'If you want food you should have brought your own,' he said, and went back to looking out of the window. Cotton was reading the notes.

The next time the two Guardia came along the train they stopped and opened the compartment door. The space between the two rows of seats meant there was room for only one of them to come in. The beefier one entered; the other stood almost behind him with his face looming over his shoulder. He murmured into the neck of the beefy one, who nodded and spoke.

'*Libro gordo.*' Thick book.

Cotton looked up. 'Yes, it is.'

The Guardia sniffed. 'What language is that?'

'It's English,' said Cotton.

'*Traiga.*' Let me see.

Cotton gave him the book, and the Guardia turned over a few pages. 'And where are you going?'

'To Cadiz,' said Cotton, holding out his hand for the book.

'What for?'

'On my government's business. I have the papers.'

'I am sure of it.' The Guardia slapped the book shut and handed it back to Cotton. 'But what are you going there for?'

Cotton considered the two men in uniform. 'One of my countrymen has died.'

The beefy Guardia shrugged. 'Important man?'

Cotton was not sure. The Guardia glanced back at his companion. Did he think he had just been witty?

'Important enough to send me down.'

'Your brother?'

Cotton checked him again. No, that was not wit exactly. 'No.'

'A friend?'

'No,' said Cotton. 'I didn't know him.'

The Guardia sucked his teeth and nodded. 'All right. Who's going to win your war?'

'The Allies landed in Normandy three months ago.'

'So why do you need the Reds?'

Cotton shrugged. 'Convenience of war?'

The Guardia shook his head. 'They'll eat you up, you know. They will.'

Cotton said nothing. From the corner of his eye he saw his hawking travelling companion shift in his seat. The Guardia lifted his chin.

'And here?' he said. 'What's going to happen here in the Peninsula?'

'I'm not Spanish,' said Cotton.

The hawker emitted a dry laugh like a cough.

'Who's that?' said the Guardia.

'Forget it,' muttered his companion. 'He's not worth the trouble.' He turned to go.

'Wait,' said the first Guardia. 'Will the Americans help us or attack us?'

'I really don't know,' said Cotton.

'Oh, for God's sake,' said the hawker – 'they might shoot *food* at us! A couple of rounds of York ham and who knows! On the other hand,' he went on, abruptly changing tone, 'we must not underestimate our *Caudillo*.' He shrugged. 'Franco dealt with Hitler and Mussolini. I don't see why he wouldn't be able to deal with Roosevelt. Or do I mean Eisenhower?'

'Shut up,' said the Guardia.

Something was happening, but Cotton was not sure what. His travelling companion was bristling.

'Why would I have to do a thing like that?' said the hawker. 'I ran behind those *moros* the *Generalísimo* brought over from Morocco to fight. Find me a man who ran in front of them!'

The Guardia turned a little, as if appealing to an invisible audience, 'But who does this man think he is?'

'Leave him alone,' mumbled the other Guardia. 'He has . . .'

'What? *Venga ya. ¿Qué tiene?*' Come on! What does he have?

'Relatives.'

The beefy *Guardia's* eyes opened. It was as if he had been punctured with a pin and then the air seeped out of him. '*Ya.* Such as?'

'Military and civil.'

The beefy Guardia sighed, gave Cotton a formal nod, and then deliberately banged the butt of his rifle on the carriage door as he went out. '*Señores.*'

'Shit,' said the man with the relatives. He was shaking. 'Give me a cigarette, will you?'

Cotton raised his eyebrows. 'Have you seen me smoke?'

The man shook his head. '*Los estúpidos son los más peligrosos.*' The stupid ones are the most dangerous.

He hawked again. Till then Cotton had been prepared to take the man as a shabby shadow provided by the Spanish authorities. Now he understood that this was by no means necessarily the case, but that it didn't really matter. The Franco regime did not have to pay people to inform. Fear was so pervasive that most would do it for free, others because they were on the right side, some, apparently, for both reasons. Evidently there were still potentially lethal squabbles between allies.

The man jerked his head. '*Oye*,' he said.

'What?'

'That part about the dead man . . . Is that true?'

'Yes,' said Cotton. 'Where are you going?'

'Seville. I'm from there.'

'How much longer is that?'

'*¡Yo qué sé!*' What would I know? The man paused, then leaned forward and whispered. 'Have you anything to sell?'

'No.'

'I'm getting married,' said the man.

'Congratulations,' said Cotton.

'You don't understand.'

'What?'

'I *need* things.'

'What things?'

The man groaned. 'How would I know? *Things*.'

Cotton smiled and shook his head. 'I have nothing to sell. I'm sorry.'

The man hawked and turned his head away. Cotton considered him, the man with the relatives, military and civil. He wore a double-breasted suit that might have been made for someone larger and then altered. His shirt cuffs and collar were frayed. But his shoes, though worn, had been of good quality. Some kind of hand-me-down relative, perhaps, but one travelling first class.

Cotton looked down at his own shoes. They were coated in dust. His suit was rumpled. His trousers were clinging to his legs. His shirt felt clammy. He was unshaven. He had another try at reading *Don Juan*, but gave up. He could hardly remember any of the narrative. He closed the book, reopened it, and closed it again. He blew out and drummed his fingers briefly on the cover. The hawker glanced at him. Cotton closed his eyes. It was getting hotter in one of the hottest areas in Spain.

When they reached Seville, at about noon, the hawker got out without a word. Cotton watched him until he had disappeared through the Moorish, brown-brick exit arch, then he himself stepped off the train and walked along the platform, briskly, like his father. It was a relief to get out of the carriage, stretch his legs, and breathe. He looked up. Waiting with a porter was an extraordinarily tall old gentleman with a beard cut like a spade and dressed in the sort of livery Cotton associated with coronations. He was from the Hotel Alfonso XIII. Whoever he had been expecting was not on the train.

Cotton had had enough of the heavy coin in his trouser pocket. He moved it to his side jacket pocket and threw the remains of the revolting chocolate bun into a bin. He couldn't see anything to eat on the platform, but he bought some *horchata* – orgeat or tiger-nut milk – from a stall. It was pleasant enough, but best of all it was cold and liquid. He drank it down, belched, and felt rather better than before. At least he was about to tackle the last stage of the journey. And he had the compartment to himself.

As soon as the train trundled off again, Cotton went to the bathroom and tried to wash. But the water had run out. 'No Spitting' read a sign. He couldn't even urinate. He wiped his face with his handkerchief. He had to bend down to see himself in the spotted mirror. His bones ached. He closed his eyes and imagined a bath and a change of clothes.

A little past Utrera they stopped once more, the engine wheezing and the carriages creaking in the heat, for close to two hours. Cotton stared out of the window and watched a man in the distance walking slowly beside a pair of yoked mules along a path towards a grove of orange trees. At last the train began to creep along again, but did not build up speed. The landscape of the Guadalquivir valley was on a huge, blank scale, the soil bald brown, exhausted-looking and dry, the trees rare and single except for infrequent houses with walled gardens and lush vegetation, like atolls on land. Cotton thought of Byron travelling through it by carriage or on horseback.

It took another hour and three-quarters to reach Jerez de la Frontera. Cotton sat up as they passed acres of vine-yards with their white clay soil that retains enough water for the grapes to make sherry. He was absorbed enough by what he saw to be surprised by a turn of the track and a sudden view of the sea. And there, at the end of a long, thin sandy spit, was Cadiz itself.

It appeared, aptly enough after so long, like a mirage in a Mediterraneanized Atlantic. Almost entirely sur-rounded by sparkling blue water, Cadiz had a pleasant, bright, crowded look, white houses showing silverish in a thin haze. Cotton blinked, despite himself, pleased as well as relieved that Byron might be right.

Then the view was almost immediately withdrawn. The train began its slow curl round the Bay of Cadiz:

Puerto de Santa María . . . Puerto Real, no longer port or royal . . . San Fernando, the Spanish naval base, with grey ships in the water and mountains of coarse sea salt . . . and then out along the sand-and-scrub spit before the train stopped again. While Cotton straightened his tie and combed his hair, he looked out at the water of the bay, no more than ten feet away, and to the other side over dunes to the open sea.

The train began again at little more than walking pace. They passed some kind of fort, a clump of trees, some milk cows across from a shipyard, became overshadowed by a rock face, and then the single track abruptly acquired companions and the train stopped.

Cotton waited a moment. A door slammed. There was no loudspeaker announcing the arrival. The ancient engine threw off steam with a long sigh. Cotton got down his suitcase, hitched up his trousers, and climbed down from the carriage. It was 7 p.m. – thirty hours since the train had left Atocha station in Madrid.

Cotton walked along the platform. There were several men waiting at some non-existent barrier, almost all of them wearing peaked hats. As he got closer, he saw that most of the hats bore the name of a hotel or boarding house. No one showed any sign of seeing him. He pointed at the man he wanted. Wordlessly, his case was taken. The man began walking. No one took Cotton's ticket.

After the railway carriage, Cotton had expected some relief and freshness from the sea, but outside the station a wave of warm, salt air settled on him. He saw two horse-drawn taxis – ancient, scrawny-looking animals yoked to open carriages. Neither of the drivers showed

34

interest in Cotton's custom, and the hotel man kept walking.

'Is it close? Do we walk?' asked Cotton.

The hotel man did not reply.

'I said, "Do we walk?"'

The man put down the suitcase. 'Are you tired?' he asked.

'Are you?'

The man spat. Cotton was not sure if he had smiled. He jerked a hand behind him at the horses. 'They're expensive and they're not horses. Just look at them. Today is not a petrol day. And here, nowhere is far.'

'Good,' said Cotton. 'Just tell me how far.'

As he spoke, he felt a tug at his trouser leg. A filthy, barefoot little boy about five years old, wearing a once-white vest that had been tied between his legs, was holding out his hand. The hotel man raised his hand in a chopping motion and mouthed, '¡Fuera de aquí!' Get out of here. There was something of a listless ritual about it. The porter simply dropped his hand. The child turned and pattered away yelling, with increasing confidence, '¡Mamá! ¡Mamá!'

'You're not from here,' said the bagman.

'No.'

The man frowned. 'German?'

'No, I'm English,' said Cotton.

'Ah. May God give you strength!'

'I'm not that tired.'

The man shook his head. 'I was referring to your war,' he said.

'Yes,' said Cotton. 'Tell me which way.'

The man rubbed his chin. 'Let's see. It's about five minutes from here,' he said, picking up Cotton's case again. 'This is the Plaza de Sevilla, ahead is what is called Canalejas. Just follow me.'

They crossed a road and then walked along by the port. Most of the people Cotton saw were short – shorter than in Madrid, but small-boned as well – looked poorly fed, and appeared to have nothing to do except look at him. They passed a legless man in a wooden box selling dented, pale-green fruit in a soft basket.

'*¡Chirimoyas!*' he called. Custard apples.

As they went past the port gates, a small group of men on crutches stopped talking and gawped until they remembered they were beggars.

'*¡Una limosna!*' Charity.

'*¡Que Dios te lo pague!*' May God repay you.

'*¡He sufrido mucho!*' I have suffered a lot.

The hotel porter continued walking. As Cotton followed him, he understood that it wasn't just his fatigue and being in an unknown place: he really was being stared at. That was the first difference between Madrid and Cadiz. In Madrid, people had obviously avoided looking at him. In Cadiz he was too tall, fair-haired and blue-eyed, was wearing a worsted English grey suit and a striped shirt, and was carrying a trench coat and an attaché case, and so people had to look at him. It was still gruesomely hot – Cotton could feel the sun grazing his face as if his skin was being scraped – and so he felt doubly uncomfortable. The staring was completely unselfconscious. They saw him, they stopped, mouths opened. There was a good deal of squinting, puzzlement, and sometimes consultation about who he might be.

'¿*Ése quién es?*' Who is that? It sounded like 'Essaykienay'.

The people smelled of warm, dusty poverty overlaid with burnt-sugar smells from some of the street stalls, a desiccated oyster-and-salt smell from the sea, and now and then a waft of cheap cologne from the combed hair of small boys.

The poverty was no surprise, but Cotton had thought it would be accompanied by elements of violence and repair – a gutted church; a patched-up house. Somehow this decay was more depressing than the damage he had left behind him in Madrid. Here, the facades had lost stucco, the paint had peeled, and the symmetry of the eighteenth-century houses had crumbled. Walls had sagged outward; parapets had rounded out or dropped away. They did not appear to have used bricks to build the houses, but stacks of clay tiles instead. The only building that stood square was a shabby palatial structure with baroque details round the windows, directly in front of them. The stone blocks were a yellowish-gold, but the stone itself looked honeycombed.

'What is that?' asked Cotton.

'It's the old customs house,' said the porter. 'Now the provincial government. That stone is from the Cadiz that lies under the sea. They chipped the shells off.'

'What do you mean?'

'The *maremoto*.'

Cotton thought for a moment. *Maremoto*. Seaquake. 'When was that?' he asked.

'Oh . . . ' said the porter, '*hace mucho*.' A long time ago.

Cotton nodded. 'They told me that Cadiz wasn't fought over in your war,' he said.

'Well, it depends what you mean by "fight",' said the porter. '*En Cádiz hubo algo de bronca pero también muchas estupideces.*' There was some violence, but also many stupidities.

'Right,' said Cotton. 'How is it you pronounce "Cadiz"?'

The man stopped for this and licked his remaining teeth. '*Ka-deeth*,' he said, mouthing carefully. He shrugged. 'Well, "Ka-ee" is what we say.'

'*Te oigo,*' said Cotton. I hear you. It wasn't quite *caí*, 'I fell', in Spanish, but close enough, and it had a kind of plaintive caw at the end, like that idiot First World War song that ended 'Good-byee, good-byee'. Here 'good-kyee'. How had Byron contrived to rhyme 'Cadiz' with 'ladies'? It was not even like 'laddies'.

The porter stopped again and, with a minimum of flourish, stretched out a hand. 'There you have it, sir – the Hotel Buenavista.'

Behind some horse carts was a tired white-and-pink construction. The name above the portico had slipped and lost letters. They crossed in front of the old customs house and went into the peeling, pale-green doorway.

There was a revolving door that let Cotton into a dark, high-ceilinged reception hall. At first look, the interior was impressive by contrast with the facade. The decoration was all 1890s gilt and red. But then his eyes grew accustomed to the gloom – there was a single light bulb in the chandelier – and he saw that the mirrors were worn and spotted, that a cherub lacked both feet and a wing, that the plush carpet was down to dun backing in places and had the more common routes marked out in bare threads. The place had a stale, unused smell, overlaid with bleach and garlic.

The welcome, after some shrill bell-banging from the man who had carried his case, was uneasy. An old woman appeared first, stopped, and immediately called. Out came an old man. And another. Round-faced and bald, the two men could have been twins, were possibly just brothers. They looked rather more like elderly retainers than hotel staff. The three of them hovered, sniffed at him, and mumbled.

'Who do I have the pleasure of speaking to?' asked Cotton.

'Evaristo Aberasturi,' said one old man. 'This is Hipólito Aberasturi. And that's Puri.'

Cotton nodded. Aberasturi is a Basque name. Who Puri was, whether sister or wife, was not mentioned. Evaristo asked for Cotton's passport.

'*Aquí falta algo,*' he said. There is something missing here. He did not sound suspicious so much as unhappy.

'I'm sorry?' said Cotton.

'*Que sólo hay un apellido.*' There's only one surname.

'Yes,' said Cotton. 'Yes.' And he offered them, Spanish style, his mother's maiden name for their form.

'*Y entonces, ¿por qué no está en el pasaporte?*' But then why doesn't it appear on the passport, they were saying. Was Cotton aware that they were responsible to the police? Cotton replied that the British were different and that the police would understand. Grudgingly, they let him sign the registration book. There was a pause. Then, in what seemed to Cotton a torrent of aggressive but toothless Spanish, the old woman Puri ran through the tariff. Cotton was having trouble with the local accent and intonation. It was thick-tongued, guttural, and the ends of some words seemed to be missing or to tail off in a wail. He nodded, shrugged, and claimed he understood. He got out his wallet and showed them the edge of his banknotes.

He asked if he could have a meal. He would bathe and shave first, he said, and then eat. There was another pause, a murmured consultation among the trio. The first old man explained that the water would have to be heated. This was a lengthy task, he said. Difficult so late in the day. Very well, said Cotton, he would shave cold and then eat. They looked stunned. Cotton wondered what Byron could have rhymed with 'hiatus'.

'¿Y qué quiere comer?' – What do you want to eat? – said Hipólito.

'I don't know,' said Cotton. 'Have you a menu?'

There was another pause.

'To tell the truth,' said Evaristo Aberasturi, 'food is a problem.'

'Do you want me to go to a restaurant?' asked Cotton.

'No, no. In general, I mean. Food is a problem. A question of supplies, I understand, señor.'

'But can you supply a meal for me? Can you give me food?'

Evaristo sighed and, as a reply, stared at Cotton's wallet.

Cotton scratched his neck. '¿*Cuánto*?' he said, and began counting out notes. They stopped him after three days' full board and lodging. Evaristo began making out a receipt. Hipólito extracted a note and gave it to the old woman. Grumbling, she left the hotel.

'Here,' said Cotton to the bagman, offering him a tip.

'No, no, no,' said Evaristo Aberasturi, 'that's not necessary. He's on a good commission.'

Cotton smiled at the porter. 'Is that true?' he asked.

'If he says it is,' said the porter, 'who am I to disagree?' He leaned towards Cotton and lowered his voice. 'Old shit.' He put on an obsequious voice and spoke up. 'If you're serious about the tip, sir, you can pay me when you leave.'

'Yes,' said Cotton. 'All right.'

The bagman threw up his hands and turned to go. 'Later! It's always the same story!'

Cotton watched him go through the revolving door muttering and shaking his head.

'Take no notice of him,' said Evaristo. 'I've never considered him a good man. Not really.' He handed Cotton a receipt in floridly inexpert handwriting made out to 'Piter Jams Beatie'. His mother's surname had been Beattie. The old man had evidently flagged with the effort or become confused enough to omit his surname as he had copied it from Cotton's passport.

'The passport will be returned to you when the police have seen it. The girl will bring your luggage up. Hipólito will show you your suite now.'

Cotton trudged after him. They went upstairs to the next floor, where Cotton was given a fusty, high-ceilinged run of rooms consisting of a large bedroom with a pale-green painted bed that had a curtain rail but no curtains, a small sitting room – which contained an empty mahogany bookcase, two enormous dried-out leather armchairs, and a marble-topped chest of drawers – and a bathroom, large and bare to the light bulb. The bathroom had no window, but there was a grille high up on one grey plaster wall, a centrally placed bath with clawed, cast-iron lion's feet, a basin in a corner, and, behind a latticed screen, a water closet without a seat. The room felt chronically damp.

'Well,' said Cotton. The place had the feel of a long-abandoned brothel. Was that possible? A small girl staggered in and dropped his case on the floor. Hipólito murmured something about finding everything satisfactory, gave a little bow, and closed the door.

Cotton shaved cold, his razor scraping painfully. He washed with the crude, strong-smelling bar of green soap provided. It barely lathered. Then he put on fresh clothes and went downstairs to the dining room. Most of the tables had been stacked; others were left bare; only one had a cloth on it, which was not very clean. He was the only person there. Was he the only guest? He heard a creak and saw the old woman peering round the door at him. It took a second or two to understand that she was waiting for him to sit down.

He was given egg soup, which looked exactly, to Cotton's mind, as if someone had served up water and the remains of an ineptly poached egg. Next came a small piece of rank, greasy fish, a very small cut of tough meat, and a tasteless apple. It was, he considered, almost miraculously bad. The coffee, however – a small cup, but thick and black – was real and good, and went some way to overlaying the meal.

Cotton left the dining room and went into the reception hall. There was no one there. He was beginning to marvel at the shabbiness and decay. He noticed that the feet of some red plush chairs – a kind of club Adam – appeared to have grubby gesso where the gilt had chipped. He looked up at the enormous chandelier; it had a thicket of electric cables, but nothing in the way of bulbs. To his left, through some double doors, Cotton saw a bar and cocktail lounge. He pushed in. There was no one there. There was one lamp on, and he could barely make out his reflection in the encrusted bar mirror. But the bottles looked used. He hit the little bell. Almost at once, he heard the scuff of feet behind him.

'¿Qué quiere usted?' said a deep voice. What do you want?

Cotton did not turn immediately. He was a little surprised that the blurry reflection that joined his in the mirror should be, with a voice like that, so short. The reflection wore a hat, and Cotton thought he could make out a moustache. He turned round. He had never seen him before, but the man looked, in some way at least, familiar. That was impossible. The man used his thumb on either side of his moustache as if checking it in the mirror. Was he clowning?

'What have you got?' said Cotton.

The man blinked, raised one eyebrow, and slowly swivelled round towards Cotton. 'Well,' he said,

43

clambering on to a square bar stool, 'I asked you amiably enough. I can say, I believe, that the question was put openly and frankly. Can you say the same of your answer?'

Cotton kept his face neutral. 'Of course I am a foreigner, and my deficiencies in such a rich language as yours may be very evident, but they will require your indulgence if our conversation is to prosper. I am entirely at your disposition.'

The man nodded as if Cotton had just said something profoundly true. '*Ya*. A man from Seville is a foreigner here.' He banged the bell and took off his hat. He was very bald, but had combed the sides back so that he looked as if he might have hair under his hat. 'Two brandies!' he called.

'I know,' said Cotton. 'I came through Seville on the train.'

The man smiled. 'Our age-old hospitality is world-famous,' he said. 'You can see for yourself! Now, if I have to raise my voice . . .'

'*¡Voy, voy!*' called the old woman. I'm coming.

'Well?' said the man, turning to Cotton.

'What?'

'Our hospitality?'

'I'm only just beginning to experience it. Of course I've read about it. Homer mentions it and . . . oh, he praised the women here. They were very good dancers, apparently. Very neat feet.'

'Oh, yes,' the little man nodded. 'I can see you're an educated man. That's quite clear. This hotel, you know, was built just before the turn of the century.'

44

'Really?' Cotton looked again at the shabbiness around them.

'Yes. It opened about two weeks before Spain lost Cuba and Cadiz the tobacco trade. Never really recovered. Did you say "Homer"?'

'Yes.'

'A Greek?'

'Yes.'

'He was lying, of course.'

'Really?'

'Yes. I regret to say that the girls in antiquity here were famous for something else. I believe one name for it is "giving head". There was actually an academy for it – truly – and the girls were exported, like olive oil or fermented fish guts. The feet I don't know anything about. That's not my kind of vice.' The little man paused. 'Do you know who I am?' he said.

'Specifically no. In general terms, I think so,' said Cotton.

The man smiled. 'That's my job,' he said, smirking modestly. 'These days I'm told it's my duty, even my vocation.' He looked at Cotton. 'What do you know about Cadiz, Mr Cotton?' he said. 'The real Cadiz.'

'Very little,' said Cotton, 'except that in the real Cadiz you know my name.'

The little man looked pleased. He reached into his inside pocket and handed over Cotton's passport. 'Let me explain Cadiz to you, then,' he said.

The old woman sidled down behind the bar with two glasses and a bottle of brandy.

'This is on the house,' instructed the man. 'Wipe those glasses.'

He leaned forward and laid his forearm on the bar, then turned the palm upward.

'This will do to illustrate,' he said. 'Make Cadiz my hand and you'll see that I don't have any trouble.' He chopped lightly at his elbow. 'I cut them off here, if you understand me.'

Cotton shook his head.

'Hah,' said the little man patiently. 'What are you waiting for, woman? Pour.' He turned to Cotton again. 'You see,' he said, running his finger along his forearm, 'this is the spit that links Cadiz – although Cadiz is really an island, as Homer knew – the spit that links Cadiz to the mainland. One roadblock and that's that!'

'What? You're telling me Cadiz is like a bottle and, like a bottle, has a neck?' said Cotton.

'Well, I don't want to take too much credit, you know. There's nowhere to hide, and there's only one way out.'

'What about the sea?'

The man blinked with genuine surprise. 'Well,' he said, 'next stop is America, if you can swim. We search the boats. With dogs. The city motto is "*Non plus ultra*".'

Cotton nodded. 'Yes, I'm getting an idea.'

The little man lifted his chin. 'You know Latin.'

'Some.'

'Go on. What does it mean?'

'No further.'

'Exactly. In Cadiz it's always *no further*.'

He drank his brandy in one gulp and thumped the glass down on the bar. 'Another!' he said. 'Now I don't want you to think that my job is too easy. There are criminal elements, pickpockets, pimps – you know the kind. But I have other responsibilities. It's also my job to handle cases in which discretion is needed. People sometimes offend against the Law of Public Health.'

'And you decide who offends,' said Cotton, feeling over-obliging.

The man nodded. 'I am not alone, though. But of course the best defence against misunderstandings, as our Mother Church always says, is openness and frankness. If you have nothing to hide, you have nothing to fear.'

'My bedroom door has no lock,' said Cotton.

The man laughed, even gave Cotton an admiring look. 'I'm glad our chat has gone so well,' he said.

'You know why I'm here?' asked Cotton.

'Yes, of course,' said the little man. 'I've been expecting you. It's something of a relief that you've arrived.' This time he took a sip of brandy and assumed a reflective face. 'Many famous people have passed through Cadiz, did you know? Hercules is said to have founded it. Caesar was here. A little more recently, and in my own experience, I accompanied Trotsky around.'

'Was he impressed with Cadiz?' said Cotton.

'Well, he wasn't here long. He was off to Mexico and, ultimately, a fatal meeting with an ice pick.' With a grunt, he got down off the bar stool. 'Oh, he said he liked the cigarettes.'

The little man put on his hat and checked it in the mirror. Then he smoothed his eyebrows and his moustache. 'Ah,' he said, still looking at his reflection. 'Do you know where Clark Gable was born?'

'What?' said Cotton. What had he said? 'Clock Gibble'? Cotton realized the little man was really trying to pronounce like an Englishman and had just risked his dignity. He shook his head. 'No, I'm sorry, I don't.'

'Cadiz!' said the man.

Cotton blinked, but said nothing. His visitor smiled.

'Cadiz O-hi-o!' he said.

'Right,' said Cotton. 'Your health.'

'That's it,' said the little man. He swallowed the rest of his brandy and gave Cotton a light clap on the shoulder. 'I'll see you around.'

Cotton watched him go. He was no more than five foot three. Cotton guessed him to be about sixty. He walked very stiffly, and Cotton saw first that he had lifts in his shoes, then that he was wearing a corset. At the door, he stopped, put a cigarette in his mouth, and, with some difficulty, cracked a match on the sole of his shoe. He combined the first puff with a sigh, and then pushed out through the door using both hands.

The old woman appeared at once to remove the bottle and the glasses.

'*Buenas noches,*' said Cotton.

'*Buenas noches, señor.*'

'Oh, give me a bottle of water, would you? And could I be called at eight?'

She said nothing, but brought him the bottle. He repeated the time question. She gave a resigned shrug.

'Till eight, then,' said Cotton. 'Goodnight.'

They were locking the main door. Cotton saw there was a lift, examined it briefly, and then took the stairs up to his room. He found that his clothes had been neatly

put away. In the bathroom, the recent ⌐
was still visible on the stone-tiled floor. Despite
Cotton smiled.

He undressed and got into bed. The sheets had been
ironed – to get the damp out of them, he supposed – and
still retained a little warmth. He opened his notebook,
wrote '7.9.44', and then a list of expenses. He had to get
out of the creaking bed to turn off the light.

3

In front of him in the dark Cotton could see a thin vertical line. Not part of a spider's web, this was a thread. Dribbling down it was a drop of something oily, the colour and thickness of perfume. When he focused on it he saw the drop was diminishing as it went, coating the thread. But when he peered at it more closely the sudden reflection of his own diminishing, distorted face startled him. Behind his head he could hear the murmur of casually insinuating voices. He woke.

Hastily, because the salt was stinging his eyes, he wiped the sweat off his eyelids, cheeks, forehead and nose. He blinked at his watch, then closed one eye. He had been asleep for no more than an hour. A little amused, mostly irritated, he relaxed and breathed in. Was he really that alarmed to be sent somewhere so remote? He shook his head and got up. He went through to the bathroom and washed his face. Absurd. He'd get on, close the office, and get away. He rubbed the back of his neck with cold water.

But back in his room he realized the voices he had heard were real. Someone outside laughed low. Then there was what sounded like a brief, lackadaisical army drill. In the dark, Cotton tiptoed over to the window, opened the shutter a crack, and looked out. A thin mist had come in from the sea, and the sounds echoed. If in Madrid there had been platoons, in Cadiz there was just a line of representative individuals from each of the armed forces plus military police, Guardia Civil and anybody else with a uniform or a fascist shirt. They had strung out across the entire frontage of the old customs house, and were stubbing out cigarettes and swinging their rifles in front of them. Then, in more an indolent demonstration of force than a serious security sweep, the line began ambling down the road. Cotton got back into bed and listened until the voices faded away. His lids came down. Later, rubbish was collected with much banging and clattering of bins, and at dawn engines started up. It was a petrol day.

Cotton dozed until about seven, and then went into the bathroom. He ran the tap. There was still no hot water. Annoyed, he touched the pipes to check for warmth and got a mild, almost fuzzy, jolt in return. The plumbing was being used as the electrical earthing system for the hotel. The tingle of Cadiz. Nevertheless, he bathed and shaved again and, still feeling slightly damp – the hotel towels were thin and wonderfully unable to absorb any moisture – he drank water and a cup of coffee downstairs at the bar.

At nine o'clock he was outside the British vice-consulate on the second floor of an office building. A piece of card on a string told him that the office didn't open until ten o'clock. So he went back downstairs and walked along the road. There were not many people about yet. A one-armed blind man with lottery tickets pinned to the front of his shirt with clothes pegs had taken up his position on a corner of the road, while, a few yards away, a woman with sores on her legs was scrubbing bleachy suds into a doorstep with a wad of raffia. Dotted along the street, men were standing in doorways. To avoid the staring and the increasing sun, Cotton decided to go into a café and have another breakfast. It didn't make much difference. The people inside the café – mostly workers breakfasting on tumblers of milky coffee and tiny glasses of *coñác* or *anís* – stared too. And those outside stared in. He ordered bread, butter and coffee. The bread steamed when he broke the crust open; the butter smelled mildly rancid. When he began eating, he saw, peering in through the window, a woman whose jaws moved in time to his. She stopped when he did, and then resumed. A beggar stood by him for some time, sporadically holding out his hand. When he had gone, another man, filthy and bleary, sat down across the table.

'Why did Dra-kay do that? Eh?'

Cotton did not understand him. 'Do what?'

'Destroy Cadiz.'

'What are you talking about?' said Cotton.

'The pirate. Dra-kay.'

He was talking about Drake. 'How do you know I am English?' asked Cotton.

The beggar looked at him in disbelief. 'Everyone knows.'

'Drake is history,' said Cotton, looking at his watch.

The filthy man blinked. 'Of course it's history,' he said. 'What else would it be? Eh?'

Cotton remembered the hotel porter and the seaquake. 'A long time ago,' said Cotton.

'What? You think that makes it better?'

Cotton saw a couple of people moving closer to hear more. 'No,' said Cotton, 'only I'm not H. G. Wells. I can't journey back in time to correct it, even if I wanted to.'

'Who?'

'Wells. A writer,' said Cotton.

'I'm not talking about *writings*,' said the man, 'I'm talking about real flames, real rapes, real destruction.'

'How long ago was this? Sixteenth century?' said Cotton.

'You can only reply with centuries!'

'Look,' said Cotton, 'what is it you want from me? Conversation? Or something else?'

'I have my pride,' said the man.

'I'm sure of it.'

'I saw you and I thought . . .'

'Yes?' said Cotton.

'Yes. I said to myself, "Here is an Englishman. I will engage him in conversation. Perhaps I will pick up a word or two of English and make my fortune." I didn't know the Englishman would try to humiliate me as his ancestor did.'

'*¡Fuera de aquí!*' said the barman. Get out of here! 'Begging is a crime.'

'I have never begged in my life,' said the man indignantly.

'Of course! You have lots of close friends anxious to save you the trouble of asking,' said the barman.

The beggar muttered something which Cotton didn't catch.

'What's that?' said the barman. 'Look. How do you think your family got along when you were inside licking

53

the soles of the prison governor's shoes? They begged. Or they whored. You take your pick. Because no baker I know would extend credit quite that long to a non-political prisoner.'

One of the listeners turned to Cotton and tittered. 'He was not a prisoner of principle.'

Cotton got up.'That's enough,' he said. 'How much is that?'

'*Hombre*,' said the beggar, 'I don't mind. Whatever you can afford.'

Some people laughed. Someone threw him a coin so light it caught in the air and dropped into the sawdust. The beggar quickly scooped it up and brushed it. 'Barman?' he said, holding it up.

The barman took Cotton's money and shook his head at the beggar. 'Not here,' he said.

The beggar hawked and spat very close to Cotton's feet. Cotton was not paying any attention, but heard an intake of breath nearby. He looked down. He frowned. 'I'm glad you didn't hit my shoes,' he said. 'If you had, I would have screwed you into that empty light socket.'

There was some laughter. Cotton walked out. He felt irritated at himself for feeling unnerved. Had they enjoyed that miserable wrangle? He had the impression they had.

He walked up to the vice-consulate a second time, but this time briskly. The door made a loud creaking noise when he opened it, and a cowbell clanked. Behind a desk barely bigger than a bedside table sat a youngish man.

Cotton introduced himself and said, 'I'd like to see the vice-consul, please. He'll be expecting me to call.'

The young man blinked. 'Um. I sorry, sir. You speak Spanish?'

Cotton repeated his request in Spanish.

'*Muy bien,*' said the young man. 'One moment, please.' He got up, knocked at the only other door, opened it as little as possible, and squeezed himself in.

Cotton looked around. There were pictures of the King and Queen on the wall, a map of the world with British Dominions and colonies in pink but everything else white, and a big Spanish religious calendar with the feast days in red and the saints' names for each day. Today was '*Adela, Caridad y Nuria*'. There was a small sofa against one wall. The youngish man came back.

'Mr Henderson apologizes but he is extremely busy just now. Would you care to wait or make an appointment?'

'I'll wait,' said Cotton.

The youngish man looked nonplussed, but then, not knowing what to do, shrugged and went back behind his desk, fiddled with a paper clip, cleared his throat, decided to write something down very slowly and with his tongue out, then got up and knocked on the vice-consul's door.

Cotton waited. At first he stood, then he sat on the sofa. Instead of a table, there was a low, glass-covered cabinet which contained newspaper clippings, selected apparently for historical interest or a kind of phlegmatic propaganda: war declared, Dunkirk, great victory at El Alamein and, the most recent, the D-Day landings. Cotton had time to read them all. He did not take offence. He was disinterestedly prepared to believe that the vice-consul really was busy.

At shortly before eleven a bell sounded, and he was ushered in to meet an elderly gentleman with watering eyes, trembling hands and a very stiff manner. The vice-consul, in his linen suit and striped tie, remained seated.

'I'm so sorry to have kept you waiting, Mr Cotton,' he drawled in what was, thought Cotton, the meanest-toned apology he had heard for some time. 'One's terribly hashed. Please sit.'

Cotton sat on the chair provided for visitors. He decided to wait for the vice-consul to begin. Henderson rubbed his chin and dropped his voice.

'You have come about May, I take it.'

'Yes.' Nothing followed from Henderson. 'What happened?' said Cotton.

Henderson jumped up from his seat at once. 'You must appreciate our position here,' he said, agitatedly. 'You simply *can't* ask that question.'

Cotton frowned. 'I'm sorry,' he said. 'Why not?'

'Good heavens! You *must* know we are delicately placed! One's *not* – how shall I put this? – *non grata*. That's our status here.'

'I see,' said Cotton. He nodded. He waited for the vice-consul to sit down again. 'But that's not the case here, between us, surely?'

'I'm trying to impress on you how difficult and delicate the matter is,' said Henderson. 'Without that appreciation on your part, we're not going to make much progress at all.'

Cotton looked impassively at the peevish, plaintive old man and waited.

'They don't give *us* parcels of land "from a grateful people",' said Henderson. He seemed to think this remark particularly enlightening.

'Are you saying the Spanish government has given the Germans land?' said Cotton.

'Yes, of course.'

'Is that linked to May?'

'Good heavens, *no*. I didn't *say* that. I was making a point. Surely I can make a general point without you leaping to particular conclusions,' said the vice-consul.

Cotton shrugged and nodded, a nicer young man. 'Ah,' he said, 'I see.'

'I'll give you an example of our attitude, Mr Cotton. You remember that terrible business when a merchant ship was bombed along the coast?'

'No,' said Cotton.

'Well!' said Henderson. 'I thought you people were supposed to be briefed!'

'Vice-consul, I arrived in Madrid three days ago. I didn't know of May then, and was quite unaware he was already dead.'

Henderson frowned. It was clear to Cotton why it had taken so long for May's disappearance to be reported, and who was responsible for waiting until his body had been found. 'Well, it's useful background,' the vice-consul said.

'Please go on,' said Cotton.

'The ship went down about twelve miles away, towards Gibraltar. Five bodies were washed ashore.'

'I see,' said Cotton.

'Well, we banded together, didn't we – the British community in the province, that is – and we buried them in the British Cemetery, commissioned a plaque, and a collection is paying for a new wall by the railway line. It was a good show: quiet, heads up. It was an opportunity, you see. To demonstrate our attitude.'

'Yes,' said Cotton. 'That was well done.'

'No, no,' said the vice-consul. 'It was *nicely judged*.'

'I appreciate that,' said Cotton. 'I'll certainly visit the cemetery.'

The vice-consul did not seem taken with the idea. 'May's there now,' he mumbled. 'He was buried two, no, three days ago.'

'I see.' Cotton bit his lip.

'He was washed up in the bay,' said Henderson.

'Yes,' said Cotton. That was the link with the dead sailors.

'He died by drowning. They did an autopsy.'

'Who did?' asked Cotton.

'The local authorities. A competent forensic chap. I know him slightly,' said Henderson.

'How long had he been in the water?'

'About . . . fifty, fifty-five hours, apparently.'

'And when was he last seen?' asked Cotton.

'The first of the month. Not by me. I hadn't seen him for some time. I understand his clothes and belongings are in your office – that's upstairs.'

'How did they get there?' said Cotton.

'What? Oh no, no,' said Henderson. 'They don't work like that. Everything will be there, I assure you.'

'I am not doubting that.'

'What do you mean?'

'They searched my room last night.'

'Who did?'

'I don't know that,' said Cotton. 'The man I spoke to was small, bald, with a moustache. He thinks he bears a close resemblance to Clark Gable.'

'Oh, that's Ramírez. He watches a lot of films,' said the vice-consul.

'Yes, I had imagined that.'

Henderson pursed his lips. 'They have called it an accident,' he said. 'And I certainly do not wish to argue with them about that.'

'I understand, vice-consul,' said Cotton. 'But it's my job to be tidy. In confidence, do you think there is a possibility that May's death wasn't an accident?'

'What do you mean?' said Henderson.

'Well, is there a possibility that it might have been suicide?'

The old man blinked with a watery kind of bitterness. His mouth tightened further. 'One wonders', he said indignantly, 'what in God's name persuaded them to post him here! The man was totally unsuitable. Highly unstable. Why, May didn't even speak the language well!' Undoubtedly he could have gone on and on, but he pulled up. He swallowed. 'I . . . erm . . . consider him to have been foolhardy.'

'I see,' said Cotton. 'Then I'll speak to the forensic man. Do you have his name? Where should I go? His address?'

Henderson told him. 'When exactly were you thinking of doing this?' he said.

'I was thinking of now,' said Cotton. 'I'd like to get the report done as soon as possible.'

'Oh, no,' said Henderson. 'You'll need to make a formal appointment. Besides, there are some rather urgent other matters to clear up.'

'Yes?'

'There's the rent for one thing. No notice, you see.'

'The rent for May's office?'

'Yes. You should see the porter about that. And then there's the matter of the funeral expenses. We paid up only very reluctantly, you know. It's really not our department, as I am sure you are aware.'

'Quite,' said Cotton. 'I'll certainly see to those things, vice-consul.'

Cotton stood up. 'Thank you very much, sir. You've been most helpful.'

'Ah, well,' said Henderson. 'You have taken my point? I do advise the utmost discretion. If I can help you with that, please do not hesitate to call in.'

Cotton shook his hand. 'Thank you,' he said.

It took Cotton the rest of the morning to deal with the rent. The porter of the building was stolidly unhelpful, and directed him to the bank. Cotton stepped out into the street, which had taken on bustle and noise while he had been with Henderson. The light was now aggressively bright, and made his eyes water. The bank, which was round the corner, just a few minutes' walk away, was a morass of paper and boredom. The bank clerk, self-important in his starched shirt behind his ledger, was as unhelpful as the porter. Cotton recognized the look. First there was alarm, then the eyes closed off as quickly as a tortoise takes refuge in its shell. He refused to consider the possibility of releasing any of the funds placed by May. He would consider accepting cash payment in pesetas, but was unhappy about providing a guarantee that the money would reach the office owner's account in less than three days. So Cotton raised his voice and banged on the counter until the manager appeared. He was then treated with courtesy and dispatch, and the necessary funds were released.

Cotton felt like asking a question, but was not sure who would give him a reply: If porters and bank clerks were frightened of any responsibility, why were they there? Or, again, why didn't they say only the manager could take decisions? Or consult with him directly when asked to do something beyond them? And then, perfectly simply, as he stood by a marbled column in the bank, one part of his brain told Cotton it was his own fault. In such a stratified society, if you wanted something done you sought out the person that that society considered was suitable to deal with you.

He walked back to May's office building, handed over the receipt for the rent, and picked up the keys from the porter. Two floors above the vice-consulate, the single room had a green safe, a desk on which sat a shrouded Imperial typewriter, a chair for him, and a visitor's chair and a sofa. Someone had dumped May's clothes and belongings on the sofa; on top of some shirts were his comb, a toothbrush and a tin of tooth powder. To one side was a pigskin suitcase with his initials. It contained nothing.

Cotton took out his notebook and looked up the combination of the safe. It opened without any problem. The coding machine was there, as was May's code book: Jane Austen's *Persuasion*. There were also work files, some circulars, some money in a tin box, some private letters, and a local guidebook in English. Cotton sighed. He closed the safe, and then wrote a note asking the forensic doctor for an appointment the next day.

He locked up and took the envelope down to the porter, who said he would see it was delivered. Now that Cotton actually had the keys to the office, he noticed, the relationship had changed. From someone defensive, Cotton now had what the Spanish call a *pelota*, a ball – but meaning someone apparently, but by no means always sincerely, grotesquely deferential. The porter smiled with a fixity Cotton had seen only at Halloween. His name was Eugenio García García, '*a su servicio, caballero, lo que sea*'. At your service, sir, for whatever you may need. '*Por ejemplo*', for example, Eugenio wondered if Cotton might consider having some lunch sent up to his office. They agreed on that, and when Cotton asked about payment Eugenio said he should pay only when completely satisfied with the food and service.

Eugenio spoke through his smile again and said he had some papers for Cotton. These turned out to be shipping lists.

'Do I have to pay for these?' asked Cotton.

'No,' replied Eugenio. 'They also come in the newspaper. This is a courtesy from the Port Authority.'

In addition he had an envelope for Cotton. Inside was an itemized bill from Henderson: for a horse-drawn hearse, a non-Catholic burial service and 'all expenses incurred in the funeral of Ronald Alfred May'. Cotton took it upstairs and put it in a drawer.

His lunch was potato omelette with Serrano ham and a cold beer. He ate and drank standing by the window. He had a clear view over the port. Men were unloading barrels and boxes from carts on to the quay. Closer to the dockyard railings he could see two men sitting on a bench playing cards. The shutters were not quite fully open. Moving them, he discovered a pair of binoculars. There was a small sticker on them with some tiny writing: 'Private property of R. A. May'. This struck him as rather schoolboyish, but the binoculars were excellent and German. He pulled his chair round, and as he ate he looked out through Zeiss lenses. He could see the card values one man was playing, but did not know the game and had forgotten that the Spanish play with different suits: gold coins, *copas*, which look like fruit sundaes, swords; and things like ulcerous-looking shillelaghs for clubs. He raised his view and picked out rusty rivets on a ship. Someone moved through his vision, and he lowered the binoculars. A man threw a bucket of slops into the water. Cotton made adjustments to the glasses and looked through them again. He picked out a patch of oil, strips of orange peel, sections of water-melon rind and a broken wooden crate floating in the water. He looked out over the bay. Across an extraordinarily calm sea just off Rota he could make out a fisherman casting a round net from a small boat. They were good binoculars.

When he had finished eating, Cotton put the plate, glass and money outside the room as instructed, then locked the door from the inside and began looking through the contents of the safe.

He looked quickly through the notionally English guidebook of Cadiz, with its strange misuse of vocabulary carrying the ghost of Spanish syntax and meaning behind it. It had been 'written by a humble scribe with no affinities of lucre, but simply and plainly a massive desire to sing his so beloved city in prose worthy of the estimated visitor'. He spent rather longer on the fold-out street map provided at the back of the book. May had written alternative street names in two kinds of ink. In blue, above the printed names belonging to the pre-Franco era of the Republic, were the traditional ones – what May called 'folk names', such as *El Cojo,* The Cripple – and below, in red, were all the street names which had been changed after the Spanish Civil War. In a lot of cases that made three names for each street. Cotton had some sympathy when he found the key to an unusual PS – People Say – written in green ink, which gave a few streets four names. A maze of streets is more of a maze when the street names shift.

The safe also contained personal letters, all from May's mother, done up in elastic bands: 'My Darling Ronnie . . .'; '. . . Your Ever-Loving Mother'. Cotton glanced briefly at them. 'So glad . . .'; 'So nice . . .' She wrote every Sunday. There were two more, unopened, on the desk. Cotton opened them. They were the same as the others: 'Such weather . . .' He added them to the pile.

The circulars were to do with art clubs. 'Would you like to draw like the Old Masters or the Impressionists? In the comfort of your own home?' These went into the waste-paper basket. Cotton then opened the cash box and counted the money. He made a note of the amount. There were also two small sheets of folded paper – petty-cash IOUs, thought Cotton. But they were not.

To Ronnie, with that kernel of myself that somehow, no matter what, remains inviolate – and yours. J.

It was in English, written in black ink, and the paper was expensive. Cotton held it up to the light. The water-mark was Spanish. Cotton looked at the other note:

Do you know how much I adore you? See you tonight. Your J.

It was the same handwriting, the same paper. Cotton decided to keep them with the petty cash.

Then Cotton turned to the files. He was a quick reader. May had been in Cadiz since March 1943, first to prepare for the changeover in Spain's status from 'non-combatant' to 'neutral', then to watch over the aftermath. 'Non-combatant' had translated as 'hostile to the Allies'. Cotton lifted the paper. Beside 'neutral' May had written something in pencil and then rubbed it out. The word looked like 'hopeful'.

May's main brief had been to report any shipping of tungsten through the port of Cadiz. There were some humble but direct notes in the margins of reports sent to him. 'How do I recognize wolfram? More to the point: how do my informants recognize wolfram?' A little further down May had written the first basic point:

'Wolfram equals tungsten.' Then came two important facts. The Germans used tungsten in precision engineering to a level and on a scale that neither the US nor Britain could match. Tungsten was also used in the manufacture of armour-piercing shells. 'And light-bulb filaments,' May had added.

And then the next big point. Germany relied almost entirely on Spain and Portugal for its supplies of tungsten. With the change in Spain's status, the Americans and British had embarked on a strategy to diminish those supplies. They were, however, faced with a smuggling problem and those ministers in Franco's government who were still pro-Axis. Germany needed some 3,500 tons a year. Allied intelligence estimated the amount that had been smuggled out of Spain in the last year as 800 tons. Watching the port to see how much of that was going through Cadiz had been May's main job.

Cotton took a little time to think. At one level he was not unsympathetic to May. Cotton knew nothing very much of his predecessor or his background, but he had begun to experience a little of what it meant to be alone in a place as closed and as distant as Cadiz. The idea of being confined to a small city island for eighteen months was not attractive. There was some evidence that May had had a relationship with someone who wrote slightly fruity English. Cotton could hardly blame him. There was also the job – important enough in terms of armour-piercing shells, but hard to make directly interesting day after day. Had May known what he was to do when he arrived in Cadiz? Cotton had been recruited as part of the British economic-warfare unit set up in response to the American Safehaven operation to stop the Nazis secreting stolen funds to regroup. That is what he had been told, and, while he remembered asking someone what it would entail – 'Mostly bribing bank and shipping clerks, I expect' had been the reply – he had not imagined he would be put to picking through a dead man's effects.

There were a couple of puzzles, though. In return for much-needed supplies – chiefly oil – Franco had agreed four months earlier to banish German Abwehr agents from Spain. The German agent had abandoned Cadiz at the beginning of July. It was after that that May's handling of finances had caused alarm, leading to Cotton's being sent to relieve him. There were no obvious clues to what May had been doing with the money. His own records had simply stopped. And the bank had merely recorded that he had made three substantial cash withdrawals on three consecutive days at the beginning of July. In theory the amounts should have been countersigned or at least queried by someone at the bank, but, going on his own experience, Cotton thought that May would have had few problems just by being in the branch and by understanding the order of command there.

Cotton read through the files until he reached the news of his own coming under the code name Pedrillo. There was no indication of how May had reacted to this. In *Don Juan*, Pedrillo (little Peter) is the name of Don Juan's tutor's dog, who is eaten by starving sailors. Cotton used his code book and sent a message on the coding machine for the first time:

Arrived. Still not been eaten. May died by drowning during the night of September 1st–2nd. Body found over forty-eight hours later. Buried September 5th. Cause of death according to Spanish autopsy. Will interview pathologist tomorrow September 9th. Pedrillo.

It was then seven in the evening. Cotton looked through the drawers of the desk. May had been writing something on Spain or 'Things quintessentially Spanish', which he described as 'part travelogue, part interior journey'. Cotton leafed through the notebook. There were about twenty pages filled with May's attempts at poetic prose, then some blank pages and, towards the back, miscellaneous jottings and quotes. Cotton leafed on. Then his eye was caught by a loose page folded inside the book. He opened it out and read:

'What's your proposal? To build the just city? I will,
I agree. Or is it the suicide pact, the romantic
Death? Very well, I accept, for
I am your choice, your decision: yes, I am Spain.'
                                        Auden (from Spain 1937)

Shit, thought Cotton. That was all he needed. It's one thing to be a poet writing of just cities and romantic deaths. It's another to be an agent with binoculars looking for shipments of tungsten in an isolated coastal town who ends up dead in the sea. He read the lines again, then refolded the paper. He shut the paper inside the pages and returned the notebook to where had had found it.

In another drawer there were an extraordinary number of bottles of coloured ink, including turquoise, red, green and a dozen blue-black. Another drawer was stuffed with blank paper. The deep drawer at the bottom contained, on its side, a chipped glass vase of some ugliness, along with a blue penknife that turned out to be blunt and a pot of glue. Then there was official paper, empty files, some much-used carbons, several packets of thin, brown envelopes, and a tangle of elastic bands. There was also a tin tied up with a piece of green string. Cotton untied it and took off the lid. Inside was a collection of wine corks – presumably mementos of treasured tastings. He replaced the lid and retied the string.

In the last drawer he found a report that surprised him both by its presence there and by its subject. Headed 'Franco's Interpretation of Freud', it was a report by a War Office psychologist called Frederick Tapster. Cotton skim-read. The report suggested that, far from being disgusted by Freud's theories, the Spanish dictator had found confirmation of and expression for what he already suspected. He had simply adapted and applied the theories to the Spanish body politic. For Franco, the unruly id and the Spanish people were equivalent. Franco himself represented the ego that would control the id. There was also 'a likely religious element' in considering himself the father of his people. There was more stuff on anal retention, prudishness and the pleasures of self-denial.

Cotton frowned. As far as he could remember, Hitler considered Freud as doubly degenerate, and he had not bothered to think Franco might be different. It was not so much whether there was any truth in the profile as whether there was any use in it. He knew various reports had been drawn up on Hitler, Mussolini and Stalin with the aim of predicting their reactions to hypothetical situations and pressures. Tapster considered Franco to be 'a combination of extreme caution and considerable ruthlessness very difficult to dislodge'. Cotton shrugged. He wondered why May should have found the thing interesting. May would have had to request it, and, since the stamp said 13 July 1944, it was relatively recent. What was May's interest in a Freudian interpretation of Franco if his job was to seek out smuggled tungsten?

Cotton glanced over the previous occupant's clothes. He held a brown suit up against himself. May had been considerably shorter and rather plumper. Inside an envelope there were a signet ring, an identity tag and a ruined wallet wrapped in oilcloth. Another envelope contained May's passport and documents. Cotton looked at the passport photograph. It showed a dark-haired little man with a flat, small-featured face and eyes that looked like a spectacle-wearer's. Cotton saw that May had been thirty-one – six years older than him. For some reason, he found that reassuring. He looked at his watch and saw it was getting on for nine.

On his way out of the building, the porter called him and gave him a note. It was from the forensic doctor inviting him to call at 11 a.m. the next day. He put it in his pocket and walked back to his hotel.

Cotton was eating – the meal decidedly better than the night before – when Ramírez clapped him on the shoulder and sat down.

'And how do you find Cadiz? No, no, you don't have to answer.'

Cotton offered Ramírez some wine. Ramírez shook his head.

'At my age,' he said, 'my drink should really be caramel water. You know that's what they use in films to look like whisky and to leave the actors sober?'

'I think I heard something like that,' said Cotton.

Ramírez smiled. 'You know you've got a nickname already?'

'No. What?'

El bombillero. 'The light-bulb man.'

Cotton looked blank.

'You know,' said Ramírez – 'when you were having breakfast this morning!'

'Ah. The beggar.'

'You should have done it!' said Ramírez. He was enjoying himself.

Cotton shook his head. He drank some wine.

'Bring me a beer,' called Ramírez. 'And keep it off this man's bill.' He coughed, took off his hat, and used both his hands to smooth back his hair on the side of his head. 'Good day?' he asked.

'I can't complain.'

'You're translating from the English! But it's an expression we use too,' said Ramírez.

'Yes?' Cotton put down his knife and fork. He had been eating *urta*, a large, local fish with firm, white flesh, caught exclusively, he was told, off the Bay of Cadiz. Ramírez pointed at the two long bones left on the plate. 'It should come without bones,' he said.

'If you say so.'

Ramírez nodded. 'My men fished May out of the sea,' he said.

'Is that their job?' asked Cotton.

'Sometimes. Of course, the dead don't really come under my jurisdiction. There's an investigating judge. But he usually likes . . . assistance.'

'Right,' said Cotton. He sat back in his chair.

'Are you ready to talk about this?'

'Why not?' replied Cotton. 'It's what I'm here for.'

Ramírez sighed. 'On the whole,' he said, 'I don't swallow suicide.'

'Right. The vice-consul is keen to have May's death treated as an accident.'

'Oh, accidents happen,' said Ramírez. 'We lose a couple of rod fishermen every year or so. They slip; a wave knocks them off the rocks.'

'I see,' said Cotton. 'What have you got against suicide for May?'

Ramírez wrinkled his nose. The beer came. Cotton watched him pick up the glass. He saw that quite a lot of his impersonation of Clark Gable was due to his large ears and chin. Ramírez blew at the froth.

'Experience?' he said. 'Instinct?' He took a large mouthful. 'Mm. Too gassy.' He wiped his mouth and smiled. 'My problem is I know I can't really rely on experience and instinct. And he was a foreigner, of course.'

Cotton nodded. He wondered what Ramírez was up to. 'I understand,' he said. 'But how much does it really matter?'

Ramírez drank, wiped foam from his moustache, but did not reply.

'I mean, if the choice is between suicide and an accident,' said Cotton, 'I'm sure his mother would prefer accident.'

'Ah, yes,' said Ramírez – 'the mother. We mustn't forget the mother. I'm assuming English mothers are like Spanish mothers?'

'Some are, I suppose,' said Cotton.

Ramírez nodded. He cleared his throat, drank some more, and suddenly smiled. 'I was thinking about you last night,' he said. 'Forgive my asking a personal question, but are you married?'

'No, I'm not.'

'But there's a girl, surely?'

Cotton sighed and pulled at his lips. 'I was engaged,' he said.

'Ah. But she didn't leave you?'

'No, I don't suppose she did.'

'What do you mean?'

'Look . . . she's dead. Some are brave ex-soldiers picking up the administration to do with a corpse in Cadiz. She was a nurse. She died under rubble. In Clerkenwell – that's in London. The hospital was bombed.'

'I am truly sorry,' said Ramírez. He nodded. 'But I suspected something similar.'

'You did?'

'Yes. My friend, I'm very sorry.' He nodded again, but then took out a small card from his top pocket and slid it face down across the table. Cotton turned it over. It read:

There was an address and a telephone number.

'Friend to friend,' said Ramírez seriously. 'Her artistic name is *La Santanderina*.'

Cotton looked up at him. He cleared his throat. 'Is this your public health?' he asked.

'My boy,' said Ramírez, 'this is discretion.'

'I hadn't thought of you and the British vice-consul sharing such an interest in keeping things quiet.'

Ramírez smiled. 'She's good honest company and a refuge. I'm not offering to pay.'

'Am I supposed to thank you?' said Cotton.

Ramírez drained his beer. 'Yes,' he said. 'You're a good boy. I knew you were. No clap, no trouble.' He got up and put on his hat. 'I'll be seeing you.'

Cotton watched him amble away, smoothing his moustache.

The old woman came to clear his plate away. 'Anything else, *señor*?'

'Just water,' said Cotton. He picked up the card Ramírez had left on the table, looked at it briefly, then put it in his pocket, got up from the table, collected the bottle of water from the old woman, and trudged up to bed, wondering how the people of Cadiz could eat so late. He was sweating again.

He wondered why Ramírez had said so little.

4

IN SPITE of being disturbed briefly by shouting and singing, Cotton slept well and awoke reasonably refreshed, or at least feeling he had sweated a little less, though when he looked at his pillow he saw it was soaked. Slowly he drank half a bottle of water. Today was Saturday. Since it was not a petrol day, he took a horse-drawn cab to his appointment with Dr Guillén at eleven. He was not used to sitting so high and, somewhere else, might have felt uncomfortable at being so much on view. The horse clopped by the Plaza de España with its grandiose monument to the Liberal Constitution of 1812 – a tall rectangular column rising from stone lions and robed ladies in helmets, surrounded by ochre soil and formal gardens. Shortly afterwards they turned left and Cotton found the pleasantest part of Cadiz so far, the open sea on one side, sunlit houses on the other. He passed a garden and an ornate, almost Mexican church, and then the sea was closed off again. Later there was a dreary barracks to his left and a formal garden to his right, but a while later Cadiz opened out again by a small harbour. It was barely bigger than a village harbour, but the stone quays were in the shape of a crab's claws, with each pincer a stone fort. Leading from the road, built on stilts on the beach, was a white *balneario*, again in the shape of a crab. It looked like a cross between a pier and a galleried tea room left over from the days when immersion in the sea was a health cure. On the other side of the road, fronted by a huge old mulberry tree, was the Hospital de Mora, a large, plain, white building. The cab stopped under the tree.

Cotton clambered down and knocked on the enormous, studded door. A flap opened.

'What do you want?'

'I have an appointment with Dr Guillén.'

A door within the door opened, and Cotton stepped in. A nun was called, and a little after he was led through cloisters to an annexe with a door marked 'Pathology'.

The forensic doctor was an amiable-looking man with a small grey moustache and neatly trimmed hair. He had a glass of sherry on his desk. There was another, half drunk, on top of a filing cabinet beside a large, ground-glass-stoppered jar containing a foetus.

'*Fino*, Mr Cotton?'

'No, thank you.'

'Brandy, perhaps. Or have you acquired a taste for *anís*?'

'Nothing just now,' said Cotton.

'Well, do take a seat. Cigarette?'

'No, thank you.'

The doctor lit one. 'So how can I be of service to you, my foreign friend?'

'I believe you performed the autopsy on Ronald Alfred May, British national.'

'Yes, yes, yes,' said the doctor. 'I did him . . . oh, about five days ago. A report was sent to Mr Henderson at the vice-consulate.'

'Quite. There's no problem there, I assure you. We're very grateful for your co-operation and speed. Only, as I am sure you will understand, I've been sent to Cadiz to make a report and . . .'

'There's another layer of bureaucracy,' the doctor smiled.

'That's it, more or less.'

'Well,' said Dr Guillén, 'from my point of view it was pretty straightforward. You do understand the body showed all the usual signs of time and salt water? We have a standard procedure in what is a fairly common business in any coastal town. There was nothing . . . exceptional about your colleague's case. Death was by drowning.'

'I know you won't misunderstand an ignorant question,' said Cotton, 'but how do you ascertain the cause of death when the body is, as I take it was the case here, decomposing?'

The doctor looked at the young Englishman in front of him and nodded. 'Excellent,' he said, smiling. 'I have a theory, you know, that the English and the Germans fight not because they are so different, but because they are so similar. It's the small differences that constitute the worst affront. Mm? Oh, I keep my theory private, of course. But there is something admirably direct about both nations. You both ask good questions. And when you don't know something, you ask. Tree of knowledge?'

Cotton smiled back patiently. 'What tree?'

'In the Garden of Eden!'

'Ah, yes.'

77

'I think the Protestant Reformation was another bite of the apple,' said the doctor. 'All the great scientists are from Protestant cultures.'

Cotton smiled. 'Galileo? Descartes?'

'Oh, yes, but they were usually tortured, whether mentally or physically, and not, when it came down to it, very practical.'

'Ah.'

The doctor smiled again and savoured his drink. 'Well,' he said, 'my job is only really difficult when the corpse has been a long time in the water and been caught amongst rocks or been in a bad storm. Normally – and this is a normal case – the physiological changes are there to see. For example, if your countryman had been dead before entering the sea, his lungs would not have filled with water like that.'

Cotton nodded. 'I see,' he said. 'And how much of your opinion is formed by the fact that he was fished out of the water?'

'This is a delightful conversation,' said the doctor, stubbing out his cigarette. 'And of course the answer is, Quite a bit. Of course, usually one knows. A fisherman is seen to fall overboard, a suicide leaves a note. In cases, however, where we have little or no background information, I certainly look at other possibilities.'

He looked up at Cotton. Cotton looked back and waited. The doctor took out another cigarette, but did not light it. Instead, he tapped it on his desk. 'I looked at the possibilities,' said the doctor, 'but there was nothing untoward. Your colleague had eaten and drunk well – I'd say very well. He was normally dressed, was not carrying anything of value, but then again was carrying a wallet and keys and so on.'

He looked up again. Cotton nodded. The doctor shrugged and lit the cigarette. 'There was bruising, but nothing not commensurate with falling in and so on. Nothing else.'

'An accident, then?'

'That's the theory. He'd definitely drunk enough to slip or fall over. What? You think he might have committed suicide? Is there any evidence for that? I suppose somebody might have pushed him, but there's no evidence for that either.'

'Everybody assumes, I see, that May couldn't swim.'

The doctor roared. He sounded as if he was always drunk enough to find people reasonably amusing, and just kept topping up. 'Very good!' he said. 'Marvellous!'

'I don't know about that,' said Cotton.

'I do!' said the doctor. 'The thing is, Mr Cotton, to imagine what happened. May is walking, perhaps stumbling, along the sea wall. He slips. There is quite a drop to the water. He is already disorientated, and he hits liquid that is several degrees colder than the air. He plunges downward, perhaps with sufficient momentum to strike the stones on the seabed. Already disorientated, he is now doubly shocked and possibly did not keep his mouth shut. Salt water has already got into his lungs. He struggles, thrashes about, but the shocks have slowed him – fatally. Do you think that's convincing?'

'I think so.'

'Of course, if you wish, I can arrange for you to speak with the investigating judge,' said the doctor slyly.

'I'd be grateful for your advice,' said Cotton.

'Yes,' said the doctor, enjoying himself, 'I think we could say that the investigating judge is . . . well, politically skilled or somebody's relative.' He cocked an eyebrow. Cotton nodded. 'Then we have an accident. Your Mr Henderson was keen – and the authorities here possibly just as much so – not to embarrass the concept of Spanish neutrality in this war, particularly with the recent changes in fortunes of the combatants. Are you sure you won't have a drink?'

'I'm sure.'

The doctor poured himself another sherry. 'It's simply a question of months before you win the war, I take it?'

'Probably,' said Cotton.

'Good. May I ask you something now?'

'Please.'

'Oh, I'm not a politician or a diplomat but . . . you know there was quite a . . . a flutter when May's body floated in.'

'A flutter?'

'Yes. You see, last year, off the coast of the next-door province of Huelva, a fisherman found he had brought up a dead British pilot in his nets. There's a rumour that this pilot was carrying top-secret plans about the invasion of Europe. With ingratiating haste, the authorities sent the plans on to Berlin. The rumour is that the plans were false and that if my colleague in Huelva had had, let's say, the right equipment he would have been able to make out that the body had been dead for some time, kept chilled, and then dressed in a pilot's uniform and dropped into the sea. He would have seen, in other words, that, far

80

from being a stroke of luck, the body was a ruse. So May, as it were, caused a flutter. His death brought back perhaps unfortunate memories. I am not sure that the then German agent survived the mistake. He was certainly removed in summary fashion.'

Cotton nodded, then shook his head. 'Well, I've certainly never heard of that, doctor. It does sound, well, rumour, if you don't mind my saying so.'

The doctor smiled again and nodded. 'Who have you spoken to about May?' he said.

'Only Henderson. And then Ramírez talks to me. He comes to my hotel.'

'Well, he would,' said the doctor. 'I don't know . . .'

'What?'

'This is what we call *un asunto bien muerto*, a dead and buried affair – or at least a number of important people hope so. Are you interested in the human condition, Mr Cotton?'

'Well,' said Cotton, 'it depends on – '

'No, no. I am referring to the human condition only as a phrase that recognizes how varied people can be. May is dead and buried. But I know Ramírez is curious.'

'About?'

'Has he told you?'

'What?' said Cotton.

'About May's special friend.'

Cotton stared at him. 'In what way special?'

'A boy – from a *very* good family.'

Cotton breathed in and shut his eyes for a moment and sighed. 'Yes, I suppose he has. In a manner of speaking, that is.' He thought of Ramírez's apparently clumsy enquiry about his own marital status, and the card he had slid across the table. He remembered the notes he had found folded up in the cash box.

'The boy was called up a couple of months ago,' continued the doctor. 'I saw May myself. He was a distraught drunk, if you know what I mean. Rather sad. That was never the point of alcohol.'

Cotton nodded. 'Thank you. You've been most kind, Dr Guillén,' he said. He stood up.

'Have I?' said the doctor. 'You're probably very busy with your war. But . . . perhaps you're like Ramírez. He always wants to know what people are hiding – though, to be fair to him, sometimes he covers it all up again, quite respectfully, you know.'

Cotton went directly to the vice-consulate, ignored the young man behind the desk, knocked on Henderson's door, and walked in. The vice-consul was standing looking out of the window in the direction of a palm tree. He turned.

'Have you come to deal with the funeral expenses?' asked Henderson.

'No,' said Cotton.

'May I ask why not?'

'Because I have no intention of dealing with the funeral expenses just now,' said Cotton.

'I beg your pardon,' said the vice-consul.

'I believe you have a copy of the autopsy report.'

'That is correct.'

'You didn't think I might like to see it?'

'You did not ask,' said Henderson stiffly. 'I need the request in writing.'

'I really don't see why you felt able to allow the dead man's clothes to be dumped in my office without any request, whether written or verbal, but kept the report. I am disinclined to co-operate with you until I'm sure that I know of all the documents pertaining to May's death and I have them in my possession.'

'I don't know what you mean, and I take very strong exception to your tone.'

'My apologies,' said Cotton briskly. 'Now, may I have the autopsy report? I will, of course, sign for it.'

'Very well,' said Henderson.

The report was, in fact, waiting on the vice-consul's desk. He merely lifted it and dropped it a little nearer Cotton. 'Sign at the top,' he said.

Cotton signed and unclipped the report. 'Is this in my keeping now?'

'Yes,' said Henderson. He sniffed. 'I suppose you'll want copies of the death certificates as well.'

'Thank you. Do you know of any other documents I need to make my report?'

'Not to my knowledge,' said Henderson.

'I see. Why didn't you tell me that May had a boy-friend?'

The vice-consul blinked. 'Because I didn't know!' snapped Henderson. 'Should I have done? It's not my business or responsibility to pry into other people's private lives. And it is not my duty to tell you!'

'Even when the death is not natural?'

'What?' said Henderson. 'Who said that?'

'May died by drowning, Mr Henderson.'

'Oh yes. Yes, I see.' What had he been thinking of? Henderson frowned. 'Who told you of May's . . . proclivities?'

'The doctor who did the autopsy.'

'He made absolutely no mention of any such thing in the report.'

'Why should he? He was reporting on the cause of death, vice-consul. I certainly don't think he was lying to me. He may just have been drawing attention to his own discretion, and perhaps offering me some help as well.'

'Quite.'

'He also said that May's boyfriend had been called up,' said Cotton.

'What is he suggesting?'

'I don't know. But it certainly removes the boy.'

Henderson frowned, mostly at Cotton. 'I am not sure I take your meaning,' he said primly.

Cotton shrugged. 'I don't know if there is one. I'm simply passing on the information.'

'Why?'

'Because by hearing your comments I can better evaluate the information and get the report done and close down the office here.' Cotton was aware that this was probably the first Henderson had heard of the office closure.

Henderson did not exactly look mollified, but he tried. 'Well, I imagine the doctor's information is accurate. It's not a thing to say lightly in this society, particularly when speaking of the dead.'

'Well, I haven't had the impression so far that May was much in the society here.'

Henderson stiffened. 'Is that supposed to be clever?' he said.

'Certainly not,' said Cotton. 'It's simple ignorance. Mr Henderson, can you not give me some of the background? If you could speak clearly, I'd be grateful.'

Henderson considered this. 'But I don't like your kind of clarity,' he said at last. 'Whether it was an accident or there was a possibility of suicide, it has been *called* an accident. I don't think we need unearth the motives.'

'My instructions were to clear things up and close the office.'

'I, however, received no instructions,' said Henderson. 'May died in a foreign country. He didn't die in a vacuum, you know. Quite apart from any other considerations, the local regulations stipulate that corpses must be buried within twenty-four hours of death. I think I can fairly say that I acted with dispatch and discretion under difficult circumstances. Having done that, I received the only instructions I have had from the embassy: to wit, to pay for the funeral expenses and to claim reimbursement from you on your arrival.'

'Yes,' said Cotton distractedly. He frowned. 'What happened to the clothes May was wearing?'

'For goodness' sake, they were burnt! Have you any idea of the state they were in?'

'You gave your authority for that?'

'Yes,' mumbled Henderson.

'All right,' said Cotton. 'Do you think there is any possibility that May's death was suicide?'

'I should have said I concur with the forensic doctor.'

'Who says May was drowned.'

'Yes.'

'Then I see three possibilities,' said Cotton. 'First, that he died accidentally. Second, that he killed himself. Third, though whether this would constitute murder or manslaughter I don't know, he was pushed. The second and third possibilities might involve his activities here. An alternative, or additional factor, might involve what you call his proclivities.'

Henderson stared at him, sucking his teeth as if sucking a very bitter lemon. 'This is quite fantastic,' he said. 'What is your game, eh? What are you trying to stir up? This is an unfortunate but simple accident, entirely caused by sending someone unsuitable to do a delicate job. The matter has, as much as possible, been decently and quietly handled, and here you are spinning some fantastic nonsense that could cause infinitely more problems.'

'You misunderstand,' said Cotton. 'It's my job to make absolutely sure of the cause of death. It may well have been an accident. But we must know. The considerations must be obvious to you. Blackmail is not necessarily financial, Mr Henderson. Surely you understand that. We must be sure for our own security.'

'Well, I know nothing of what he was doing here.'

'That is exactly as it should be,' said Cotton.

Henderson pursed his lips. 'In theory, I can appreciate what you are saying, but . . .'

'I'd be grateful for any information, Mr Henderson.'

'I won't have the consulate mixed up in it.'

'That's exactly what I want too, Mr Henderson. But some background information on May . . . ?'

'I hardly knew him, Mr Cotton.'

'But obviously you formed an impression of him.'

'I told you what I think,' said Henderson. 'He didn't give the impression of doing anything particularly valuable.'

Cotton raised his eyebrows.

'Oh,' said Henderson. 'But he was not discreet! He was . . .'

'What?' asked Cotton.

'I was going to say "of a rather fawning cast", Mr Cotton. He said he came from Worthing. I don't know if that is useful to you.'

'Mm,' said Cotton. 'Anything else?'

'The man was . . . extravagant. His behaviour. He liked to recite poetry in a loud voice.'

'What kind of poetry?' asked Cotton.

'Keats,' said Henderson. 'That kind of thing. Oh, and Hopkins . . . A lot of Hopkins. He had a kind of rolling Welsh voice for that.'

'Welsh?'

'Yes, especially when he was drunk. Declaiming Hopkins the worse for wear in a Spanish bar hardly counts as discretion. He was becoming a joke.'

'In what way a joke?' asked Cotton.

'They made effeminate gestures at him in the street. He'd laugh.'

'Ah,' said Cotton.

'He was letting us down,' said Henderson.

'Yes,' said Cotton. 'I see. Well, thank you very much, Mr Henderson.'

Henderson blinked at him.

'Oh,' he said. 'You're going?'

'Yes,' said Cotton.

'But you will see to the funeral expenses?'

'Yes,' said Cotton.

He checked he had the autopsy report and the death certificates, Spanish and British, and offered his hand. Henderson looked at it.

'I don't think we have to stand on any more formalities, Mr Cotton.'

Cotton smiled, admitted to himself that he had enjoyed discomforting the old man, and trotted cheerfully upstairs to his office. An envelope had been pushed under the door. Inside was a large card:

WILLIAM ALEXANDER SIMPSON
NORA MARY COOPER DE SIMPSON

On the back in a florid hand was the date – 9 September 1944 – and the following message: 'We should be so pleased if you could dine with us tomorrow evening, at 9 p.m. Nora Simpson.'

Cotton sat down. Should he know who the Simpsons were? He took out a sheet of paper and wrote, 'I should be delighted to accept your kind invitation. Yours sincerely, Peter Cotton.'

He took the note downstairs to the porter and asked for it to be delivered.

'Without fail,' said Eugenio.

Cotton paused. 'Who actually takes it?' he asked.

'Well, one of my children,' said the porter.

'How many do you have?'

'Eight,' said Eugenio. 'Five boys and three girls.'

'Ah,' said Cotton. 'Is there no charge for doing this?'

Eugenio pushed out his lips and shook his head. 'No, sir.'

Cotton waited. Eugenio raised his eyebrows. 'Lunch?' he said.

Cotton nodded. 'I see,' he said. 'May I ask you a question?'

'*Sí, señor.*'

'How do they pay you your commission?'

'Mostly food,' said Eugenio. '*Cosas que sobran.*' Leftovers.

'Of course. You have a lot of children,' said Cotton. 'All right, Eugenio, you choose for me,' he said.

Years before, Cotton's mother had told him that the word 'caddie' for the person who carries golf clubs round a course comes from the name given to men who carted water, ran errands and delivered mail in the old town of Edinburgh before there was 'proper plumbing and a postal service'. Evidently Cadiz had a version of this. Presumably it wasn't inconvenient for Ramírez either.

Back in his office, Cotton looked over May's autopsy report. There were a lot of pages to it but not many words on each page, and most of those were couched in a very old-fashioned 'By the Grace of God' Spanish and had nothing to do with what Dr Guillén had found. The findings took up only two and a half pages of nineteen, and added nothing to what Cotton already knew.

'*Rico, rico, rico*,' said the porter when he arrived with Cotton's lunch tray. *Rico* means 'rich' – in terms of food, good and tasty.

Cotton paid him and saw what he had brought. The *almejas*, tiny clams, were excellent, but the fried peppers and the *atún encebollado*, a tuna stew, he found rather rich in the English sense. Having eaten and placed the tray outside his door, Cotton tried to stretch out on the sofa, but soon got up.

He opened the safe, took out the petty-cash box, and looked again at the notes in it. He checked the notes against May's codebook, but they were indeed purely personal. He put the notes back in the cash box and put that back in the safe.

Next he sat at the desk and looked at May's notebook. The annotations at the back were disjointed, glum little remarks in the main about Cadiz – 'Churches? Packed. Prisons? Crowded. Hotels? Empty.' Cotton also appreciated 'Without the local language you are the village idiot.'

Cotton sighed and got up. Cadiz was siesta quiet. He closed the shutters and sat down again. Nothing about May's death made much sense. There were no other foreign agents in Cadiz. The Spanish authorities would have no interest in getting rid of May. The only possibility along that line was if May had run into a smuggling operation, possibly run from somewhere in the Spanish government.

And then there was the person Dr Guillén had called May's 'special friend'. If May had been distraught and drunk, he might not have been suicidal, but he could have been wilfully careless. Again, the boy 'from a *very* good family' might have compromised May or been compromised himself. The missing money could have gone on blackmail. But to what end?

Cotton breathed out and shook his head. Was he missing something simple or obvious? He thought again and got out the shipping lists since 31 August. From a smuggler's point of view the first few days of September would have been the time to act, without an Allied witness. But Cotton found there had been little traffic in the port. He made a note of three ships, and sent details of claimed cargoes and destinations to D to have checked. That took him a little time at the coding machine. Then he took rather longer over his next decision. He decided he would say nothing yet to D of May's special friend, having to admit that he had no good reason but was relying on instinct. Or maybe just caution.

Around six, he heard the squeaking and clanking of shop-door grilles and the growing murmur of voices from the street. He got up, pulled back the shutters, and looked out of the window. Tree sparrows squabbled in what he now thought of as Henderson's palm tree. He needed a walk. Cotton locked up and went downstairs. He stepped into the street, turned down an alley, and came to San Francisco.

He ambled, paused, looked. He smelled something fried and sweet, just short of pineapple. This was replaced by fusty ink and paper dust from a stationer's. Then the smell of black tobacco as he passed an *estanco*. Across a small side street was a shop on a corner, one window displaying leather goods, the other ornate fans, lace mantillas, and silk scarves. He looked up. The shop had an Italian name. He went in just for the smell of the leather.

Immediately by the door were two glass-topped cabinets. One contained haircombs in tortoiseshell, black lacquer, ivory and what looked to him like black wood. The other contained hatpins – some very long; some with fantastic heads. He was looking at a miniature silver galleon placed on a pin as long and as wicked-looking as a stiletto, wondering what kind of hat or person that would be for, when a woman close by spoke in German.

'*Was machst du hier?*' What are you doing here? Cotton's German was confined to a number of financial and shipping terms he was happier to read than to say and enough elementary grammar to be confident that the informal or familiar form of 'you' would not be used on him. He looked round to see who she was talking to.

'Yes, you. What are you doing here?'

Cotton considered who was asking him. A very tall, very pale woman of about thirty dressed entirely in white – white dress with large white buttons; close white hat – was frowning at him. She would have been tall anywhere, but in a dark Cadiz shop, with that pallid skin, she looked like a peculiarly imposing ghost. 'I'm looking,' he replied in what he hoped was German. He took a step closer, and the woman became uncomfortable. He wasn't sure if that was the heat or a flush of embarrassment against all that white. She spoke again. Now Cotton was not at all sure. Had she really said, 'You're dishonest'?

92

'Not in my own language,' said Cotton.

She sighed. He was half amused that she should be so deliberate in her manner, as if the puzzle she wanted to solve was impersonal, somehow did not concern him. She raised her chin and spoke again, this time in formal Spanish, but with no shift at all from her German accent, intonation and manner.

'*Usted. ¿Quién es?*' Who are you?

Cotton replied in a Mexican accent. '*Un servidor,*' he said. Your servant.

As Cotton inclined his head in a little bow, he took in that the shop assistants, though ostensibly not looking at two tall, blond foreign people possibly involved in a scene, were beginning to seem alarmed. The German woman paid no attention to them, but concentrated on her problem. Cotton was struck that she had no vanity or pose, but wrinkled her nose and stuck out her lower lip.

'Argentinian?' she asked doubtfully.

'*Tampoco.*' Not that either.

'Well, are you going to tell me or not?' she demanded, using the informal 'you'.

'Isn't it evident?' asked Cotton. 'I'm British.'

Judging by her reaction, it had not been so clear. She frowned. She shrugged. 'I don't know why you have been so coy' – *tan remilgado* – she complained. 'It's not as if we are uncivilized, you know.'

Cotton bowed a little again. 'Peter Cotton,' he said.

They were interrupted by the manager scurrying out. '*Señora, señora,* a thousand apologies for the delay.'

She gave no sign at all that she had seen or heard him. It was, thought Cotton, one way of navigating Cadiz.

'I'm looking for a wallet,' she told Cotton. 'For my husband.'

'I see,' said Cotton. He didn't shrug, but nodded instead.

'Well,' she said, 'you're a man. Help me.'

'We have all kinds of skins,' said the manager – 'snake, crocodile . . . '

'Something plain, something elegant,' said Cotton.

'Black or brown?'

'Oh, black,' said Cotton, as if it mattered to him.

The German woman considered. She nodded. 'Yes,' she said. 'I agree.'

There was a pause. She blinked, then very slowly turned her head and looked at the manager as if it were beyond her that he was still there. As he rushed off, she said, 'The thing for cards.'

The manager pulled up, turned, and acknowledged the instruction. Cotton saw that she had set all the shop assistants in motion, and smiled.

'Have I said something funny?' she asked.

'No,' said Cotton. 'Is your husband German?'

'No,' she said. She thought for a moment and then began to speak in English. 'My husband', she said, 'is a Spaniard.' Her English suited her unvarying German accent rather better than her Spanish did.

'Right,' said Cotton.

'He is a naval architect.'

Cotton nodded.

'He is a very good one.'

'I am sure he is,' said Cotton.

She raised a hand, as if to stop him interrupting. 'We were married in 1939. We have two children, a boy and a girl. I met him first in Germany, where he was finishing his studies. My father is an aeronautical engineer with Junkers. We met again when my father was posted to Spain.'

Cotton felt his eyebrows going up again. Junkers had provided aeroplanes for Franco's forces. But mostly he was impressed by her very serious manner and by her habit of speaking in sentences and of pausing between them. He waited a little to make sure she had finished before responding.

'I am only here for a few days,' he said. 'I am not married.'

For the first time the young German woman smiled – but not, Cotton was clear, at anything he had said. 'My husband is a . . . *tall* Spaniard,' she said, as if reading from an exercise in intonation. 'Actually, his own mother is German.' There was a slightly longer than usual pause after the full stop. 'But she is an unpleasant woman, and we have little contact with her.'

Cotton blinked. The woman looked reasonably content now. He saw that patches of her face powder had melted in the heat. They gave some planes of her face an almost transparent gleam, but some areas looked flushed and dry, almost sore. He doubted that she would match Ramírez's version of open and frank.

She turned towards the counter. '*La cosa de las tarjetas*,' she said. The thing for cards.

She was shown a small red leather box. She opened her handbag, took out some cards, and fitted them in. She slipped one card off the top.

'This will do quite well,' she said, and handed the card to Cotton. He took it and read

IGNACIO DELGADO MAURER
ILSE STROTHE

'I'm very sorry,' he said, 'I don't have a card with me.'

Ilse shrugged, began looking at the wallets. 'You gave me your name. Cotton.' It sounded like 'Gotten'. 'This one or that one?'

One wallet was black and soft, the other blacker, more glazed, and with gold strips at the corners.

'I'd take the plain one,' said Cotton.

'It's not too soft?'

'Not for me.'

She prodded at it, looked slightly doubtful, but nodded. 'The soft one,' she said to the manager. 'Deliver it.' She turned to Cotton. '*¿Cuál es su graduación?*' What is your graduation?

'I graduated in economics.'

'No. In the armed forces.'

'My rank? I was an army captain.'

'Good,' said Ilse. 'Come. I will take you home. You can meet my husband. He would like that.'

'He would?'

'Yes. I said so. In Cadiz we don't meet many sophisticated people.'

Cotton had never thought of himself as particularly sophisticated, but doubted that her idea of sophistication included much in the way of irony or humour. He ushered her out of the shop.

'Our house is quite near,' she said indicating that they walk towards San Juan de Dios. 'Why is it that you are not fighting?'

'I was injured,' said Cotton.

'Wounded,' she said, as if correcting him. She frowned. 'Did you say you weren't married?'

'Yes.'

'Passion is essential in a marriage. You should remember that.'

'I will,' said Cotton. He looked sideways at her. Years before, he had had to spend some school holidays with a maiden aunt. Her old tom cat had developed the habit of depositing voles and mice on the doormat. His aunt had the acquired stiffness of having lived years alone and found the habit distressing, but not for any reasons to do with dead rodents. 'You don't think it is an offering, do you Peter? It's not a *token*, is it? Oh, I do wish you could get him to stop doing it.'

Ilse did live near, in a whole town house. It had nothing ornate around the windows or door, and it was only after a blink that Cotton realized it was relatively new.

'My father-in-law gave it to us as a wedding present,' said Ilse. 'He and my mother-in-law now live apart. It was surplus to their requirements.'

He looked at her. She was still not joking.

A uniformed maid let them in. Instead of tiles there was polished grey granite on the floor, and the inner patio was much more of a reception hall. The stairs were built round three walls in what Cotton thought of as a canti-levered curl with a plain handrail.

'The house is cement and steel,' said the German woman, 'but the steel is rusting. In Cadiz everything rusts.'

At the top of the stairs another maid took their hats. Cotton saw that Ilse had short, very straight, very fine, blonde hair, only darkened where she had sweated. He had to wait for her to rub at her hair and dab some more powder on her face before she pushed open a double door.

They went into a very large room now in near-dark because the three floor-length windows had been shut-tered. At one end were fitted bookshelves and an oil por-trait of Ilse in formal evening wear. At the other was a formal arrangement of furniture by a fireplace. In the middle, sitting in the near-dark in a beige-leather chair by a round table, was a man in pale-blue pyjamas and a dark-blue silk robe. He looked barely awake, but Cotton saw that he had not slept in what he was wearing.

'Look,' said his German wife, 'I've brought someone for you to meet.'

Her Spanish husband rubbed at the bag under his right eye.

'This is Cotton,' she said. 'He is English.'

Very slowly, Ignacio Delgado Maurer hefted himself to his feet. He was indeed tall, was now putting on weight, had rounded shoulders, and was losing some of his wavy hair, particularly at the front of his head. He looked very tired, but was amiable enough.

'*Mucho gusto,*' he said in a hoarse voice, and with one hand on the table he leaned over to offer the other.

Cotton shook his hand. Ignacio pointed him towards a chair and dropped back into his own.

'I bought you a present,' said Ilse. 'They'll deliver it.'

'Have you? Good.' He turned towards Cotton. 'Are you here on war business, Mr Cotton?'

'*Sólo de manera accidental,*' answered Cotton. Only in an incidental way.

Ignacio nodded and cleared his throat. 'Yes, this war of yours,' he said. 'It's a tragedy, an absolute tragedy.'

Cotton stifled a polite shrug. The naval architect raised an index finger.

'It's a tragedy,' said Ignacio, 'because, in a way,' and here he paused for a small smile, 'though I'm surprised to say it, Marx *tenía algo de razón.*' Was part right. 'The educated, the civilizers, of any nationality have more in common than they do with the workers of their own lands. Our civil war was about class, values. England and Germany should not be fighting. Unless against the Russians, of course.'

This was not what Cotton remembered from Marx. Having had the pious platitude about tragedy and war, was he now getting what someone had called 'the steel helmet inside the skull': resolute deafness? Ignacio scratched his cheek. He needed to shave again. Cotton could smell limes and ginger, cologne perhaps, from Ignacio Delgado Maurer, and beeswax polish all around them.

'Well, just look at us here,' said Ignacio, holding out his hands palms up. 'We're talking; we're civilized.'

Evidently civilization, or a fear of being thought uncivilized, mattered equally to both members of this Hispano-German marriage.

The maid came in, bobbed, and put down a silver tray.

'Coffee, Mr Cotton?'

'Thank you. That's very kind.'

'You pour,' said Ignacio to his wife. 'Do you believe you'll win this war?' he asked Cotton.

'Yes,' said Cotton.

'What? You're quite confident about that?'

'Yes.'

Ignacio frowned. 'I see. But what exactly is your confidence based on?'

'The arithmetic.'

'What kind of arithmetic would that be?'

'Britain plus the USA plus the USSR.'

Ignacio blinked, but then smiled and wagged a finger at Cotton. 'Ha! You have a dry sense of humour, Mr Cotton.'

'Not really.'

Ignacio smiled again and shook his head. He knew better. Cotton wondered how much he had annoyed him.

'Still,' said Ignacio, 'the Germans have truly excellent scientists.'

Cotton could not disagree. 'Without any doubt.'

'In my opinion,' said Ignacio, 'the best trained in the world.'

'That's entirely possible,' said Cotton.

Ignacio nodded. 'They have improved the V-1,' he said. 'The doodlebug, no? Isn't that the name you give it?'

'Yes, doodlebug.'

Ignacio smiled at this quaint name, raised his right hand palm down over the table, and waggled it. Cotton took this as a reference to wing-tipping, when a manned British fighter plane endeavoured to send an unmanned V-1 off course by 'tipping' its wing. He guessed that, as a counter-tactic, Ignacio would think that as quaint as the name.

'I understand', said Ignacio, 'that the Germans have just started launching the V-2 at London. A much more advanced and deadly affair. A breakthrough. Certainly technologically.'

Cotton knew nothing of this, but he nodded. 'The Nazis still don't have enough time,' he said.

'But in negotiations?' said Ignacio.

Cotton shrugged. Then, to his surprise, Ignacio shrugged too.

'Oh, you're probably right,' Ignacio sighed. 'Leaders must know their own limitations and what their people can do.'

Cotton looked at him. He was hearing someone adjust his terms of reference to new circumstances while being very anxious to reassure himself he had not been wrong. Then there was another pronouncement.

'A weak country with an authoritarian leader is accept-able to the world. A strong, acquisitive country run by an erratic genius is not.'

Cotton said nothing. He could imagine Ignacio as a tall, plump, obedient boy getting excellent marks in science subjects. He stifled a belch. 'Acquisitive' and 'erratic genius' were presumably references to 'invasive' and 'Hitler'.

'What really worries me', said Ignacio, 'is the concept of democracy.'

Cotton glanced up. The maid and Ilse were putting small bowls on the table.

'Try these,' said Ilse.

They were tiny biscuits. Cotton dutifully took one. It was very sweet, and tasted of coconut. Ignacio looked at the bowls and shook his head. His wife and the maid consulted in whispers. The maid nodded and almost ran out of the room.

'Democracy favours mediocrity and compromise,' said Ignacio. 'That's the point of the arrangement. Kowtowing to and manipulating any idiot with a vote. But tell me, why should my vote count the same as that of a welder? He is obeying my instructions and he has little knowledge of the fuel that powers the flame and none of the stresses a hull is subject to. He doesn't understand what is at stake!'

Cotton was not sure. Here was a rich man in a dictatorship expressing apparently sincere worries about the concept of democracy – there was alarm in his tone – while waiting for his wife and a maid to work out what it might be that he wanted to eat.

Cotton had no wish to get involved in a debate on universal suffrage, nor any particular reason to be rude. 'You are suggesting that democracy has to be developed over time?'

'But that's exactly my point,' said Ignacio. 'In Spain, we're not ready yet. Our lower classes are uneducated; our middle class is small. And we have the complication of religion. Your man Chesterton put it well: when people cease to believe in God, they believe anything. The Reds know this. It has made the rest of us religious for not very good reasons. Our war has put us back a quarter of a century. Your war has put us back another decade. But Franco could give us the foundation to advance if he can consolidate things.' He paused. Perhaps he thought he had sounded too plaintive. 'And you British owe him something.'

'What is that?'

'If he had allowed the Germans access to Gibraltar, you would have lost already.'

'I've heard that theory. Why do you think he didn't?'

Ignacio smiled and looked round as if he had not heard. The maid brought in a bowl of salted almonds. He nodded, picked up an almond, and licked it. Ilse and the maid smiled.

'You British, who think you are winning, are almost as ruined as we are. You'll pay for that confusion later.'

Cotton sighed. Mercifully they were interrupted. Someone began shepherding two small children into the room.

'¡Ah, niños!' exclaimed Ignacio. '*Venid, venid. Tenemos visita. ¿Qué se dice?*' Come, come, we've a visitor. What do you say?

The person shepherding them in was a very striking young woman with red hair. The children were called Adolfo and Inmaculada – Adolf and the Immaculate Conception – the boy blonde, the little girl very dark. Cotton shook hands with them and smiled. The little boy then buried his head in his father's side and muttered something. The little girl took her mother's hand. Cotton looked at the striking red-haired girl, but she was not introduced.

'*¡Que no!*' said Ignacio to his son. '*Papá tiene que trabajar aún más!*' No. Daddy has to work even more. He looked up and smiled. 'If I don't, there will be a big disappointment on Saturday for the *Generalísimo*.'

Cotton smiled back at how important Papa was, noted the point of pride in the naval architect, almost at once felt his smile was becoming fixed because the skin on the back of his neck was contracting. What was it that Marie had said? Franco's movements were kept mysterious. He recalled the Freudian report on Franco at his office. But mostly he remembered what D had said. 'There is a kind of human arithmetic. You may not see the whole sum, but people will give you parts of it. It's probably the most exciting part of the work. Nothing exists in isolation, and someone, whether wittingly or not, will help you put the parts together.' He smiled some more, took part in the handing out of biscuits to the children, looked at a drawing Adolfo had made of Papa's big ship, but then got up to leave.

'I really mustn't keep you,' he said as casually as he could. 'We all have things to do. Thank you very much indeed for all your kindness.'

'*¡Hombre!*' said Ignacio. '*No pasa nada.*' That was nothing.

'I'll get his hat,' murmured the red-haired girl, already moving.

'*La gobernanta*,' said Ignacio, raising his eyes heavenward. The governess. 'From the only English-speaking theocracy in the world. Ireland.'

Cotton nodded and smiled.

'Please call again,' said Ilse. 'We'd like that.'

Cotton smiled again. '*¡Adiós niños!*' Bye-bye children. 'Thank you.'

At the top of the stairs, as he was about to introduce himself, the Irish girl bobbed forward with his hat and whispered.

'Inside the hat.'

'Well, thank you,' said Cotton. His 'You're very kind' was addressed to her back.

A maid saw him downstairs and out of the house. He ran his fingers over the inside hatband, took out the folded note, and put his hat on. He unfolded the note. The handwriting was large, round and uncomplicated.

My day off is tomorrow. I shall be near the Playa Victoria Hotel from 11 a.m. to 2.30 p.m. I would be most grateful if you could meet me there.

Miss Deirdre Carroll

Cotton refolded the note and put it in his pocket. He looked around.

The people of Cadiz were now out in numbers for their Saturday-evening stroll and the murmur of voices had thickened, though still relatively subdued. To his left, his eye was caught by a slim young girl with thick, sleek, almost black hair hanging down her back to her waist. He saw that her arm was firmly under that of a vigilant, girdled matron wearing a black dress, her hair pulled severely back and gathered with a comb in a carefully coiffed bun at the nape of her neck. The girl lifted her free arm and turned her head to point out something to her mother or grandmother. Cotton caught a glimpse of the curve of her neck. Perhaps Byron had been right about the girls of Cadiz, he thought – and then he saw her face and was shocked to see that she could have been no more than twelve or thirteen. The Irish girl had stirred him.

'What have you been doing?' asked Ramírez.

Cotton turned round and looked down. 'Talking about wallets and civilization,' he said.

'What?' said Ramírez. '¿La alemana?' The German woman?

'And her husband. The naval architect.'

'Ya,' He shrugged. 'Do you know what a señorito is?'

Cotton was surprised. Señoritos, or arrogant, rich, landed brats, were famous – and feared – in Andalusia.

'Oh, he's not . . .'

'Es un señorito docto y educado.' A polite, educated brat.

It wasn't a bad description. Not that Cotton showed he thought so. 'Social life for foreigners is exhausting in Cadiz,' he said. 'Tomorrow I have to have dinner with people called the Simpsons.'

He wanted very much to check the polite, educated brat's information on Franco's visit and to consider just how conscious the naval architect had been of his indiscretion, but he knew Ramírez was not going to let him do that. There was nothing specific about Ramírez's intention: he simply had other plans, his own pace, his own way of doing things.

'You've been having a stroll?' said Ramírez.

'Yes.'

'Yes, it helps clear the mind. Good day?'

Cotton nodded, but decided to push a little. 'I really was going back to the hotel,' he said.

'No. That's a dreary place. Come for a walk first,' said Ramírez. 'You could find this interesting. It will give you a better idea of Cadiz.'

Cotton nodded and smiled. 'I am in your hands then.'

Ramírez led the way. They strolled towards San Juan de Dios, but almost at once turned down a street to the right and started threading through a maze of narrow back-streets. The deeper they went into the maze, the stronger the smell of drains. Women were hanging their heads out of the windows above or leaning over the wrought-iron balconies, watching for things to happen. It was so dark at street level some women looked like silhouettes against the sky. A group of three girls walking arm in arm in a dingy, narrow street giggled and nudged each other as they unfurled and passed them in single file but with their arms still linked.

Ramírez paused by a doorway and looked around and up. 'Can you see a number?' he asked.

Cotton stepped back. Numbers were often just above the door, set into the facade. 'It's rather faded, but it says twelve, I think.'

'Yes,' said Ramírez. 'Do you want to see inside?'

'What's there?'

Ramírez smiled. 'You might find it interesting,' he said.

'All right,' said Cotton.

They went in. There had never been anything grand about this place. It was small and shabby and smelled of

mould and limewash. It had the usual central courtyard –
this one small and sloping, the tiles cracked, crumbling
and loose. To one side, in the crook of the stairs, was a
whitewashed well, now peeling and mouldy. Ramírez
pointed upward. 'The rainwater gets channelled down
and is stored in here,' he said.

They looked up. The skylight had several broken panes.

'I suppose they put pots down on the floor here,' said
Ramírez. He smiled without showing his teeth.

'Maybe,' said Cotton patiently.

Ramírez nodded and raised his voice. 'Are you there,
Conchita? It's me.'

A tiny, bony, black-dressed old lady, her back hunched,
what was left of her grey hair scraped back in a bun,
stepped out, then slowly raised her chin so that she could
see them. 'I knew it was you,' she said. 'What do you
want?'

'I want to show my young friend here something.'

'Is he the Englishman?'

'That's it.'

The old lady shrugged. 'You can let yourselves out,' she
said. 'You've no call to disturb me.'

'Wait!' said Ramírez. He turned to Cotton. 'Do you
have any change?'

Cotton put his hand in his pocket and brought out a
few coins. 'A peseta?'

Ramírez shook his head. '*Hombre, no.*' He picked a
twenty-five-centavo piece off Cotton's palm. 'Where shall
I put this, Conchita?' he said, holding up the coin.

Conchita gave him a look. 'You come closer,' she said.
'Now give it here.'

'We won't be long,' said Ramírez.

'It's all the same to me,' said the old lady.

Ramírez and Cotton trudged up the narrow, uneven stairs. The steps were not big enough for his feet, and Cotton had to crouch at the turns so that his head did not hit the steps above. They stopped on the third floor by a thin door that no longer hung straight on its hinges. Ramírez used the handle to lift it up, and then pushed in.

The room was light but basically a wooden shack or shed tacked on top of the house, with an angled roof and a row of small, square windows to the outside. It contained a small table covered with an oilcloth, two rush-seated chairs, and an armchair. Next to an interior window was a birdcage with a moulting canary on a perch. It looked like a sad impostor.

'They don't sing when they're moulting,' said Ramírez.

'No?' said Cotton. He couldn't remember having seen a canary before. The bird looked somehow rudimentary and pale, with nothing of the solid brightness he had seen in tropical birds in Mexico.

To one side of the canary's cage was a kitchen barely bigger than a cupboard. Off the other side was a narrow bedroom containing an old-fashioned hospital bed, another chair with a rush seat, and a sloping wardrobe with no doors but a cheap curtain.

The only other piece of furniture in the room was what looked to Cotton to be a worm-eaten pot stand, here holding a tin basin and jug.

'What do you think?' said Ramírez.

'Monkish,' said Cotton.

'I hadn't thought of that,' said Ramírez. 'I don't think the monks would like you saying that.'

'No? I thought they liked simple things.'

'Oh, there's simple and there's poor,' said Ramírez. 'This is what there is. Everything else is in your office. Poke around. There's nothing.'

They went back into the main room, and Ramírez went to the small, interior window. The pane had been broken, and it had a patch of oiled paper on it. He opened it. 'There's not even much of a view,' he said.

Cotton bent down. The window gave on to a damp blackened wall about six feet away. 'Privacy?' he suggested.

Ramírez laughed. 'I thought you'd like to see it,' he said.

Cotton looked around. 'Why?' he said.

'Mm. Why would May do it, do you think? Why live here like this?'

Cotton shrugged.

'He began in the place you are,' said Ramírez.

'Ah, in that case . . . '

Ramírez shook his head. 'I'll tell you what I think,' he said.

'Do.'

'The hotel made him uncomfortable.'

'It is,' said Cotton.

Ramírez touched his own chest above the heart. 'Here,' he said.

'What? You're not suggesting he felt guilty,' said Cotton.

Ramírez wrinkled his nose and shook his head. 'I think it was worse than that,' he said. 'He tried to get too close. I think he wanted to be one of us.'

He said this so solemnly that Cotton laughed. Ramírez blinked. 'But', he said, 'that's just not possible.'

'I can accept that,' said Cotton. 'But then people do say things to foreigners that they wouldn't say normally . . .'

'Yes, that's very true. But they keep on being foreigners,' said Ramírez.

Cotton smiled. 'I don't think I'm going to be here long enough to find out all the details. The foreigners I'm meeting seem anxious to find out what is happening outside Cadiz.'

Ramírez grudged him a smile. 'Let's go,' he said. 'This is a dosshouse. It depresses me.'

They went downstairs.

'Conchita! We're off.'

He was answered by a grumble, and he smiled. 'She was a whore of some distinction once,' he said as they walked out. 'Now she rents out rooms.' He paused in the doorway. 'I still don't know why May chose this. Any number of people would have been pleased to give him lodgings. And he had a generous allowance.'

'He liked imported whisky,' said Cotton.

'Yes?' said Ramírez. 'Would you like me to accompany you back to your hotel?'

'If I'm not keeping you from anything.'

'No, no,' said Ramírez. 'You're probably right.'

'About what?'

'That May was a spendthrift. I did worry what he was doing with his money.'

'We have an allowance,' said Cotton, 'but it's not that much. He probably rearranged his expenditure according to his priorities.'

'I wasn't sure if he was being charitable or if he was being robbed.'

'A bit of both?'

'Yes. Terrible thing. He wanted so much to be liked. It's a weakness.'

'Mm,' said Cotton.

Ramírez put a hand on his forearm. 'You can't replace knowledge of a place with sentiment about it.'

They had barely moved from May's old lodgings when Ramírez stopped and turned round.

Coming after them down the street was a man . . . what was the word? Sashaying? Shimmying? He had one hand on his left hip and the other extended outward, and he placed each step directly in front of him. Though dressed in a man's suit, those were black suede pumps he was wearing, and his shirt looked like a blouse. He was wearing more than a little rouge on his cheeks, and had kohl on his eyes. But most remarkable was his dyed hair. The man was bald, but had grown the hair at the sides of his head long enough to tie up as a topknot.

'¿Me encuentras atractiva, guapo?' he said to Cotton as he passed. Do you find me attractive, handsome?

'Hoy no, Gloria,' said Ramírez. Not today, Gloria.

Gloria laughed, pitching extravagantly between false and falsetto, but when past he spoke up in a firm, natural voice. 'Puto cabrón.' Fucking bastard.

'Ése sí que quiere morir,' sighed Ramírez. That one does want to die.

Cotton saw that Gloria had parted the back of his jacket and tucked the two flaps into his waistband. This revealed the shiny seat of his trousers and gave a kind of bustle effect. He sighed.

'What?'

'Nothing,' said Cotton, but he did wonder if Ramírez had arranged this too.

'I can only do what I can,' said Ramírez.

'Yes.'

But Ramírez had not finished. 'I keep things quiet. I can cover them up. But I can't change them.'

'I understand,' said Cotton.

'You do? Good,' said Ramírez. He nodded again, stopped nodding, looked down the street again. 'I can't provide solutions,' he said. 'I can know what is happening, but I can't solve things.'

'I understand,' said Cotton.

'This way. It's easy to get lost here.'

'Yes, everyone says it's a maze.'

Ramírez shook his head. 'Not if you live here,' he said.

Strolling back, they saw a priest with a handbell outside a church. He rang it three times, paused, rang three times again.

'Late Mass?' said Cotton. He looked at his watch. It was just after 10 p.m.

'No,' said Ramírez gloomily. 'Open-air cinema.'

Cotton looked at him.

'Censorship,' said Ramírez. 'He doesn't approve of the film. He thinks Judy Garland is a bad influence.'

Cotton smiled.

'The *Generalísimo* likes cinema. They say he even scripted a film – under a pseudonym, of course.'

'Really?'

'Yes, yes. Called *Raza*.' *Raza* means 'race' or 'breed'.

'Good?'

'Not bad. Of course, soldiers usually swear.'

'I don't think they swear much in English films.'

'Ah, but do they speak in *ñoñerías*?' *Ñoñerías* are euphemisms. Ramírez gave him an example. '*Dicen córcholis por cojones.*' They say 'blast' instead of 'balls'.

Cotton thought. 'I think the British prefer the officer using polite irony.'

They were near San Francisco again, and the noise level was now strident. The street was crowded enough to make movement without contact impossible. The din was good-natured enough, but some of the children were fractious, and quite a number of adults had drunk too much. Suddenly Ramírez tensed up. Against a wall a drunk was muttering at anyone female. Cotton heard, '*Te como. Patata. Conejito.*' I'll eat you. Potato. Little Rabbit. Spanish has a long tradition of *el piropo*, of males paying compliments to young women as they pass by. This man had gone directly to the long list of words provided by Montserrat Gil – as she had put it, 'as long as the incredible offer to satisfy the female parts alluded to'.

'*Perdóname,*' Ramírez said, and he leaped across the road to smack the man across the face. '*¡Tus soeces a casa! ¡Ya!*' Take your filth home! Now!

Cotton blinked. The strollers of Cadiz did not stare at Ramírez. Muttering, but now indistinctly, the man shuffled away. Ramírez sniffed. He was a little out of breath. When he came back, Cotton nodded.

'When do children in Cadiz go to bed?'

Ramírez looked genuinely surprised. 'When they're tired, of course. What else?'

After he had said goodbye to Ramírez, Cotton went directly to the dining room and ordered something to eat. He was still the only person there. The light was wretched, but he noticed that he had been given a clean cloth and, unasked, the old woman brought him a dish of olives while she was preparing his supper. She gave him gazpacho, a swordfish steak and lemon rice.

He went to bed about eleven thirty, and found the maid turning down the bed. She was very young – no more than eleven or twelve – and looked very scrawny under her uniform. One side of her straight, black hair was kept back by a cheap hair clasp.

'Are you the person who unpacked my suitcase?'

The girl looked alarmed.

'¿Señor?'

Cotton smiled. 'No, no, there's nothing wrong. I wanted to give you a tip for looking after me.'

The poor girl gave an anxious little bob-cum-curtsy.

'Is that your grandmother downstairs?'

'No, señor,' she whispered. 'I'm from the *Casa del Niño Jesús*.' The House of the Baby Jesus. 'I'm an orphan.'

Cotton smiled and gave her the money. 'Keep it for yourself,' he said. 'Will you do that?'

'I will, *señor. Gracias,*' said the girl, and fled.

Cotton closed the shutters but opened the windows and sat in the dark in his little sitting room. He could hear hushing, the hiss of frying, and the loud clatter of plates. A couple of drunks were giggling and singing. For the first time he thought there might just be a touch of chill in the air, or at least something less brackish. He breathed in and shook his head. There was no trace of any chill. How did the people of Cadiz sleep enough to think? This was not the intimacy that Marie and Houghton had mentioned. It was more tall houses, very narrow streets, and many open windows. '*¡Que te calles!*' a woman shrieked. Shut up – at full volume. Then the sound of a slap and a child wailing. Cotton thought he would sleep with earplugs.

Since he had left the army, Cotton had had the habit, when he was thinking of sleep, of mulling over his day. There was nothing structured about this. He thought of it as trawling, to see if he had missed anything. He relaxed, and viewed what came to mind.

He was now struck that Ignacio Delgado Maurer's German wife, Ilse, had spoken peremptorily in the leather shop, but had barely said a word at home – instead, had been modest and attentive. He was not sure whether or not Ignacio himself was more than a gratefully conservative beneficiary of Franco's victory. And then there was the appetizing Irish girl. He didn't know if all those well-rounded letters in her note meant she had anything to say, but he was quite happy to see her again. He toyed a little with the word 'governess', but shrugged and put his feet up on the low table. His back started sweating against the

116

leather of the chair. He took off his shirt and placed a towel behind him.

Mostly, however, he considered May. He had heard the pathologist say May was distraught, he had heard Henderson's opinion that May was 'letting us down', and now he had seen where May had chosen to live. He mulled a while. Had May suffered some sort of breakdown? Come unravelled in Cadiz? And why just then – why in July? Well, there was his friend's call-up. But how did the German agent's going influence things?

Suddenly he knew. The German had gone because of Allied pressure on Franco. From May's point of view, it meant that the Allies were dealing with Franco in ways they would never deal with Hitler. If you are dealing with someone, you give him a degree of legitimacy. Was that why he had requested the Freudian report on Franco? More to the point, had that 'I am Spain' business from Auden meant something to May? Was Ramírez right in his reading of May as someone with more sentiment than knowledge? Had May thought the Allies were betraying the Spanish people by negotiating with Franco?

Cotton grimaced. It did not make sense then that May had spent enough money to attract his bosses' attention and had then not justified his expenditure, drawing enough attention to himself to end up getting replaced. If he had had a plan for something, surely he could have disguised it. Never stifle your instinct. D had said that. It's often right.

Cotton sighed and rubbed his eyes. He listened. It was a little quieter perhaps, but not much. He felt tired. He thought he was having to invent too much of May. At the same time, he had no intention of being bitten by a dead man, however distraught or confused. He got up, wiped down his chest, and went looking for something that would do for earplugs.

5

ON SUNDAY morning, Cotton woke at first light. He had the sensation of something odd and unfamiliar. He removed his earplugs and listened. Nothing. He blinked. That was the point. There were no sounds. He listened carefully. Cadiz was silent.

He got up and looked out and, apart from a drunk asleep on a bench, the view was empty of people. Pleasantly surprised, he decided then to go for a walk before the city had woken and while the air was at its freshest.

By the time he was out – he had already heard a loud yawn nearby – there was some noise, but the sounds were relatively sparse: someone brushing a street some distance away; a creak as someone opened a front door and stretched. He set off along Canalejas, and turned into Plaza de San Juan de Dios. A little to his left in front of him was the town hall, but it was the view ahead of him to his right – the cathedral, with its dull yellow cupola showing above roof level – that he concentrated on.

At first he looked up at the four-, sometimes five-storey houses, some with elaborate wrought-iron balconies. Some balconies had been glazed and shuttered in. Some simply had a rudimentary blind stretched out from the top of a window over the balcony railing.

When his route narrowed in the streets off the square, Cotton realized the city combined a sundial and maze. There were streets in Cadiz that were fully lit only when the sun was overhead. In the early morning it meant that sunlight reached only the upper floor of the buildings on one side of the street – occasionally more when a building to the east was lower. It made for very sharply drawn shadows, and sections of street that were both marginally chilled and very dark. It meant that he stumbled on uneven cobbles if he didn't keep his eyes on the ground. So he walked on head down, registering changes through the shadows that fell on him – like that of a cross-beam propping up two houses on either side of a street as narrow as the distance between his outstretched arms. Drainage was obviously a problem in a place so near sea level. In one place the pavement was not so much up as missing, and he saw that the undersoil was simply sand. As he walked, he stopped from time to time to take his bearings, looking out for a glimpse of the yellow cathedral cupola at crossroads, to see if he was on track.

In the event he was already too close to see where he was, and almost thought he had gone wrong when he saw a dour expanse of grubby stone in front of him. From close up, without the benefit of light and distance, the cathedral was an inelegant blending of two stones and styles as cash and architectural fashion had come and gone. The building was ugly, still not finished, but suffering erosion where softer stone had been used. Some nets had been hung around the towers, presumably to catch or brake falling stones. The main door was studded and resembled the entrance to a castle, so that there was something stolidly religious and fancifully military about it.

Cotton did not linger. He turned right, and found himself walking on cobbles so potholed and uneven that he banged an ankle. He must, he thought, have looked like someone trying to cross a river on stepping stones.

And then he found himself looking across a bright, tongue-shaped open space at the Post Office. He had never thought of a post office as being an aggressive building before. This was pseudo-Moorish brick, a little fortress with shot holes, letterboxes in the shape of lions' mouths and, on one wall, another black stencilled portrait of a Spanish Civil War hero. Thinking of firing angles, Cotton looked past the Post Office to the left and saw the central market, a large, low, shabby structure decked about with bleached awnings. It was lit by the sun as if in a kitsch sepia print of an Arab street market.

Cotton turned right again and then kept going. The street was dark but relatively straight. He turned down a short side road and then, blinking, stepped out into dazzling light and space. In Cadiz, the only real vistas were out to sea or across the bay, and then he had to squint. You could have walls or you could have sun.

He took his bearings. His hotel was to his left; his office down to his right along the avenue that faced the port and the bay. Canalejas was, for most of its length, divided down the middle by a garden with a fountain at one end. This was the only street he had so far seen in Cadiz that was comfortably wide enough for cars and trolleys in both directions. He looked at his watch. His walk had taken no more than twenty-five minutes.

However maze-like Cadiz might seem at first, it was a tight, compact maze. Church bells began ringing, though tolling was probably a better description.

Cotton turned right and went directly to his office. There was a message to decode. It was a routine contact, and included the usual sort of joke – this one about Don Juan's tutor, also eaten by sailors. By now he was getting accustomed to the code and was taking much less time to decipher and to draw up his own messages.

He sent a message about Franco's visit: 'Check Lambro in Cadiz next Saturday 16th. Unconfirmed report. Pedrillo.' He looked out at the port. One thing about the binoculars: they sharpened a view of nothing much happening. There was no visible maritime traffic, but he could see a group of dockers waiting to be selected. Some of the houses in Cadiz had lookout towers for merchants waiting for the sight of a sail returning from South America. Cotton turned away. He had breakfast sent up. He traced his route of that morning on the map, and checked some of the street names: Prim, Columela. Then he heard a ship's whoop. He went to the window. Out in the bay a tramp steamer from Argentina was calling for a tug and a pilot to bring it into port. He watched the tug cast off, then locked up and went down to the avenue and across the garden to the taxis. Today was a petrol day.

'*¿Adónde?*' said the taxi driver. Where to?

'*Al cementerio británico, por favor,*' said Cotton.

'Hm. No favour about it,' said the taxi driver huffily.

Cotton had forgotten that in Spain, please – *por favor* – can be taken as sarcastic. He got in.

'Are you the Englishman?' said the taxi driver.

'Yes, I'm English,' said Cotton.

'I knew it,' said the man, looking at Cotton through the driving mirror.

They drove up the Cuesta de las Calesas, the only thing resembling a steep slope in the town, with the railway station and the bay down to the left, and the tobacco factory – another pseudo-Moorish brick building – to the right. There was a steady trickle of people walking up the dusty hill towards the sound of church bells. The women, wearing black veils and carrying rosary beads and missals, herded and scolded their children. The men had replaced their working overalls with white shirts and uncomfortably fitting suits, and were walking at a dignified distance ahead of their families. The taxi drove on past a large convent and church, and some shabby houses. At the top of the slope on the left was the Palacio de Justicia – the law courts – and a little further on stood a wide, stone city wall, with turrets, a flag and two cherubic saints in armour on high plinths. They drove though the left-hand arch.

'*Puerta de Tierra*, the city gates,' said the taxi driver. 'They killed some Reds there in what they call a glacis or something. Like a very big ditch.'

Cotton saw that the ditch had been filled in. 'Are they still there?'

The driver laughed, and Cotton saw him glance up at the rear-view mirror. '*No creo*,' he said chattily. I don't think so. '*Ahora tenemos orden.*' Now we have order. 'We needed it.'

Cotton nodded. In one way it was something of a relief to find someone not frightened or anxious to show that, while they lived in a dictatorship, they were not part of it.

'I owe everything to General Varela,' said the taxi driver.

'¿*De veras?*' Really?

'*Hombre, el coche.*' The car. 'He kept his word, put me at the top of the waiting list.'

Cotton wondered vaguely what service the driver might have provided to be so rewarded, but did not ask.

They were now out of Cadiz proper, but, despite the newly reinforced limits to the old city, the spit was undergoing some sort of development. There were shabby marine warehouses and workshops, a munitions factory to the left, a few villas and gardens behind walls, some scruffy allotments, some milk cows in a pen, a school for girls, and then a large army barracks on one side of the road and a bullring on the other. As they passed the barracks, Cotton saw '*Todo por la Patria*' – Everything for the Fatherland – in gold letters above the main entrance. Soldiers with rifles were standing in sentry boxes on either side.

And then, a little before a sandstone eighteenth-century church, they turned left down a dusty, rutted road with single-storey houses – reminiscent of a western film, thought Cotton. They went all the way along and stopped just before a level crossing. To the left were a wine bodega and a wrought-iron gate in a high wall that had not been limewashed for years.

'You've arrived,' said the taxi-driver. 'This is the British Cemetery.'

'Will you wait?' asked Cotton.

'*¡Hombre!* I have the car. What I need is business. Of course I'll wait.'

When Cotton got out of the taxi, he was assaulted by a rancid smell of old sugar and stale vinegar from the bodega. He held his breath and tried the gate. It was locked. To one side was a square hole in the wall, and, by bending, he saw there was a bell pull. He pulled. Something like a cowbell clonked. Nothing happened. He squinted through the gate. There appeared to be more vegetation in the British Cemetery than in the rest of Cadiz. He could hear, rather than see, a dovecote. The pigeons thrummed and cooed; the leaves seemed to increase the reverberation, make it a distilled, liquid accompaniment to the silence.

'*¿Qué quiere usted?*' said a voice.

'Who is that?' said Cotton.

An old man with a broken straw hat reluctantly stepped sideways into view. 'What do you want?' he repeated.

'I want to see a grave, please,' said Cotton.

The old man squinted. 'Have you permission?'

'Yes.' Cotton showed his ID.

'It's Sunday.'

'Yes,' said Cotton. 'Is that a problem?'

'I need a paper from Mr Henderson.'

'I have already spoken to Mr Henderson. You have a new grave.'

'That's true,' said the old man, peering. 'Is he a relative of yours?'

'Look,' said Cotton, 'this is undignified. Open the gate, please.'

The old man considered him. 'Well,' he said frankly, 'I'll let you in because of your manner and your clothes.'

'Very kind, thank you,' said Cotton.

'I have to get the key,' said the old man.

Cotton waited. The pigeons thrummed. The old man returned with a large, very rusty key, which he was rubbing with an oily rag.

'It stuck at the funeral,' he said. 'Mr Henderson was angry.'

Cotton could imagine that. 'I'm sorry to hear it.'

But the key worked, and Cotton was let in.

'I have to lock up at all times,' said the old man.

'I understand,' said Cotton.

Between the bodega wall and the old man's shack-like house there was a narrow walk. The bodega wall was thickly covered with vines the old man had trained on to overhead wires in a kind of pergola. Bunches of nearly ripe white grapes hung down like weird lanterns. Cotton had to move his head to avoid them. At the end of the short walk, between the last pergola post and the end of the old man's one-room house, there was a small vegetable patch of tomatoes, peppers and *habas* or beans and a paved area for stonemasonry. On a gravestone, someone had drawn out 'RONAL AL MAY' in blue chalk.

'Will you do the stone-cutting?' asked Cotton.

'No,' said the old man. 'There's a man who comes in. They just paid for ten letters.'

Cotton nodded. He thought he should ensure that May retain his name at least, and, after some fiddle and wipe he produced 'RONALD A MAY'.

'Is that clear?'

The old man shrugged and scratched his forehead. 'Well,' he said obligingly, 'It seems all right to me. The grave is this way.'

The cemetery was not much bigger than a suburban garden, and in no way big enough for the massive, mottled trees that inhabited it. Tree roots had pushed gravestones aside, cracked slabs, and invaded the paths. It was almost like being in a rank, green room. Leaves shrouded the view to the sky and filtered the light like a lamp Cotton remembered in his maiden aunt's house: she had called it art nouveau, but it had always struck him as modified Moroccan, being made of stained glass with a kind of close-fitting fretwork metal cap.

'This is the nicest garden I have seen here,' said Cotton. 'It's marvellous.'

'There's no gardener just now,' said the old man. 'Mr Henderson is looking for one. Do you wish me to show it to you?'

'Yes, thank you.'

The old cemetery guard pointed to a newish patch of earth, which was already drying out. 'Your relative,' he said, and took a step backwards.

Cotton was about to correct him, but decided to do May some sort of justice. He paused for a minute or so of silence, mumbled 'Poor bastard', but then could not come up with anything more fitting. He did think, What were you doing? What did you think you were doing? He nodded. 'Well,' he said with a try at a sigh, 'show me the graves.'

The old man took him around. Although it was called the British Cemetery, it was where all non-Catholic foreign nationals were buried. There were some interesting graves. There was a wonderful white marble slab, entirely covered in cursive French, for the Russian consul of his Imperial Majesty the Tsar of all the Russias. Cotton noted that he had died on 17 October 1917. He was not sure about the precise dates of the Russian Revolution and the difference in calendars. Had this florid-sounding person died without knowing? They walked on and stopped at a curious brick grave, round at one end, square at the other, built into an angle of the path. It bore no name.

'*Judío*,' said the old man. A Jew.

'Surely it's pointing towards Mecca,' said Cotton.

'It's all the same to me,' said the old man simply. 'I was told he was a Jew. You've got to walk on him in any case, to get round.'

There were stones with lists of children – Cotton saw one with the names of nine infants engraved, followed by their mother – and there were stones that complained: 'Sent here for his health, 6 June 1876, but died 9 June 1876'. Cotton saw that an angel had lost its head over a slab on which the lettering had worn away; a lizard basked on the neck. A little further on there was a rusty, cracked cast-iron grave, absurdly like a fanciful water cistern, commemorating an engineer. And then, slightly separated from the rest, was a clump of markers in rotting wood: 'Fell from the main mast . . .', 'Fell from the quay in drink . . .' Cotton counted nine men who, on shore leave, had fallen into the sea and drowned. Six others had been knifed – 'Who met his end in a common brawl . . .' And there was one in which a word had been cut out of the wood and a blank section substituted – an eight-lettered word preceded by 'foully'. And then, finally, on the wall by the railway line, barely visible in the shadows, was the commemoration in blue and yellow tiles of the five drowned sailors, donated by Henderson's British Community in the Province of Cadiz.

'*Gracias*,' said Cotton to the old man as they turned back.

When they got to the gate, he put his hand in his pocket.

'No, no. I am an employee of the British government,' said the old man.

Cotton acknowledged this with a small bow. 'Well, many thanks.'

'Not at all,' said the old man.

The taxi had turned and was waiting for him. Cotton got in.

'Our cemetery is over there,' said the driver, pointing a finger through the windscreen – 'a little way along from the bullring. Yours is a lot quieter.'

'Yes.'

'Back?'

'No. Take me to the Playa Victoria.'

'The hotel?'

'Yes. But pull up short.'

'Done,' said the taxi driver.

As they drove further down the spit, away from the town, Cotton looked left across the bay to Spain, then out to sea on his right. Inland the sky was a darker blue; out to sea the blue was paler, but high above the horizon were touches of faint yellow and rather more patches of pale rust.

'That's African dust in the air,' said the driver.

They turned right into a square in front of the hotel, a stolid, white edifice with side wings and a pseudo-Moorish dome on the main block. Constructed half on the beach, it had the look of a disproportionate bunker. Cotton paid the driver, got out, and walked towards the hotel.

Miss Deirdre Carroll was standing just to the right of the entrance in a fitted green dress with yellow lozenges on it. She raised her arm, but not for him. It was to secure her hat from the small gusts of wind coming in on the tide.

Cotton raised his own hat and smiled. 'Miss Carroll,' he said. 'I'm sure it will be less windy inside.'

'What?' said Miss Carroll. 'Oh, I'm not going in there, Mr Cotton.'

Cotton was already looking in. There was a palm room set out with plants and round tables and wicker chairs, and he could see a pair of elderly ladies wearing old-fashioned hats with the kind of hatpins he had seen in the Italian shop. Serving them ice cream were waiters, while beside them two army officers wearing shiny riding boots looked round at him. They looked like adult grandchildren rather than gigolos.

'No?' he said, though already half in agreement.

'No,' said Miss Carroll.

Cotton smiled. She really was remarkably pert and pretty. 'Well, shall we walk then?'

'Yes.'

So they turned and strolled along the promenade towards Cadiz. Despite the heat it was no longer the bathing season, and there were few people down on the beach: some fishermen mending nets by some upturned boats, and a group of men repointing the retaining wall. From this angle there was a clear view down the spit towards Cadiz itself. At that distance and in that light the dome of the cathedral gleamed, and the blue sky above the town looked contained by a violet and silver strip in the shape of a croquet hoop.

After the British Cemetery, the comparison cheered him. He glanced at his companion. What was the word? *Apetitosa*.

'Mr Cotton.'

'Yes?'

'I'm just desperate.'

'What?' said Cotton. He pulled up, and so did she. Behind her the sea flickered. No longer quite calm, the water was catching sunlight in a kind of rapid fire.

'It's my *moral* status,' she pronounced, half mouthing her indignation.

'Your what status?' said Cotton, though he had heard what she said.

She began walking again, but this time tilting towards him as though she were confiding to the top pocket of his jacket. She had put her hair up, and he could see small beads of sweat on the fuzz of her neck.

'I need a good moral report to *stay* here,' she said. She took a deep breath. 'I need a good moral report to *go*!'

Cotton nodded. 'You'll have to explain that. A sort of good-conduct certificate? Is that it?'

She straightened up. 'That's it. And it's official. It's from the authorities, and I can't move on without it.'

'I see. And where is the problem?'

'My employers have to sign the paper and put it in.'

'And they won't?'

'It's that man! He's an absolute satyr!'

Satyr? She was talking of Ignacio, the naval architect with an interest in civilization, married to the German Ilse with a similar interest.

'He's careless with his hands, if you take my meaning. It's as if I'm a soft part of the furniture.'

Cotton's eyebrows came up at her language, but he nodded.

'Well, I know the Spanish are much more physically demonstrative than we are,' she said, 'but I am sure this is not right.'

'I see,' said Cotton. What was it D had said? You think you are looking for facts, but you are always dealing with people. 'But are you really saying you won't get a good moral evaluation unless you – how do I put this? – compromise your morality?'

She did not reply, but she did blush.

'I am so sorry, Miss Carroll,' said Cotton – 'have I got that wrong?'

She did not reply, but blushed even more.

'Miss Carroll?'

'You don't understand!' she burst out. '*She* doesn't think highly of me either. She thinks I'm weak.'

Cotton frowned. 'Now why would she do that?'

'She seems to think I'm neither one thing nor the other. I talked to her, as discreetly as I could, you know. She just looked at me. In that way she has. Told me to grow up. Take things in my stride. As if morals were innocent! Or something just for children!'

Cotton nodded. 'Oh, dear,' he said, mostly to himself.

'I'm living in a purgatory, I am.'

Just then there was another, quite sharp, gust of wind. The Irish girl let out a yelp and thrust her skirt between her legs with one hand and clapped the other just below her rear. It is difficult to be prim and elegant at the same time.

Miss Carroll next had to tackle her wobbling hat, and she did that by crouching cross-kneed to trap her skirt and free up a hand.

Cotton grunted. 'Let's get out of this, shall we? Would you like some coffee?'

She surprised him. 'Oh, I'm really a tea drinker,' she said.

'We'll see what they have then,' said Cotton.

'Maybe juice,' said the girl.

'Possibly,' said Cotton.

They crossed the road and sat in the shelter of a wall outside a café. Miss Carroll decided on *tila*, an infusion from the linden leaf – 'For my nerves,' she said. Cotton had never heard of it. Politely he asked her if she wanted something to eat. She said she wanted angel-hair cake. Cotton looked at her again.

'Angel hair?' he said. '*Cabello de ángel?*'

'Oh, it's made of pumpkin and sugar,' said Miss Carroll. 'I've a very sweet tooth.'

Cotton ordered the infusion and the cake for her, and coffee and water for himself. Despite himself, he was depressed sitting opposite the very pretty girl. He remembered a conversation with his dead fiancée.

'Could you explain the difference between lust and love?' she had asked him.

'I think people say "passion" instead of "lust", and get over it that way.'

She had laughed. He had met her in the summer of 1943 in Peaslake on the northern slope of the Hurtwood Forest on the Surrey/Sussex border, when she had been visiting her aunt and he had been convalescing at the Arts and Crafts house his father had bought in 1932. 'Peaslake,' she had said: 'home of smugglers, Quakers and a refuge for suffragettes.' Her aunt, then 'a potter on a private income', had once been a suffragette, 'That's why I have this terrible name. Emmeline.'

'Do you want salts in the water?' asked the waiter.

'What? No. Thank you.' He turned his attention back to Deirdre Carroll. 'What is it you think I could do to help?'

'Well, you've met them. At their level. You could maybe intercede?'

Cotton looked at her. 'Did they tell you to talk to me?'

'No! If they knew I was speaking to you they'd have a fit!'

Cotton closed one eye, then opened it again. He was not sure if he had just performed a demure wince or not. It was clear she had nothing to do with his job in Cadiz, and all this trite, prudish, down-to-earth innocence was driving him to distraction.

'Quite what action do you want to take?' he said.

Miss Carroll thought. 'I think I just want to get out of here, Mr Cotton. I do. But my options are severely curtailed.'

Curtailed? Cotton nodded. The waiter approached and served them. To Miss Carroll he gave a small, square slice of what looked like honeyed pastry. On top of it were some silvery and transparent strands, and on top of those a red glacé cherry. Miss Carroll used her pastry fork to spear the cherry, and started nibbling at it with very white teeth between her rather full lips.

'It's just too sticky to eat with fingers,' she explained.

Cotton cleared his throat and stirred at the coffee. 'Why did you come here in the first place?'

She pulled the cherry off the fork, chewed, and swallowed. 'Mr Cotton,' she said, looking askance at him, 'I am from County Cork. I had this or being a nun.'

'I see,' said Cotton. He breathed out. 'A simple choice can turn out to be complicated.'

'Oh,' said Miss Carroll. 'There you have it exactly.' She used her fork to cut into the cake. 'I sometimes wonder, you know, if my parents had any idea of what I was letting myself in for.'

'I don't imagine they did. Tell me, did you ever know a man called May?'

'What? This is a very small place, Mr Cotton. I knew *of* him, if you understand me, but I'm not one for gossip – not of that kind.'

'He didn't come to your house?'

'No, no,' said Miss Carroll.

'Who does?'

Miss Carroll thought. 'Well, not that many people actually. Señor Delgado works a lot, and . . . well, she doesn't have many friends really. I don't think she's very popular, you know, with the locals.'

'But some people come to the house.'

'Rich people mostly. Engineers, lawyers. Oh, and his brother. He's a doctor in the navy.'

'What do they talk about?'

Miss Carroll shrugged.

'Franco?' said Cotton.

Miss Carroll showed a little shock. 'Oh, they are not very respectful. But he is the head of state after all.' She leaned forward. 'They call him "shortlegs" in private, as if that was vulgar.'

Cotton sighed. He almost said, 'Well, that's privacy for you.' He chose something else instead. 'But what is it I can actually do for you, Miss Carroll?'

'Help with my moral papers, Mr Cotton. Then I can leave. But I need the moral papers for my reputation. You do understand that, don't you? It's all a girl has. Ireland is a Catholic country, like Spain. Any employer will want the two years I've been here properly accounted for.'

Cotton nodded. 'I see.' The imprimatur on a good girl.

'And you do move in different circles,' said Miss Carroll.

'I'll do what I can,' said Cotton. 'But you do know I'm only here for a few days, and that I'm British and you're Irish and Ireland is a neutral country.'

'Like Spain,' said the girl. 'It's just nice to meet a gentleman who is one, if you know what I mean.'

He obliged with a brief smile, and watched her finish her cake.

Miss Carroll wiped her rather full lips on the tiny paper napkin provided and suffered what Cotton had seen with some smokers: a layer of paper stuck to her lower lip, and she had to lick her finger and unpick it.

'I can only do what I can do, Miss Carroll.' Cotton thought he was beginning to sound like Ramírez.

'Oh, I know,' said Miss Carroll. She began using her upper teeth on her lower lip.

Cotton called the waiter and paid.

'Thank you so much, Mr Cotton,' said the girl. She leaned forward. 'I've nothing on my . . . ?'

'No.'

She sat back. 'Then perhaps it would be better if I waited.'

'What?' said Cotton.

'You get the first tram. I'll wait for the next.'

Cotton nodded and shifted his chair back. It made a grinding noise he had not intended.

'Right,' he said, as he got up. 'Let's do that.'

'I'm very grateful, Mr Cotton.'

'I haven't done anything yet,' said Cotton.

'Truly grateful,' said Miss Carroll.

'Do take care, Miss Carroll.'

'Oh, I will. Thank you again for the tea and cake.'

Cotton strode briskly back to the square in front of the hotel and jumped on a tramcar. He tried to sit down, but he was not built to scale and could not get his knees into the gap between his wooden seat and the back of the one in front. So he stood and held on to a strap that ended below his shoulder level.

'¡*Que no veo!*' complained someone. I can't see!

So Cotton sat as it were side-saddle, bringing in his legs when someone else got on or off as the tram clanked back

137

to Cadiz along the scruffy spit. He saw he was gripping the seat in front of him hard enough to make the knuckles of his hand white. He closed his eyes. He would never know whether or not his marriage to Emmeline would have worked. He opened his eyes. Think simple. Think plain. Don't get distracted.

A little before the city gates the tram passengers quietened down. Cotton looked round. Ramírez smiled.

'*Buenos días, Don Pedro*,' he said. 'Enjoying your Sunday?'

'I've been talking to an Irish girl.'

'The governess?'

'Yes. She wants to leave.'

'What? *¿Le han metido mano?*' Someone has been free with their hands? '*¿Él o ella?*' Him or her?

'She says him.'

Ramírez shook his head. '*Es una pava aún.*' She's still a turkey – meaning an excitable, silly adolescent.

'She needs what she calls her moral papers.'

'*Claro*,' said Ramírez. On that she is right. He looked round and smiled. 'That one needs to put her finger through a ring before you can put . . . '

'Thank you. She asked for help.'

'Can you give it?'

'No.'

Ramírez nodded. 'All right, I'll see what I can do.'

'Thank you.'

Ramírez sighed. 'Have you learned anything new?'

Cotton knew he meant more than about the governess. 'Not much. Perhaps that foreigners get confused and overly dramatic.'

Ramírez smiled. 'You see. I have to get off now. I'll see you around.'

Ramírez got up and hissed at the driver. The tram halted between stops. Ramírez clambered down and started walking towards the law courts. Cotton saw that it took a few minutes for the noise level to rise again. The only other person he had seen in Cadiz who had that effect was Ilse.

Cotton got off at the first stop on Canalejas, so that he could stretch his legs on his way back to his office.

'Please, I don't want to be disturbed,' he said to Eugenio on his way in.

The little man straightened up and looked serious. 'Rely on me' was the reply.

Cotton used the lift. He felt heat-weary. The pace and the pettiness of Cadiz were getting to him. But there were some simple compensations. His body was getting back into balance. On his floor, he went to the WC and urinated in a quantity and colour he recognized. He washed his hands and let himself into his office. He was half amused at how nervous he was. He wanted to find messages waiting for him, so that he might know he was in touch with someone outside. He was asking for luck on a Sunday.

And he got it. He had a message from London.

Madrid cannot confirm Lambro visit. But Lisbon says Iberian Summit definite and can confirm Portuguese navy preparing flotilla. D.

Cotton knew that Lisbon was a much better place than Madrid to acquire information. He was now certain

Ignacio's information had been accurate, was fairly sure the naval architect had merely been boasting of his status in Franco's Spain, had had no other objective.

There was another message waiting: '*Rumor. Malbro se va a tu Puerto. Baba.*' Rumour. Malbro is going to your port. From Houghton. Cotton blinked. The message was a variation on the French song 'Mambru *s'en va-t-en guerre*'. Houghton's 'Malbro' was a rearranged 'Lambro', or Franco. It wasn't much of a joke, but Cotton was grateful.

There was even a third message, this one from Houghton again:

Marie has report of Jewish refugee near you who could need help. If need arises, could you assist? B.

Cotton replied at once.

Of course. Have you more details? P.

He took the porter's advice and, for lunch, had a dish of monkfish – poor man's lobster, Eugenio called it. Cotton couldn't remember ever having eaten it before, but this was cooked with mussels and saffron. It was light and firm – just what he needed.

That afternoon, he read over the harem part of *Don Juan*, in which Juan is disguised as a woman in a Turkish seraglio and, while welcomed as a pretty face, finds his presence proves oddly troublesome to some of the other inmates. He also looked at some of May's writings and found that May had had an odd way of drafting, a sort of written stutter: 'It was at the beginning of July. It was at the very beginning of July, a hot July, a July so hot any leaves other than the spiky sort had withered,' and so on down the page. At a rough guess, July cropped up about twenty-seven times, all with some smallish descriptive variation.

At the back of the notebook, what Cotton had taken for sketches turned out to be doodles. May had had the habit of placing a name in the centre of the page and then branching off all over the paper. There was one for Cadiz, complete with a tower and a tree. Another name might have been La Cartuja. A third looked like *Flor de Canela*, possibly *Carrela*. *Canela* is cinnamon. In the corner of that one was the name Ramón. He remembered something, and flicked through the shipping news. *Flor de Canela* was a ship out of Cuba, a regular caller at the port of Cadiz. From the consignments, it sounded like a tramp steamer.

Cotton raised his eyebrows, shrugged, and carefully put May's stuff back in the drawer. It was time he caught up with his letters. He wrote to his father in Peaslake, then to his older sister, Joan. She had married an American banker called Todd, had three children, and lived between Manhattan and Shelter Island. She felt, she said, 'uncomfortable out of it, but not that much', and most of her discomfort was because of their father, retired and on his own. He also wrote to the army bank, Glyn Mills, where he had opened an account when he had been commissioned. They still insisted on addressing him as 'Captain', even though it was a year since he had been in the army.

Around seven thirty in the evening he received a new message on Marie's matter:

Source good but report imprecise. Information some days old. Subject in hiding, probably in Seville. Subject code: Don José.

Cotton checked his copy of *Don Juan*. Yes, Don José was Don Juan's father.

> A true Hidalgo, free from every stain
> Of Moor or Hebrew blood . . .

That was Marie, all right.

Later, he returned to the hotel, took a leisurely bath in, if not hot, at least tepid water, and changed.

At nine he presented himself at the Simpsons' house. A brass plate on the outside wall told him that Mr William Simpson OBE was the agent of a maritime-insurance company that foreigners sometimes confused with a government department or the BBC. A uniformed maid showed him into an enclosed patio with black and white tiles, a small fountain, and wicker furniture. Simpson came out to meet him – a small, neat, balding man, whose perfunctorily charming manner sat oddly on full Highland fig: kilt, sporran, velvet jacket, and ruffs.

'My dear fellow,' he said, 'so glad you could make it. This way, mm?'

Simpson led Cotton through a narrow, high-ceilinged room, down some steps, and into a long drawing room that overlooked a small, formal garden. Mrs Simpson, a fat, ginger-haired woman, was sitting with one lightly bandaged foot on a stool. She held out her hand. Cotton bowed over it. Mr Simpson watched him approvingly.

'Well, this one knows the ropes all right,' he said. 'Probably knows something of Spain too, I daresay.'

'You'll have to forgive me', said his wife, 'if I don't scintillate tonight. This ankle of mine is really too much.'

'How did that happen?' said Cotton.

'Damned cobbles,' said Simpson. 'Drink?'

'I slipped on the stairs,' said his wife plaintively.

Evidently, thought Cotton, they have started without me.

'Whisky and water, right?' said Simpson.

'Thank you,' said Cotton.

He had barely taken a sip of what turned out to be lukewarm and almost neat whisky when the maid announced that dinner was served. Simpson turned at once.

'Follow me,' he said.

'Can I help you?' Cotton asked Mrs Simpson.

'What? Yes. Get my stick.'

Patiently, Cotton helped her through to the dining room.

'William's been here fourteen years, you know. Far too long for someone of his calibre. It's all the fault of this wretched war, if one's allowed to say that sort of thing without being accused of treason.'

Cotton twitched out a smile. His face felt stiff. He sat Mrs Simpson down. At once she picked up and rang a small, shrill bell. Cotton sat down. There were three decanters of red wine on the table. With the fish, however, they drank a bottle of chilled *fino* sherry. He noted that Mrs Simpson had difficulty keeping her eyes open, but from time to time would frown and fiddle and tug at the bust of her dress.

'This is delicious,' said Cotton.

Simpson seemed surprised.

'Oh, good,' he said. 'I'm glad. But of course it's all relative these days. Some of them are starving out there, you know. Particularly the other side.' He seemed suddenly tired of that line of conversation. 'Where are you?' he said.

'I'm sorry? said Cotton.

'Where are you staying?'

Cotton told them.

'Ha!' said William Simpson. 'It's entirely relative then. The poor chap hasn't had a decent meal since he arrived. So don't get too cocky, eh, Nora dear?'

Cotton looked round at Nora, who had certainly not done the cooking. She was massaging her left breast and picking at her neckline. She looked up, swayed a fraction, and spoke.

'Don't get on my wick, Bill.'

Cotton shot her a quick look, but she appeared unconcerned.

'I'll try some of the red, dear,' she said, and rang the bell.

Her husband obliged and poured. 'Mustn't mind our joshing,' he said to Cotton.

Mrs Simpson suddenly appeared to remember something. 'Are you married, Mr Cotton?' She drank some red wine from her glass. 'Yes, that's fine, dear.'

'No, I'm not,' said Cotton.

'Well, there's time enough, I suppose,' said William Simpson.

'I was engaged,' said Cotton.

'What? Dear John stuff?'

'No,' said Cotton. 'She died in a bombing raid.'

William Simpson nodded. 'Ah. Awful business,' he said. 'Here.' He poured more wine into Cotton's glass, and then waited for the maid to serve the main course. 'Oh, do you know about those sailors? Five of them were washed up after their ship went down along the coast. We did something. I said to Henderson . . .'

'Oh, Henderson is like a cat that's lost its whiskers,' said his wife.

Cotton blinked at her. Her husband simply carried on.

'I said to Henderson, I said, "Doesn't it strike you as odd, to say the least of it, that not one of those poor devils was carrying so much as a penny on him?" Stripped, you see – they'd been stripped. "Oh," says Henderson, "we don't want to cause any bad feeling." Bad feeling! "You sound like Chamberlain's pisspot," I said – you'll pardon me, but I was exactly right. So I took the trouble to see a man called Ramírez. He's the man to see if you want anything done. And, without going into the ins and outs of it, I put a number of considerations to him. You know what he said? "Wouldn't that come under the spoils of war?" He said that to me! "No spoils of war, no acts of God," I said. "You don't use that terminology to me." "But what are you going to do," he said – "send it to England? It wouldn't get there. *They'd hear the coins rattling!*" Well, I pointed out to him that we could send the money to Gibraltar. And the fellow began to moan, quite literally, about Gibraltar being the thorn in Spanish hearts. Quite extraordinary. I couldn't get him to admit right out that stripping corpses is repulsive. Well, of course we got most of the way in the end. I persisted, you see. First they sent a couple of coins, said they'd found them in the sand. Naturally I sent them straight back, offered them the use of a spade. Finally, however, we got a bit over three pounds ten shillings. Not bad, don't you think?'

Cotton nodded. Mrs Simpson rang the little bell again. William Simpson poured more wine. Cotton saw that they had eaten only a little of the main course: while they had cut at the meat, they had not actually consumed very much. He thought the meat was pork.

'That port sauce was a bit rich,' said Nora Simpson. 'We'll have dessert now,' she told the maid.

Dessert was meringues and cream and chocolate sauce. Mr and Mrs Simpson picked up their spoons and forks and began to eat with rather more enthusiasm than before.

'And how are you getting on clearing up after May?' asked Simpson. 'I don't think "rum fellow" quite meets the case.'

'Now, now,' said Mrs Simpson, through meringue.

'No more than the truth, my dear.'

'I've been hearing a little of the circumstance,' said Cotton.

'Not from Henderson,' said Simpson.

'The vice-consul has been as helpful as he can.'

There was a sharp noise from Mrs Simpson's end of the table. She was scraping her plate. She paused with her spoon in the air. 'Please,' she said, 'I have nothing against them.' She licked the spoon and placed spoon and fork neatly together on the plate. 'But not in sensitive jobs, Mr Cotton. Not in sensitive jobs.'

'I think perhaps you are overestimating the sensitivity,' said Cotton.

Mrs Simpson smiled. 'Whose?' she mouthed.

Cotton nodded dutifully. 'What do you think the problem was?' he asked.

'Respect,' said William Simpson.

'Pride,' said his wife.

There was a pause.

'You know, May had no sense of humour,' said Simpson in a baffled voice – 'no sense of humour at all.' He shook his head. 'Actually, in some ways they are a remarkably tolerant, practical people, the Spanish. You can skip work, keep mistresses, fiddle the petty cash . . . and nepotism is rampant here. But you can't be ridiculous. It took me time to work out, but their honour and their humour go together. Why in God's name did they send him?' It was a rhetorical question. 'You see, it's such a small place,' Simpson went on. 'Mind you, I'm not saying May was in any way discreet, but discretion almost doesn't matter. You'll find that out. You're always being watched. We'll have coffee and brandy on the patio, shall we?'

Cotton helped Mrs Simpson to rise. It was meant as a token politeness, but she used him as support until she got herself up.

'Thank you,' she said. 'It's nice to meet an English gentleman again after the Spaniards. They overdo it, you know.'

Cotton gave her her stick.

'I'll tell you what it is,' she said. 'They're touchy.'

'Ah.'

'You see, Cadiz has a reputation for being liberal. And the rest of Spain tends to think of liberalism as a sort of effeminacy. They're touchy about it.'

'I see,' said Cotton.

He accompanied her through to the patio. High above, through the glass roof, the night looked clear but starless. Cotton felt overfed, too warm, and dry from the alcohol. Simpson was seeing to the brandies. His wife was frowning at her bust again. A telephone sounded. Simpson handed over the drinks.

'This Spanish stuff's much underrated,' he said. 'Our man in Lisbon prefers this to sherry. He sends us port.'

A maid came and whispered in his ear.

'Will you excuse me a moment?' he said.

He went out of the room, kilt swinging. He had a dagger in his stocking. From the back, his neck looked very pink. Mrs Simpson told the maid to pour the coffee. Cotton could hear a murmur from William, a low chuckle, and a light clatter from the kitchen. The maid served them coffee and left.

Nora Simpson sighed. 'He's no good in bed,' she said. 'I'm the hot one.'

Cotton looked at her. For a moment he closed his eyes. When he opened them he found she was staring at him.

She blinked. Then, high above, the glass panes rattled. Both of them looked upward.

'Ah,' said Mrs Simpson.

The panes rattled again; there was a shrill wail of wind.

'That's the Levante. It's a hot, dry wind. Usually lasts three days,' she said wearily. 'You'll see.'

William had finished his call. 'Bad for the nerves,' he said as he came in.

'What?' said his wife, not looking round.

'This damned wind,' said Simpson as he sat. 'Are you still on your first brandy?'

Making his way back to his hotel was an unpleasant experience, what with the drink, the uneven cobbles, and the noisy wind buffeting and playing pressure games with his ears. Some gusts were so strong that Cotton had to tilt forward to stay his ground, and squint against blasts of sand. He finally got inside the door out of breath and irritated. He wiped his eyes and blew out.

'Ah, there you are,' said Ramírez. 'I was wondering where you'd got to. Drink?'

'I've drunk quite enough,' said Cotton.

'Bring him water,' said Ramírez. 'Yes, your eyes look terrible.'

'That's the grit.'

'Yes? Come, sit down with me.'

Cotton sighed and complied. 'Don't you get any time off?' he said.

'I have something for you,' said Ramírez.

Cotton blinked. His eyes were still watering. He blew his nose. 'All right. What is it?'

It was another visiting card.

'I can hardly see to read,' he said.

'Do you want me to read it for you?' said Ramírez patiently.

'No.'

Cotton picked up the card.

AGUSTÍN ROMERO VELAZQUEZ
ANTIQUARIAN BOOKSELLER

On the back, in English, was written:

I would be most grateful if you could spare me some time tomorrow at your earliest convenience. My respects, A. Romero.

'What does it say?' said Ramírez.

Cotton told him and drank the water down.

'Another one?' said Ramírez.

'No, thank you.'

'It was waiting for you.'

'Yes,' said Cotton.

'You look tired.'

'Yes. No. I'm more the worse for wear than tired.'

Ramírez smiled. 'Have you been with Antonia?' he asked.

'Who?' said Cotton. He remembered another card. 'Ah, no.'

'It was sincerely meant,' said Ramírez.

'I know, I know,' said Cotton.

'So? Where were you?'

'I was with the Simpsons.'

'I know.'

Cotton blinked. 'So why are you asking me?'

Ramírez smiled. 'Where did you learn your Spanish?' he asked.

'What? Ah. Colombia and Mexico.'

'What were you doing there?'

'Growing up. My father worked for a British bank. I lived there until I was eight.'

'You lived a sheltered life?'

'What do you mean?'

'You had a beautiful garden and there were maids?'

'Yes, I suppose so.'

'I thought that. You have gardens and maids in your accent. It's not unattractive. And I know what purists say about Ibero-American accents.'

'Really?'

Ramírez smiled. 'Are you up to talking?'

'The Simpsons called you a corpse-stripper,' said Cotton.

'That's a good one,' said Ramírez without enthusiasm. 'This man – the one who left the card – he's the grand-father.'

Cotton said nothing. Ramírez leaned across.

'Let him come. See him.'

Cotton raised his eyebrows.

'He's a brave old man,' said Ramírez, 'and I have no wish to afflict him more.'

'What can I do?' said Cotton.

'The boy has deserted. May's boy, for want of a better description – but don't use it with the old man.'

Cotton nodded. 'I see. But I still –'

'Do not cause the old man more pain. Let him talk.'

Cotton shrugged. 'All right.'

'Good,' said Ramírez, and he patted Cotton's forearm. 'Thank you. Tomorrow I'll talk to you about May.'

'Why not now?' said Cotton. '*Estoy harto de tanta vida social.*' I'm fed up with so much social life.

'Because you're drunk and congested.'

'What?'

Ramírez stood up and smoothed his hair over his ears. 'You're pissed and your sperm's curdling,' he said, checking his reflection in the mirror.

Cotton laughed. 'Is that your diagnosis?'

'You have to clean yourself out. Regularly. It stands to reason. What's it for, otherwise? I'll see you tomorrow.'

For a while after Ramírez had gone, Cotton sat. The wind was howling. He drank another glass of water, pulled himself up and went to his room. The maid was there.

'Ah,' he said. 'Good.' He put his hand in his pocket for a coin. He paused. 'What's your name?' he asked.

'Mari-Ángeles,' said the girl.

'How old are you?'

The girl looked doubtful. 'Eleven, *señor*?'

'Have you worked here for a long time?'

The girl thought. 'Months,' she said.

Cotton nodded. 'And where were you before that?'

'I cleaned,' said the girl simply.

Cotton smiled. 'Here you are then.' He gave the girl her tip and received a little smile.

As soon as she had gone, Cotton stripped off his clothes and went straight to bed. He felt grim – not as if he were about to sleep, but about to pass out.

6

Around 2 a.m. Cotton was woken by his own violent vomiting. Hot, rank stuff spurted out of his nose and mouth. He scrambled out of bed and skidded on his own vomit on the marble floor. He managed to get his feet into some shoes, then shuffle-ran into the bathroom and heaved and heaved. After a while there was only bile, but he kept on retching. He stood, head bowed, and waited. His ribs hurt; his nose and throat felt raw. The bathroom smelled of old bleach, damp, clammy mould, and his sick. He rinsed out his mouth. His stomach grumbled, contracted, and spewed a little more mucus and bile into his mouth. He listened. He could hear the Levante wailing outside and, behind that, the frantic rattling of the window frames. He belched. He waited. His pulse gradually settled. He put a hand on the wall and rested.

Bit by bit, mostly by sensation – the stiffness in his knee when he had hit the bedroom floor, a bruise when he had stumbled into the chest of drawers, a sore wrist when he had grabbed for the door jamb, and a tendency to shiver – he reconstructed what had happened. He turned and groaned, and followed a trail of vomit back to his bed.

He stripped off the sheets. The smell of his own sick was being warmed by the wind. Crouched, sometimes crawling – like an embarrassed house guest it struck him later – he used the sheets to mop the stuff up, then went back into the bathroom, rolled the sheets up, tied them into a bundle, and dropped them into the bath. Then he brushed his teeth and retreated to the sitting room. He tugged the armchairs round and curled up between them. His forehead was cool to touch; he felt burning hot except for his legs and feet.

At about five he saw to his diarrhoea. If the Mexicans had Montezuma's revenge, what was this? El Dorado, he thought. It was the nearest he could come to a joke. Dehydrated and exhausted, he waited. Sometimes he even managed to doze.

He found he was so stiff he could barely move. He saw that his right knee was bruised and swollen. Shivering, he pushed the sheets up the bath, stepped in, and washed and sluiced himself down in cold water. The wretched towels, though he tried to rub, provided no heat. But he contrived to shave. His face in the mirror was repulsively pinched and pale, the whites of his eyes yellowish and bloodshot. He got himself dressed and sat again in his sitting room, hugging himself for some time, until morning sounds began to be heard.

The hotel acted promptly. The sheets were changed at once. He did not ask them to do so, but they called a doctor, who was there within a quarter of an hour – a plump, balding little fellow, who checked him over and prescribed *manzanilla* – camomile tea.

'When you feel like it,' said the doctor, 'have some more of the tea and some dry bread. Unless you get these attacks frequently, that is.'

155

Cotton could not remember the last time he had vomited. Not since he was a child, certainly.

'Good,' said the doctor, examining Cotton's eyes. 'Yes. You're quite sound. But stay in today. I'll call in tonight and see how you're progressing.'

'Thank you,' said Cotton. 'How much do I owe you?'

The doctor shook his head. 'At the end of the treatment,' he said. 'Rest now.'

Cotton was enough of a hypochondriac to decide to feel encouraged by the doctor's casual chattiness. He disliked the flowery smell of the camomile, but dutifully drank the infusion. His stomach rumbled, but the stuff did not come up. After a while he began to feel queasy again, then he thought he was beginning to feel a little better.

For something to do, he asked the hotel to deliver a message to the antiquarian bookseller. They were pleased to do so. He wrote the note, and the hotel took the opportunity to present their next bill. Quite shortly after, he had to visit the bathroom again: no, he was not getting better. The sound of the wind and what felt like pressure changes were making him feel decidedly peculiar. His ears were singing and popping by turns; he felt as if his head might take off.

The antiquarian came immediately. He was the kind of old man that made Cotton think he had been sitting, dressed for outdoors, waiting for the message to arrive.

'It is unforgivable of me to trouble you when you are unwell,' he said in precise but wheezing English. He stood in the doorway with his hat half raised in greeting, but waiting for permission to come in.

'It isn't at all,' said Cotton. 'Come in and sit down.'

'I insist on knowing how you are,' said the antiquarian. 'I can easily come again.'

'I ate something that disagreed with me, that's all,' replied Cotton. 'The doctor said I should stay in today. I don't mind at all with this wind, and I'd be bored if you went. Please, come and sit down.'

Just then, there was a particularly violent gust that made the window panes judder and trickles of dust dance paisley patterns on the floor. The old man waited for calm. 'If you're absolutely sure,' he said.

'I am,' said Cotton.

The old man finally removed his hat, to reveal a large, bald head with something odd in the pigmentation of the skin. There were white, almost luminous patches among the normal stuff, so that the top of his head appeared mottled. The patches looked soft, and had an almost baby white to them. He sat on the edge of the offered armchair and put his hat down. He cleared his throat.

'I am eighty-two years old,' he began. 'I find that if I tell people that I was born in 1862 it can be useful. It helps them to gauge not so much what I say, but how I say it.'

Cotton nodded. The old man hitched up his trousers at the knees and unbuttoned his overcoat. He was dressed as for midwinter. He sniffed.

'It is at least forty years since I was here,' he said. From an overcoat pocket he extracted a small tin. He opened it carefully.

'Little peppermints,' said the antiquarian. 'Would you like one?'

'No, thank you.'

'I think in another pocket I have some liquorice.'

'No, no. Please.'

'If you're sure,' said the old man, popping a pepper-mint into his mouth. 'It's the glucose, you know.'

'Yes,' said Cotton.

'I lived in England from 1886 to 1890,' said the anti-quarian. 'My father had an extravagant regard for British engineering. Of course, in those days one obeyed one's parents. I'm an engineer only in the sense that I am qualified. Then he sent me to the north-east of England. Armstrong's.' The old man laughed. 'Absolutely hated it,' he said. 'Liked the people, though. Then my father died. Apoplexy. It may seem a terrible thing to say, but in one respect having to take over as head of the family was a relief. I already had a passion for books. It's quite separate from reading, of course, which I also enjoy. So I took over the business. And, just so as not to mislead you, the antiquarian-bookseller business is a bit of a frost. The busiest years were spent helping North Americans acquire a great deal of armour and religious artefacts. Trading in the past for present profit,' he said.

'I see,' said Cotton.

'But in English I do have a first edition of *Treasure Island*,' said the old man. 'And the odd thing from Kipling and Chesterton. Are you a reader, Mr Cotton?'

'Oh, recently I've been looking at Byron.'

'Really? I should have thought he was notorious rather than read nowadays. Well, of course, he was here, in Cadiz. A few days only, let's not get excited about it. They tell a story that he was awfully impressed with a pair of shoes a cobbler made for him. So he ordered another pair. "Not till I've spent the money from the last pair," said the cobbler. Quite apocryphal, of course. But it's meant to illustrate the character of the townsfolk here. I'm not at all sure it does, unless it illustrates that rather self-destructive wit they enjoy. At its best, they manage a weird hilarity at having nothing.' As he spoke, the old man trembled and swallowed and licked his lips.

'Why do you think the story is apocryphal?' asked Cotton.

'Because the story makes no mention of Byron having a club foot,' said the antiquarian, and a moment after Cotton realized that the arrangement of his face had formed another pattern. The old man was weeping.

'Shouldn't do that,' he said. 'My son's dead. They shot him in July 1936. Out there. I had to go out and cut him down. They had strung him up from the bullring walls. They used wire. Nobody has been able to tell me why. And it was such a pity. He was such a nice man. That may strike you as strange for a father to say of his own son.'

'No,' said Cotton. He waited.

'I enjoyed his company, you see. Much better fellow than me. Much more energy and generosity. He stuck to things.'

Almost as suddenly as they had begun, the old man's tears stopped. He fished out a handkerchief and began dabbing and blowing.

'Can I send for something? Coffee?' offered Cotton.

The old man wiped his eyes. 'Why, yes,' he sniffed. 'A glass of water, perhaps.'

'Nothing stronger?'

'No, really, a glass of water would be perfect.'

Cotton stretched and rang the service bell.

159

'And now my grandson . . . ' said the old man, and stopped. Cotton turned. The old man had a knuckle in front of his lips; he caught the right side of his mouth between knuckle and thumb and squeezed. Then he nodded.

'When I was in England,' said the antiquarian, 'there was a horrible expression. "Bum-boy".' The old man swallowed. 'Don't you think it's a horrible expression, Mr Cotton?'

Cotton nodded and waited.

'Oh, I'm trying to say something,' said the old man, sounding irritable with himself. He shook his head. 'The problem is *here*. I don't mean they've never heard of the Greeks. But for them, *pan* is bread, which they'd like to be daily, and not some pastoral god and goat at the other end of the Mediterranean. You know of the poet Lorca?'

Cotton nodded.

'They shot him because of it.'

'Yes,' said Cotton. 'Wait a moment, please.'

The antiquarian looked up and grunted. The old woman was at the door.

'A bottle of water for my guest, please,' said Cotton.

They listened to her feet shuffle out, and then there was a shrill shout: '*¡Niña! ¡Agua!*'

'Spanish can be thought of as a prolix language,' said the old man. 'But it can also be most economical and simple. "Girl. Water".'

Cotton was surprised at the chatty tone, but then he understood that the old man was simply waiting until they were properly alone again and was taking advantage of the break to compose himself. They heard the girl's quick feet on the stairs, then the old woman's shuffle. She brought in a bottle of mineral water and a glass. She poured it, and handed it to the old man.

'Thank you.'

'Anything else, *señor*?'

'Nothing else,' said Cotton.

The old man drank a little and put the glass down as the old woman left the room. 'I have been informed', he said, 'that my grandson Javier has deserted from the army. He was doing his military service.' He looked up at Cotton. 'I don't know if they usually tell you.'

'It's in case he tries to come home,' said Cotton.

'I see,' said the old man, though Cotton thought he would surely have known that. The old man said nothing more. He was staring down at his hands as if he had never seen them before.

'Do you know when he deserted?'

The old man shook his head. 'They gave me the fact, not the date.'

'I see. Where was he doing his military service?' asked Cotton.

'In Seville.'

Cotton nodded. Ninety miles was not so far away. 'Was there anything special about his service?'

The old man blinked at him, then shook his head. 'No, no. Javier was with the conscripts in the usual thing. He was . . . I don't know how you say *soldado raso*.'

'A common soldier. A private. Did he know that his . . . that . . . ?'

'Of the death? I don't know,' replied the old man. 'I wrote to him when I knew. But I cannot say whether or not he received the letter. There is censorship, of course, but the post is incompetent as well.'

'Did he have any money?' asked Cotton.

'What do you mean?'

'Did he have funds on him?'

'I see. Yes. Well, they are hardly paid, you know. He had his allowance from me.'

'Can I ask how much that was?'

'Does it matter?'

'It might,' said Cotton.

The old man told him. It was a very comfortable sum. 'It's the same as when he was studying law at the faculty in Seville.'

'Had he finished his studies?'

'No,' said the old man. 'He's eighteen, no, nineteen years old.'

'He was a poor student?'

'No, no, on the contrary. He had excellent marks.'

'I had understood that military service could be postponed for students and then reduced to a token term, usually served as an officer on graduation. Or even fitted into the summer vacations,' said Cotton.

'That is correct,' said the old man. 'But not in all cases.' He paused. 'You need a clean bill of health.'

'I'm sorry?' said Cotton.

'You need a good background. Friends on the right side,' said the antiquarian.

'Did your grandson have problems?'

'What?' The old man squinted at Cotton. 'No, not *him*,' he said. 'But if your father's body was strung up on the bullring walls you have problems enough.'

'Of course.'

'In Seville he was in view, as it were, of his fellow students – people he had been studying with. I suppose it is a kind of humiliation. Perhaps a marking out of someone not to speak to or someone to jeer at.'

Cotton sighed. 'Do you mind if I speak frankly?' he said.

'Of course not.'

'What do you know of my ex-colleague, May?'

'Very little,' said the old man firmly. He blinked and looked away. 'Oh, he ate at my house once or twice. I mean there are standards of hospitality, aren't there? No matter what. Javier is not a . . . promiscuous boy.'

'Do you really mean that?' asked Cotton.

'Oh, my English?' queried the old man. 'I mean that he had few friends.'

'You mean he wasn't very sociable, outgoing.'

'Really? Perhaps. Yes, I suppose I mean that.'

'Very loyal to the friends he had?' suggested Cotton.

'I'd have to say devoted.'

'Señor Romero . . .'

'Yes?' said the old man.

'I don't know whether or not I have the right to ask this . . .'

'Go on.'

'Did they have a plan of some sort?' asked Cotton.

The old man paused, then nodded. 'I think, no . . . I gather, yes, the word is "gather", that the idea was for my grandson to go, to make a run for Gibraltar and then . . . I don't know. This dead man thought the war would be over very soon.'

Cotton winced. 'I am so sorry,' he said. 'This is something I know nothing about. If a plan existed, it was entirely my ex-colleague's private initiative. And when I say "ex-colleague", please understand that I didn't know him. All I know is that he is dead, what you have told me, and some bits and pieces other people have thought to pass on to me. I don't even know whether or not your grandson's entry to Gibraltar could have been arranged. Does your grandson speak any English?'

'He was brought up speaking English. I taught him myself,' said the antiquarian. 'But of course, with the wars, he hasn't had the chance to visit England.'

'I see.'

'Mr Cotton, I am here not just for myself but for his mother and his grandmother. Do you understand that?'

'Yes.'

'I am not asking you to honour an arrangement you cannot know. In any case, I'm pretty sure your ex-colleague was acting outside the confines of his job.'

'Stop for a moment, please,' said Cotton. 'Do you know if your grandson was ever employed by my government or one of its agents in some capacity? I might just be able to work on that. At risk because of his services, etcetera.'

The antiquarian shook his head. 'I don't know. No. I'm the wrong person to ask,' he said.

'There's no record I've seen. Normal, though, I suppose,' said Cotton. 'Have you spoken to Ramírez? He gave me your card, told me your grandson had deserted.'

'Yes,' said the old man. 'There's nothing he can do about a desertion from the army. But Ramírez is not all bad, you know. He understands what people are.' He paused. 'He doesn't pretend to have principles much beyond an elementary sort of justice. And what do the British say? "He knows his place and keeps his nose clean"?'

Cotton nodded. Was the antiquarian snobbish as well as sharp-tongued?

The old man sighed. 'Perhaps that is why he has survived. He doesn't threaten the clever and ambitious, and he is respectful enough to the dolts. It must work. He has survived King Alfonso, the regime of Primo de Rivera, then the Republic, and now Franco. And he's still here.' He looked up. 'I suppose he is always useful to authority because he clears up mundane things they want cleared up but can't be much bothered about. And then sometimes awkward, intractable things they don't want to know about in the first place.'

'I see,' said Cotton. He held up his hands. 'Look, I'll do my best,' he said, 'but you must understand that this amounts to almost nothing at all. I'll need time, and I'm not sure –'.

'That Javier has any. I understand, Mr Cotton.'

Cotton blinked. The old man smiled.

'But you are our only hope,' said the antiquarian, cheerfully specific and doom-laden.

'Please don't think like that,' said Cotton. 'I can give no guarantee whatsoever. Offhand, I really haven't the faintest idea of what I could do to help. Of course, I'll think about it, but please – don't put your hopes in me.'

The old man was imperturbable. He shook his head. 'Thank you so much. Unpardonable intrusion on my part, and I am most sorry to have imposed on you when you are ill.' He got up. 'Sit where you are,' said the old man. 'I insist.' He did up his coat and picked up his hat. He held out his hand.

'God bless you,' he said. 'Good day, Mr Cotton.'

7

'I MET HIM on the stairs,' said Ramírez.

'Yes,' said Cotton.

'I was waiting. I came round here when I heard you were ill. What's wrong with you?'

'The doctor's baffled.'

Ramírez was unimpressed. 'Is that English humour? I never quite saw the point.' He sat down on the arm of the chair the antiquarian had just vacated. 'So, what did he say?'

'You know what he said.'

'Do I?' said Ramírez. 'You don't know what he said about you.'

'It doesn't matter,' said Cotton.

'He said "a magnificent specimen".'

'Of what?' said Cotton.

Ramírez laughed. '¡Hombre! It's a compliment! Don Agustín is famous for his excellent taste.'

'In furniture and books,' said Cotton.

Ramírez tutted. 'You're out of sorts,' he said.

'You give answers to your own questions,' said Cotton. 'Do you enjoy your job?'

'Of course. Don't you?'

'I didn't choose it.'

Ramírez shrugged. 'So? What did he say?'

'That his grandson had deserted. Could I help?'

'You told him no.'

'I hope so.'

'Ah,' said Ramírez, nodding. 'That's good. That's honest. You're an honest man.' He scratched his forehead and cleared his throat. 'Let me make this clear. Desertion is a capital offence. I've heard the army doesn't often bother about a trial for *maricas*. They prefer to kill them by giving them a vagina with a bayonet.'

'Oh, for God's sake,' groaned Cotton.

'So the British always behave well?'

Cotton shook his head. 'That's not what I meant. And the answer is no. I was thinking of the old man. Do you know what happened to his son?'

'The son?' said Ramírez. He thought, then shook his head. 'I think both sides would have got him. He had a clear mind, and insisted on speaking it. Never a good idea. Would you mind if I smoked?'

'No,' said Cotton.

'Good,' said Ramírez, 'because I want to talk to you.' He lit a cigarette, and inhaled with pleasure. 'Mm. Do you know where I was before I came here? I went to see the Italian agent, Lusardi. I was struck the other day that you arrived almost exactly a year to the day after Italy surrendered. September the 8th, 1943.'

'Why is he still here?'

'Excellent question. He likes it. And why not?'

'What?' said Cotton.

'Ah, you're slow today,' said Ramírez. 'That's your stomach. The poor devil's marooned. He's got no money. He's frightened to go back in any case.'

'I don't know what it's like in Italy just now,' said Cotton.

'And nor does he,' said Ramírez cheerfully. 'It doesn't matter. We're removing his residence permit. It's a long time since Italian ships were welcomed here and their plumed soldiers cheered and applauded.'

'Has he no friends or contacts?' said Cotton. 'Ideologically I should have thought –'

Ramírez pulled a face. '*Ni ideologías, ni leches.*' What fucking ideology? 'He began courting one of the girls here when he arrived in 1942. There are a lot of Italian names in Cadiz – mostly from Genoa, when the merchants settled here. And he picked on one, Conchita, from a well-off family called Massarella – they have a number of very nice leather shops. You'd know about that. You met that German woman in one. But he never got round to marrying her. And then Italy surrendered, and he told the family he was no longer in a position to marry her.' Ramírez shook his head. 'I think that if he had gone ahead and married her, he would have been welcomed in and given some sinecure in the family business. Nobody would have cared at all about his lack of prospects. But he allowed his fear and his self-importance to cloud his judgement. Now the girl is, as it were, used but unused.' Ramírez shook his head. 'It's a crime. Lusardi failed to understand that, if you court a girl in Cadiz, you marry her or you get out at once.'

Cotton shook his head. 'Why are you telling me all this?'

'Because', said Ramírez seriously, 'I think I've got him on a boat to Portugal.'

Cotton nodded. Was this Ramírez's roundabout way of telling him what the naval architect with the German wife had told him? Would the Italian be going away with the Portuguese after the meeting with Franco? 'Does he want to go?'

Ramírez laughed. 'I've no idea,' he said. 'It certainly adds up to movement in his circumstances. I know somebody on a Cuban ship, and they've agreed to take him. *Flor de Canela.*'

'What?' Cotton had read that name somewhere.

'The name of the ship.'

'Pretty name.' Cotton recalled May's intricate but rather clumsy doodle.

'Good riddance,' said Ramírez.

Cotton closed his eyes and rubbed.

'Are you all right?'

'Yes.' He could hardly call Ramírez subtle. He had the clear impression something had just closed off. He decided to try something from the doodle. 'Is the person you know called Ramón?'

Ramírez laughed. '*Cabrón eres.*' You clever bastard.

Cotton was not convinced he had been clever at all.

'The last German wasn't at all bad,' said Ramírez. 'A little stiff, perhaps, which gave him an unfortunate appearance, as if he were trying to be superior. But now he's gone. I think I'd like them to send an American. Not for too long. But a rich Yankee would be nice for a month or so.'

'Why don't you tell me about May?' said Cotton.

Ramírez smiled. 'I was just chatting,' he said.

He leaned over and took an envelope out of his side pocket. He withdrew a small photograph and handed it to Cotton. It showed May standing beside a very hand-some boy at least a head taller than the little Englishman. The boy had an arm draped over May's shoulder, and was smiling confidently. May looked a rather portly little man, his smile timid and lopsided.

'Good-looking boy,' said Ramírez. 'Waste of a good cock, that's what my mother said.'

Cotton blinked. 'She must be a very remarkable woman.'

Ramírez smiled. 'Strong as an oak. Older than the antiquarian.'

Cotton nodded. 'Who took this picture?'

'One of those little men in the street who develop film in buckets.'

'A friend of yours?' asked Cotton.

'*Primo*,' said Ramírez.

Primo means 'cousin', thought Cotton. First or second, once or twice removed. It can also mean someone gul-lible, easily misled. But who was being misled here? Cotton examined the picture. 'When was it taken?'

'July 16th.'

'That was about when the German left, wasn't it?' said Cotton.

Ramírez smiled and shook his head. 'This was two days before the boy had to report to barracks.'

'He seems very cheerful,' said Cotton. He peered more closely at the photo, at the huge rock that, from a dis-tance, resembled a reclining woman. 'Is that Gibraltar in the background?'

'Yes,' said Ramírez. 'It was taken in Algeciras, by a hotel or English club they have there.'

'A what?' said Cotton.

'It's a hotel. Lots of white. Somebody told me it was British colonial style,' said Ramírez. 'The English around there go to play bridge and drink tea and gin.'

He put his hand out for the photograph, and Cotton gave it to him. Ramírez put it back in the envelope and into his pocket again. 'I want to tell you about May's last day,' he said.

'All right.'

'Well, he rose late. That was his custom. Breakfast in the Bar España – that's the one in the Plaza San Juan de Dios – with coffee and brandy. Then he went for a shave in the barber's behind the bar. Entered his office at eleven ten. Came out at eleven forty and met a man known as *El Palo*, who works as a shoeshine boy and occasional docker. The conversation was about ship movements and cargo details. They had a drink together – wine. At one o'clock he moved on and contacted a man they call Jaimito, a male prostitute. Do you know the Calle Plocia? It's full of whores and rooms. Then he had a beer and a sandwich in a nearby bar, alone, and returned to his office. He was there until 8 p.m., on his own except for one little outing, at about six thirty, when he met *La Cabra*, a man well known to the police.'

'Well known for what?' asked Cotton.

'Oh. He's always waving a knife, and we always have to make him confess because nobody will testify against him.' Ramírez shrugged. 'It's not too inconvenient, and it saves having to organize witnesses. Now, do you know what his business with May was?'

'No,' said Cotton.

For the first time, Cotton saw Ramírez look abashed. 'I have to tell you', he said, 'that this man also uses his knife to some effect at the postal depot.'

Cotton shook his head. 'I don't understand,' he said.

'*Hombre*, he's a *soplagaitas*!'

'A what?' Cotton did not know the word. *Soplar* is 'blow'. *Gaita* is 'bagpipe'. What was he talking about?

'The postman, well, he's a sorter, he's full of air!' said Ramírez, throwing up his hands.

Cotton nodded. OK. A windbag. A tedious fantasist? A grass? 'Wait. This man, *La Cabra*, accuses himself?' said Cotton, puzzled. 'Ah. Yes. *Está como una cabra*. Of course.' It meant 'mad as a hatter'. He shook his head again. 'Listen, I'm sorry. When I'm off colour my language abilities suffer.'

Ramírez looked solemn. 'Is that true? Then forgive me.'

'Why don't you tell me more about May.'

'Well, May and this . . . person, *La Cabra*, talked for half an hour,' went on Ramírez. 'May gave him something.'

'What?'

Ramírez waved his hand dismissively. '*La Cabra* imagines he *is* the Post Office. Your colleague was, let's say, gullible.'

'Right.' Cotton wondered how much La Cabra used his paper knife for Ramírez. But then, again, *La Cabra* could have access to areas of the postal service he kept secret from Ramírez. Was there a postal service within the formal state-and-police-run arrangement? Cotton thought it likely.

'At eight, May left the office and went to a couple of bars on his way to the Alameda. Do you know where that is?'

'Well . . .' said Cotton.

'It's a garden and a walk. Up there,' he said, pointing. 'By La Iglesia del Carmen. That's the colonial church where the rich get married. Just go through the Plaza de España – where all the pigeons are and the monument to the Liberal Constitution of 1812 – and turn up and left. The Alameda overlooks the sea. May met the Italian there.'

'Right. But the Italian. Is that another nickname?' said Cotton.

'What? No,' said Ramírez patiently. 'The Italian agent here. I just told you about him. Lusardi. Remember the girlfriend?'

'Yes, yes, I'm sorry.'

'Look, if you're not well . . . ' said Ramírez.

'Go on.'

'It was the first time they had talked. The first. May bought him a drink and a tapa.'

Cotton raised an eyebrow.

'Don't you believe me?' said Ramírez.

'If you say so.'

'I do. They talked about the war. The Italian did most of the talking. That's another story. He has nothing to do with this. He's far too wrapped up in his own misery.'

'All right,' said Cotton.

'May got rid of him, and then went to eat seafood. He ate alone. He drank a bottle of sherry. He was cheerful.'

'Cheerful from alcohol?'

'Yes, what else?' said Ramírez. 'But now things become interesting. He left the restaurant before a quarter past eleven. About a quarter past, we have two contradictory sightings. One says he was walking in the Alameda. The other says he was by the Parque Genovés. I prefer the park.'

'Why?'

'The current, mostly. You can never really tell. But he was a long time in the water for here.'

'You'll have to explain that,' said Cotton.

'OK. The Alameda . . . ?'

'Yes, I've got that. Through the Plaza de España and up.'

'That's it. Well, the Alameda and the Parque Genovés are ten to fifteen minutes apart, going round the sea wall. Do you know what a bulwark is?'

'Not exactly, but it's a kind of military fortification,' said Cotton.

'That's right. Cadiz still retains a lot of the fortifications built against your ancestors.' Cotton smiled and nodded. 'You remember my hand?' Ramírez went on. He held out his right hand so that only the middle three fingers showed. 'The index finger is the park and the penultimate finger is the Alameda. In the middle is the bulwark. Do you understand? If May had gone into the water at the Alameda, wouldn't he have been washed round into the bay a little quicker?'

'Ah. Would he? I don't know,' said Cotton.

Ramírez sighed. 'Right. I agree,' he said. 'You can never really tell with currents. And on land, to get to the Parque Genovés, you have to pass by the military governor's house, and the park itself is directly in front of the barracks. There are sentry boxes everywhere.'

Cotton said nothing. He remembered his horse-drawn-carriage ride to the pathologist.

'It was something of a relief when his corpse came in,' said Ramírez.

'Yes,' said Cotton. 'Do you mind me saying that you seem more irritated than interested?'

'It's because I like to know,' said Ramírez. 'I have my pride. And there's something in all this that worries me.'

'That nobody saw him jump?'

'Among other things.'

'Mm. People here keep late hours,' said Cotton. 'It was hot. Windows must have been open. People walk. Weren't there any lovers about?'

'Too late for good girls,' said Ramírez. And then he mumbled something.

'What?' said Cotton.

Ramírez bit his lip. 'There was a power failure at eleven fifteen,' he said finally.

Cotton was hard put not to burst out laughing. For a moment he stared away in disbelief at the window, still rattling in the wind. He was talking to a small, elderly man who modelled himself on a much younger Clark Gable, in a town that seemed somewhere between maze and stage, with a very observant audience and a little Italian light relief, about a well-tanked man who had fallen into the sea during a power cut. It was a very long way from tungsten, armour-piercing shells, and smuggled gold. He looked back at Ramírez.

'I see. So if May was rather drunk and got on the sea wall before the power failure, when the lights went out he would very likely have been disorientated and stepped the wrong way. And there we have our answer, don't you think? It's the simplest explanation. The delay in finding him might be caused by his jacket catching on a rock or something.'

Ramírez blinked at him. He sighed. 'It's plausible, I suppose.'

He sounded almost disappointed. Cotton frowned. He already had experience of Ramírez's kind of clowning.

'Unless, of course, there's something I don't know,' said Cotton.

Ramírez seemed to him to be overdoing the simple provincial. He made an ape mouth and rubbed his chin. 'No, no,' he said. 'You know as much as I do.'

Cotton switched tack. 'The old man seemed to think the boy might have done some work for May,' he said.

Ramírez stuck out his lower lip and shook his head.

'Well, you'd know, I suppose,' said Cotton. 'The old man thinks they had some scheme for getting the boy into Gibraltar.'

Ramírez let out a long sigh. 'It's good of you to tell me. I'm very grateful.' He looked at Cotton for a moment. 'Why did you betray the old man's confidence?'

Cotton sat back in his chair and crossed his arms. 'Did I?'

'Ah,' said Ramírez. 'Now you're being English.'

'You showed me the photo of them at Algeciras.'

'Mm,' said Ramírez. 'That's true. But you know you have to go quite a few kilometres further along the coast, to La Línea, to get into Gibraltar by land.'

'Do you think they could have done it?' asked Cotton.

'It's possible. La Línea suffers from the proximity of so many British troops.'

'What does that mean?' said Cotton.

Ramírez threw up his hands. 'The whole place is a brothel!' Ramírez stopped for a moment. 'I don't know, but it's possible . . . The boy speaks English, after all. I suppose that with papers and a uniform he could have stumbled into Gibraltar with everyone else – just another British soldier going back. You would know more about that than me.'

'I don't,' said Cotton. But he probably did in one way. He thought of Marie in Madrid and the 'Jewish run'. She had managed to get people into Gibraltar. It made him think Ramírez was limited to Cadiz town in ways even Ramírez did not quite appreciate.

'No?' said Ramírez. 'Well. Once in La Línea it might be easy enough, but you've got to get there first. The Guardia Civil control the country outside the towns. There are roadblocks, and the road is bad. Between Tarifa and Algeciras the road rises from sea level right up to where the buzzards keep you company, and then goes all the way down again.'

'You're saying it was a fantasy?'

'Perhaps it was a lovers' fantasy,' said Ramírez, without much conviction.

There was a knock on the door. One of the old men of the hotel brought in a curiously shaped parcel.

'I've been asked to deliver this,' he said to Cotton.

'What is it? Who is it from?' asked Cotton.

'They didn't say,' said the old man. He handed it to Cotton.

'Go on. Open it,' said Ramírez. 'I like surprises.'

Cotton tore at the brown paper. Inside, he found a beautiful piece of walnut. It was carved, from one piece of wood, in the shape of a large, almost fully open book. The spine was barley-twist, and on the pages there were carved, wavy lines. There was also a matching piece of wood carved in the shape of what looked like an extravagant pipe. And there was an envelope with a note inside. Cotton took it out and unfolded it.

Dear Mr Cotton,

As a token of my appreciation for seeing me and as a rather more beautiful memento of Cadiz than the affair that brought you here, I am sending you this curio. It is seventeenth century and is a lectern designed so that the traveller could read on horseback. I can only assume that the horse plodded. The attachment would have connected the lectern to the saddle.

Many thanks again.

Yours,

Agustín Romero

'I can't accept it,' said Cotton as soon as he had read it.

'Why not?' said Ramírez.

'I mean, I'm not allowed to accept it.'

Ramírez looked unimpressed. 'Are you going to offend the old gentleman? Don't be ridiculous. Besides, he's got plenty of that kind of stuff.'

'I haven't done anything for him,' said Cotton.

'You spoke to him,' said Ramírez. 'This is his thanks.'

Cotton was silent for a moment. 'What would you do if you caught his grandson?' he asked.

'Hand him over,' said Ramírez. '¡*Joder!* Do you think I have authority over the military? *Venga, hombre.*'

'All right,' said Cotton.

Ramírez stood up. 'Keep it. It will do no harm. I've enjoyed our talk. The English and the Spanish get on well, don't they?' he said cheerfully. 'The French I'm not so sure about. Still. I'll be seeing you. And don't forget about Antoñita, eh?' Ramírez stiffly patted Cotton's shoulder and left.

Cotton's head hurt. He felt weak. Sweat was trickling down his back. He wondered how Ramírez bore the corset in that heat.

The hotel brought Cotton some more camomile tea and some fresh bread. He broke off a small piece. It smelled good. He chewed it slowly and thoroughly, and sluiced it down with some of the tea. He belched. He did feel a little better.

To give himself something to do, he decided to tackle the rattling windows. The Levante was still blowing. Three days, Mrs Simpson had said. He got some paper, folded it up, and slipped bits of it into the cracks worn in the window frames. Between windows he ate more bread and drank most of the camomile tea. When he had finished, there was still a sporadic whistling noise across the floor and the wind still let out howls outside, but the windows did not rattle quite so much. When he touched the chest of drawers, he saw that there was a thin layer of dust on all the furniture and on the marble floor. The stuff felt slippery, almost greasy.

There was a knock on the door, and almost immediately it opened.

'So, how are you feeling now?' said the doctor.

'Thin,' said Cotton. 'Please, come in.'

The doctor put his bag down on Ramírez's chair. 'That's only natural,' he said.

'Dry,' said Cotton

'That's the wind. Open your mouth. Yes. Your tonsils are a little swollen. Have you been vomiting much?'

'Only rumbling. I haven't vomited since early this morning,' said Cotton.

'Have you been drinking the camomile tea?'

'Yes. Horrible stuff,' said Cotton.

'Is it?' said the doctor. 'But it's useful. I also use it to treat eye infections, conjunctivitis, nothing serious, you know. Its advantage is that it's mild,' said the doctor.

'I'll remember that,' said Cotton. 'Can I drink something else now? How about water?'

'Are you going to be here long?' asked the doctor.

'I don't know,' said Cotton.

'Well, if you're just passing through, have them boil it. Typhus is endemic here, and foreigners sometimes get it. It's para-typhus, really. If you're going to stay, you might as well get accustomed to it.'

'I hadn't thought of that,' said Cotton.

'No? Let me see your chest.' The doctor listened. 'Smoke?' he asked.

'No.'

'Good,' said the doctor, rolling up his stethoscope. 'You have to be careful with bronchitis and tuberculosis here.'

'You should advertise the place.'

The doctor smiled. 'Oh, these things are relative. I was twenty years in Tarifa, along the coast by the Strait of Gibraltar. The wind is infinitely worse there. Highest rate of suicide in the peninsula. Lovely little place, though.' He stood up. 'Well, Mr Cotton, I think you're on the mend.'

'Thank you, doctor,' said Cotton. 'Oh, may I ask you a question?'

'Yes, of course.'

'Why are there so many cripples in Cadiz?'

The doctor laughed. 'Ah,' he said after a moment. 'You're serious. Is that the case? Are there so many? Compared with England, perhaps?'

'Compared with Madrid, for example.'

'Really? And you are aware, I assume, that in our war there wasn't fighting to speak of here?' mused the doctor.

'Yes,' said Cotton.

'Then I suppose', he said, 'that it's down to tuberculosis and gangrene. Some of my colleagues are very eager to use saws. And of course, we mustn't forget the *curanderos*. They're a kind of witch doctor, I suppose you would say. They do abortions, set bones, prescribe their own potions. They do a lot of damage, but of course they do it cheaper.'

'Perhaps that's it.'

The doctor smiled. 'I think you'll be all right, though,' he said. 'Constitution like a horse!'

'I know the one you mean,' said Cotton, nodding. 'It stands outside the railway station.'

The doctor laughed, and Cotton smiled. Even as he was smiling, he felt a sensation of doom come over him. It was appalling precisely because it was so thorough-going and, at the same time, almost serene. There was nothing dramatic about it. It was as if someone was kindly pointing out the next full moon, when he knew he would already be dead. On one level this was absurd. The surrealism of fear. But then Cotton knew perfectly well that physical state affects moods and thoughts.

'How much do I owe you, doctor?' he said.

The doctor shook his head. 'Get a good night's sleep,' he said. 'Eat gently for a day or two. Do you want a prescription for anything?'

'No, thank you,' said Cotton.

'Have them call me if you get any worse,' said the doctor, closing his bag.

'Of course. I will. Thank you very much, doctor.'

Cotton sat down as the doctor shut the door behind him. He found his hands were sweating. That sensation of doom had irritated him. It made him feel he could not trust himself. So he rationalized. First there was the journey and the purpose of his being there. Then there was the language. He had spoken Spanish since he was a child – well enough for people to assume he understood everything. But right now he was tired, and it was grating on his ears. It was almost as enervating as the Levante wind. And then there was the vomiting. But this rationalization itself was agitated. Cotton gently shook his head and worked his jaws, trying to clear his ears, which were blocking and popping with the pressure.

Cotton had never considered himself brave. Years before, an uncle had given him Conrad's *Lord Jim* to read, and he had understood, without experiencing it for himself, that a desire to be brave could be a ridiculous curse. He had himself watched people cut off all thought and hope for the sake of strength and speed. But he also knew that the concept of bravery was largely propagandistic. When immediate danger threatened, he, and a number of others he had seen, had behaved with a kind of brisk detachment and very sharp eyes in a situation that, looked at rationally, was violent and entirely random, making the detachment a kind of denial and the sharp eyes something just this side of desperation. Others had performed apparently brave acts with no notion at all of what they were doing. And he remembered seeing one man act with a kind of incredulous, reckless hilarity. That had impressed Cotton, because the man, considered old at thirty-six, had been awarded a medal for bravery. 'There was a kind of delight, a relief, in giving up and letting go of myself.' The man had paused and in a very quiet voice, almost a murmur, had said, 'Couldn't do that again.' This had impressed Cotton as, if not quite true to training, honest.

He looked rather sheepishly around his hotel room and managed a soft smile. He was, as it were, listening to himself. You know you are shaky when you doubt everything. He shut his eyes and breathed in. What was it that was actually getting to him? First was probably the spread of fear through his body – not that different from the water he had drunk in Houghton's office when he had been dehydrated. Then there was the sensation that others – Ramírez mostly – were making puppet gestures at him that he could not understand. Last, possibly worst, was a desire not to die in an absurd way. Falling off a sea wall in a blackout. Slipping on his own vomit on a marble floor. In one way, he could recognize that he was alarming himself to preserve himself. After a while he began listening to and taking comfort from the howling of the wind, remembering pleasant things, usually to do with food and girls.

Later, when the maid came in to turn down his bed, he put his hand in his pocket and gave her the usual coin.

'Oh, wait a minute,' he said. 'Give me that back.'

'What?' said the girl.

'Mari-Ángeles, isn't it?'

'Yes,' said the girl. She was still clutching the coin.

'Sh,' said Cotton. 'I'm just trying to be fair. Give me the coin.'

The girl did nothing.

'Put out your hand.'

The girl did. Cotton took hold of her wrist and gently pulled her fingers off the coin. 'There we are,' said Cotton, putting his hand and the coin back into his pocket. He paused. 'What? Don't you think I've given you more work today? Those disgusting sheets?'

'*Señor.*'

'How much more work do you think I've given you?'

'*¿Señor?*'

'How old did you say you were?'

'Eleven.'

'When are you twelve?'

'In December.'

'All right,' said Cotton. 'What would you say to double the work?'

'*Señor.*'

'Double the work means double the tip, wouldn't you say?'

'I don't know,' said the girl.

'I do. Here.'

Cotton held out his fist. The girl stared at it.

'I don't know, *señor.*'

'Sh,' said Cotton again. 'It's only fair. I don't think we need to tell anyone. OK?'

'*Señor.*'

'Here,' said Cotton – 'take it.'

The girl still didn't know what to do. Cotton waggled his fist. The girl took hold of it.

'Go on,' he said.

The girl giggled and began to prise up his fingers. Cotton offered no resistance. He smiled at her. 'You see?'

The girl stared at the coin revealed on his palm. For a child it was a lot.

'Thank you very much, *señor,*' she said.

'Not at all,' said Cotton. 'Take it.'

The girl did. He waved his hand.

'Buy some sweets or something.'

'*Señor.*'

'Good night, Mari-Ángeles.'

8

Cotton woke warily, as if from a hangover. It took him a long moment to remember where he was and that he had been sick. He listened. The Levante was still tugging outside, but had slackened. His throat felt very dry, and his stomach, when he sat up, felt stiff, as if he had been bruised. No, on the whole, he was set on feeling quite well, even spry. It did take him a while with one eye closed to work out what day it was. Tuesday.

Still cautious, he got out of bed. He could feel the dust under his bare feet. He was decidedly better. He walked through to the bathroom. He tried to enjoy his cold bath, and then shaved as carefully as he could. He dressed, and considered breakfast. He would have liked a boiled egg and some toast, but in the event he was quite content with two mashed bananas and some still-warm bread provided by the surprisingly solicitous elderly people who ran the hotel.

He took the antiquarian's gift and went directly to his office along the avenue. The sky still retained a few traces of white cloud, and the sea was a green-blue colour he had not seen before. The scruffy trees rustled when the hot wind tugged.

'Oh,' said Henderson. 'Mr Cotton?'

Cotton turned. Politely, but with some difficulty because of the parcel he was carrying, he held the door open for the vice-consul.

'Thank you,' said Henderson. 'A better day today, don't you think?'

'Less wind, yes.'

They greeted Eugenio, the porter, who handed them both their mail and the newspaper. 'Reich launches new and terrible weapon against London' was the headline. It was about the V-2 rocket, launched on 8 September. Cotton nodded, mostly at Ignacio's prompt, privileged sources. Henderson shook his head and tucked the paper under his arm.

'Bad business,' said Henderson. 'Though of course they always rather over-egg it.'

'Yes,' said Cotton, 'I'm sure they do.'

'Oh,' said Henderson again, 'I just ran into Bill Simpson. He was rather surprised not to have had a note from you.'

Cotton looked at him briefly. The spirit of etiquette was alive and sniffing in Cadiz. They turned up the stairs.

'I take it you did send one,' said Henderson.

'No,' said Cotton. 'I didn't. I began vomiting, you see, shortly after I left them. Yesterday, I was, well . . . rather indisposed.'

'I see,' said Henderson. 'Well, I wouldn't leave it too long if I were you. They are possibly a little touchy about good form.'

'Do you think I should invite them back, Mr Henderson? Only it's not easy to invite people to restaurants one doesn't know and . . .'

'No, no, no,' said Henderson, 'that's not necessary at all. In their position, they rather like . . . *giving*, if you follow me.'

'And receiving thank-you notes? I understand,' said Cotton. 'I'll do that, of course. I had already appreciated that they liked formalities.'

'Well, yes. By the way, I forgot to ask, were you a soldier before this?'

'I was.'

'Where?'

'West of Scotland, mostly. Ah. Here's your door. Good morning, Mr Henderson.'

'Mr Cotton.'

'Yes?'

'How's the funeral bill coming along?'

'I'm attending to it, vice-consul. I'll be in touch shortly.'

Cotton went up to his office, put the antiquarian's present on top of May's clothes, sat at his desk, and pulled out a sheet of the best paper. He uncapped his pen and tried a few practice strokes. Then he wrote:

Dear Mrs Simpson,

I am sorry not to have written to you sooner to thank you for a most pleasant evening with you and your husband but was prevented from doing so by odious circumstances.

Dinner was a delight and I was particularly grateful for the kindness you both showed me as an ignorant foreigner in a new place; such disinterested generosity is all too rare.

With my heartfelt thanks again and my very best wishes to you both,

Sincerely,

Peter Cotton MC, MA

Cotton felt pleasantly mean having done this, but waited for a while and drank some bottled water, letting it sit, in case he had gone over the top. He rather liked 'odious circumstances'. In the event, he had just finished the water and made his decision to send the thing when Eugenio came up.

'From the vice-consul's diplomatic bag, *señor*.'

Cotton gave him the note for the Simpsons and took the waterproof pouch. In theory the contents of the dip-lomatic bag would not have been examined by any Spanish authority, but that was not something Cotton felt he could take as certain. Inside the pouch there were two separate buff envelopes sealed with red wax.

He tackled the fatter one first. There was no obvious sign of tampering. He broke the seal. Inside he found three more envelopes, also sealed.

The first envelope contained a Spanish death certificate. The dead person had no name, but had died of a pulmon-ary embolism as testified by a Spanish doctor who had signed and stamped the death certificate, Dr Rafael Muñoz Molina, number 439 of the Madrid College of Physicians. Cotton slid the nameless death certificate back into the envelope and opened the next one.

It contained a Polish passport in the name of Kott, Josef, born in Kraków. Date of birth and everything else had been left blank.

The third envelope contained two notes from Marie in Madrid. One was formal, from MI9, Escape and Evasion, setting out the technique used for identity change. The death certificate should be completed in the real name of the Jewish refugee and returned to her. Cotton should fill in the passport details that were missing, using the equipment for that purpose in his office, and give it to the refugee. In the event that 'Don José' did not make himself known, Cotton should return everything 'using diplomatic channels'.

The other note was more personal.

Dear Peter,

I hope that they have not left you feeling too abandoned. And I hope you do not feel that now I am pressing you too hard on something that is not, I appreciate, your main task.

You must understand, however, that the Franco regime allows transit to some Jews but no consistent collaboration or guarantee is offered. If the Spanish authorities can squeeze money out of the refugees, they will, but again, any money paid does not guarantee safe passage. The refugee has to take his or her chances when moving through Spain and has to avoid corruption, bloody-mindedness and the groups under Franco who are allowed to persecute the disadvantaged. It is a gauntlet. But what we are dealing with is some chance against none.

In this case, as in many, we are dealing with bare snippets of information. Your refugee may be in a poor way – we've had Poles WALK to Gibraltar – may not speak Ladino, the old Spanish that Sephardic Jews use, may not speak any of your languages, may not even have received his code name.

I know Douglas thinks I get too involved, but every refugee we get out is an individual victory. No, it is not a solution, but it is something and that is about all we can hope for – or manage to get done.

The Pears soap is wonderful.

Love, Marie

Cotton sent Marie a reply through Baba.

Have received documents and notes in diplomatic bag today, Tuesday. Did my predecessor in Cadiz collaborate with you? Did he ask for help or advice on Jewish refugees? Will do what I can. P.

Cotton then opened the last envelope. It was what D's office had sent Madrid when May had been posted to Spain – little more than a form. Cotton learned that May's father, Lieutenant Alfred Bertram May, had been killed in the Dardanelles in 1915. His mother had converted to Catholicism in 1922, but had sent May to a non-Catholic school, Brighton College, where he had distinguished himself by becoming the school chapel organist and organizer of the choir competition. May had begun a degree in theology at Durham University, but switched to mathematics. On graduating, he had spent a year, 1934–5, in Ávila in Spain, and then spent three months in Salamanca, studying religious music. On his return to England he had lived in Wimbledon (1935–7) and Croydon (1937–9), been a reader for the publishers Lindsay Drummond Ltd, and taught at an adult-education college in Clapham. Called up in- 1939, he had been declared unfit for active service, but was drafted into work 'with Signals', based in Catterick. From there he had been sent to Hanslope Park 'to train in codes', and subsequently put into 'fieldwork in Cadiz'.

It was for Cotton a dispiriting account of a shortish life, the kind of thing that could be done to just about anybody. It had a touch of confusion in the middle and of failure at the end, going from the breaking of codes to something desultory in Cadiz. How had May contrived to do that? And what did 'unfit for active service' mean? Irritably, Cotton scratched his cheek. There were organists and choir organizers in all schools. He remembered the bespectacled look of the chubby boy at his old school, but couldn't remember his name. Had they called him Hughie? He closed his eyes and breathed out.

Doublets, Emmeline had called them, from Lewis Carroll. Move one letter of a word, change a whole meaning. She had introduced the game with the sequence lust–lost–lose–love. Cotton opened his eyes. Code–mode–made–maze. The CV gave him little he could actually use, and added little to what he already knew.

And then there were the other things. Had Cadiz been some sort of face-saver for May? Exchanging codes for a pair of binoculars? Indeed, who had first thought May suitable for the job? If D had picked him, why had he picked him? Had D not known May was homosexual? And how was D now handling May's possibly accidental, possibly suicidal death?

193

Someone knocked on the office door.

'There's a man downstairs waiting to see you,' said Eugenio. 'Will I tell him to go?'

'But who is he?' asked Cotton.

'Your predecessor saw him sometimes.'

Not Don José then. 'Send him up,' said Cotton.

Eugenio was unhappy. 'He'll have to be accompanied.'

'Then accompany him.'

While the porter was going down and coming up with his visitor, Cotton collected together the documents and letters and reports and put them into the safe. He sat down behind his desk and waited.

Eugenio appeared first. 'The person you have agreed to see.'

A skeletal-looking man shuffled awkwardly into his office. Cotton saw that the upper of one shoe was adrift from the sole. The man had no socks, his trousers were holed, and he was holding his jacket up to his neck with dirt-encrusted hands. His hair had a spurious, matted neatness. Cotton guessed this was *El Palo*. The Stick.

'What can I do for you?' asked Cotton.

'I did some things for the one before.' His voice was deep and hoarse.

'Yes?' said Cotton unhelpfully.

The man rubbed at his nose. 'What I said.'

'This office is a small one,' said Cotton. 'I'm here to close it. I don't need any things done now.'

The man blinked. 'I'm owed money,' he decided.

'Have you any proof of that?' asked Cotton. 'There's no record of anything like that here.'

'Well, ask anybody. Everybody knows,' said the man.

'What's that supposed to mean?' said Cotton. 'I can't act on that.'

'I'm owed,' insisted the man.

'Well,' said Cotton, 'I would of course honour any bona-fide arrangement between you and my late predecessor in this office, but, in the absence of any such thing, I would be disloyal to my employers if I paid out money on an unsupported claim.'

The man cleared his throat. 'What's happening?' he said suspiciously.

'I beg your pardon?' said Cotton. 'I'm simply making an irregular situation regular.'

The man squinted at him. 'This is Ramírez. This is what he has done.'

'What? No, certainly not,' said Cotton. 'Of course, I can understand why a misunderstanding might arise, but let me assure you that I am . . . well,' he swallowed, 'rather like Mr Henderson. Or Mr Simpson, perhaps.'

The man almost spat.

'Of course, at the moment, I'm busy making a report on my predecessor's unfortunate death . . .' said Cotton.

He paused. If the man had anything to say on that, surely he would say it now. But the man said nothing. 'But, having done that, there's no need for this office,' he continued.

The man clutched tighter at his jacket, but still said nothing.

'Well?' said Cotton.

The man shook his head. 'I have no money. My family has no bread.'

'Charity is another matter,' said Cotton. 'I am always willing –'

'Keep it,' said the man.

'As you wish,' said Cotton. 'But you will not come here again. Is that clear? Now go.'

And before the man could properly react, he repeated, 'Go.' Then, without any hurry, Cotton got out May's guide to the city and opened the street map. In spite of himself, he had to control his hands from trembling. For a while, there was silence. Then he heard the man shuffling away.

Cotton stood and stared at the floor for a moment. He bit his lip. He had not expected the man to react like that. After a while, he went downstairs. Eugenio was spitefully delighted.

'Well done, *señor*!' he said. 'He deserved it!'

'Did he usually come here?' asked Cotton.

'Nah! I assure you, he must have been desperate,' said Eugenio, and he tittered.

Cotton ordered lunch, at Eugenio's suggestion 'for a delicate stomach', and went back to his office. He looked out of the window. There were no new ships to be seen. He sat down and read a little of *Persuasion*, but paused when the food arrived. He had been given almond soup and grilled chicken. He tasted the soup, ate rather more of the chicken. He felt a little better, then a little queasy. Unbidden, snippets from his training sessions floated into mind: 'Do not dwell . . . Concentrate on the next task . . . Everything you need is usually in front of you.' Perhaps. And of course there had been 'Be patient.' He found a tear of newsprint in one of the drawers, and saw that one side was a crossword. It had been partially completed by May. He had got seven across wrong. It had been some time since Cotton had looked at a crossword, but it didn't take him very long to remember why. He put it back in the drawer. May's copy of *Persuasion* came with both of the endings provided by Jane Austen. The first was weak and surprisingly crude, written when she was ill; the second, rather more fluent and convincing, when she was, if not well, at least better.

Then he read a canto of *Don Juan* – the one in which Juan is washed ashore on a desert isle and rescued and loved by Haidée. The notes suggested that this canto was Byron's vision of an ideal world, 'as much innocent as amoral'. Cotton was not at all sure what the annotator meant. Indeed, he wondered if Byron would have understood. Cotton got out a sheet of paper. He still had to comment for D on Eliot's 'schoolboy or accomplished foreigner' charge against Byron's English. Cotton jotted down, 'Have met accomplished foreigner. Schoolboy agrees with Eliot.' He rubbed his head, got up, and went over to the window. He looked out over the bay and the port again. The water out in the bay was still a little choppy, and there was a slight swell in the port itself.

When he heard the shops opening, he got his hat, went downstairs, and walked to the Italian leather and luxury-goods shop. He examined the hatpins in the display case by the door. They were remarkable. Presumably the length of some of them had something to do with not losing a hat in wind, but he was most taken by the craftsmanship extended on them. That was a lot of work for some very kitsch things. There was one nearly as ornate as a Fabergé egg. Another was like an encrusted crescent moon. But the one that really caught his attention was a wicked-looking pin surmounted by tortoiseshell in the shape of a bow. He was about to look up for a shop assistant when he was spoken to in loud, peremptory Spanish.

'What are you doing with my governess?'

Cotton didn't wait. 'Nothing!' he snapped. He raised his hat to Ilse and smiled. 'Good afternoon. How are you today?'

'We invited you into our home. That is not commonly done in Cadiz.'

'And I am grateful. What is the problem?'

'You met her.'

'I did. And I was polite to her, having been very briefly introduced at your home. She has been away from her own home for some time, and wanted to speak some English. It is perfectly natural.'

'I don't want you turning her head.'

'This is absurd. I don't know whether you consider her an employee or a servant, but the problem is between yourselves. To upbraid me in public when I have nothing to do with the arrangement and no interest in it other than courtesy during what is a very brief visit to Cadiz is . . . well, I don't know what your definition of civilized and uncivilized is. Good afternoon. My best wishes to you.'

Cotton walked off without buying anything. He was unsure if his use of touchiness in manners would have any effect. Had he 'outcivilized' her? Touchiness is not the same as sensitivity.

He took the lift up to his office, went back to his desk, and reconsidered what he had written about Eliot. He did not like it. He was not a doodler, but decided to try it, and was carefully shading in a triangle when, neglecting to knock, Ramírez came in. Cotton had expected him sooner.

'You're on British territory now,' said Cotton, turning over the sheet of paper.

Ramírez stopped and considered. 'No,' he said. 'That's only diplomatic offices, like downstairs.'

He closed the door and sat down in the visitor's chair. 'How are you feeling today?' he asked.

'Better, thank you,' said Cotton.

'You have a very nice office here,' said Ramírez, looking around. 'It's better than mine.'

'You deserve more,' said Cotton.

Ramírez smiled. 'I don't let it bother me. Busy?'

'Oh, you know,' said Cotton.

'Writing?' asked Ramírez, looking at the turned-over page on the desk.

'A draft of something,' said Cotton.

'Do you really like writing?' asked Ramírez. 'I avoid it if I can. It's a lot of trouble. It makes my fingers stiff.'

'I spend most time organizing my thoughts,' said Cotton.

'Really? It's the person I'm writing for that I find most difficult,' said Ramírez. 'I mean, just how much do I want to say?'

Cotton nodded. 'Yes, I know what you mean.'

'I didn't know you were a brave man,' said Ramírez.

Cotton smiled. 'I'm not at all brave.'

'They tell me you have a very good medal,' said Ramírez, sitting back in his chair.

'Who does?'

Ramírez smiled. 'My sources.'

'Must be good sources.'

'Well,' said Ramírez, 'if I don't know something, I ask.'

'Who?'

'Henderson.'

'No,' said Cotton, smiling and shaking his head. 'I put that in for you. MC is *mucho cariño,* and MA is *mucho afecto*' – much love and affection. 'In fact I'm not sure which way round the degree and the medal should be. I can't remember the priorities. Is it scholarship before gallantry in the field, or the other way around?'

Ramírez smiled. 'Yes, you definitely sound better today. Why did you want to annoy Mr and Mrs Simpson?'

'Well, "annoy" isn't the word exactly.'

'Is it an English custom?'

'What? Writing thank-you letters?'

'No,' said Ramírez patiently. 'Needling people by being very polite.'

'"Needling" is very strong,' protested Cotton. 'I hope they're pleased with the letter.'

'You want to pinch them without them knowing, or maybe without them being able to reply? That's perfidious.'

'Does it shock you?' asked Cotton.

'No. I want to know why,' said Ramírez.

'Because they are exceptionally mean and boring people. And I vomited. And if I did get the degree and the medal the wrong way round they'll notice and be pleased. But they probably won't doubt the existence of either one.'

Ramírez looked at him. 'It's interesting to see the customs of other lands,' he said mildly.

'I don't think it's confined to Britain,' said Cotton.

'But you are the masters.'

'Not any more,' said Cotton.

'Be serious, now,' said Ramírez. 'People are complaining that you don't pay for information.'

'Do you?'

'My situation is entirely different,' said Ramírez. 'If you don't pay them, they steal, get caught – and that's another charge on the state.'

Cotton smiled. 'I hadn't thought of it like that,' he said. 'Was that *El Palo*?'

'Yes. Why were you so hard on him?'

'He offered me no information. He wanted a retainer, I think.'

'Yes, that would be it,' said Ramírez.

'But I'm not May.'

'Ah. May never won a medal.'

'Do you think I did?' said Cotton.

'Well, one day you will tell me about it,' said Ramírez. 'Now, what happened with *El Palo*?'

'I told you,' said Cotton. 'It was probably my fault. I wanted to make something clear. I thought he'd be tougher, show more spirit.' Cotton shrugged. 'I wanted to get him out of the way. I'm looking ahead.'

'Looking ahead to what?' said Ramírez.

'To the end of the war, of course!' said Cotton. 'Who isn't?'

There was a pause. Ramírez sighed and blew out. He suddenly looked tired.

'The theatre is elsewhere,' said Cotton.

'In Cadiz it almost always is,' said Ramírez wryly.

Cotton smiled. 'If it hadn't been for May . . . ' he said.

Ramírez winced. '*Ya*. We don't merit you,' he said.

'I wouldn't say that at all,' said Cotton, shaking his head.

'Why are you so cheerful?' asked Ramírez.

'I honestly don't know. Perhaps it's feeling well again.'

'All right. So why did you come here?' asked Ramírez.

'You know,' said Cotton.

'Tell me.'

'To close up and tidy up here prior to the transition,' said Cotton.

'Transition to what?'

'To peace. At present, peace is a somewhat abstract concept bobbling between the Board of Trade and the National Debt. I've spent most of the last two months reading papers: "Opportunities in the Post-War Period". Before I came here I was given a paper called "Agriculture in Andalusia". Someone had underlined the section on sherry.'

'And what about May?' asked Ramírez.

'Honestly?'

'Yes, honestly,' said Ramírez.

'Well, I think they forgot about him. And now I think they want to make sure that any damage he did is minimized. I was already in Madrid when they heard he had died.'

'So we really don't merit you.'

'I don't merit *you*,' said Cotton. 'I'm here by chance. I'm small beer, an undistinguished ex-soldier who happened to speak some Spanish and who at least did a course on economics at university.' He shrugged.

'Oxford?' asked Ramírez.

'Cambridge,' said Cotton.

Ramírez nodded. 'I see. Can I ask you a question?'

'Go ahead,' said Cotton.

Ramírez leaned forward. 'What do they call you? Your job, precisely, here I mean. Not the formal name.'

'Right. I understand. Yes, in this case I think they'd call me a fireman.'

'A what?' said Ramírez.

'A little fireman. I think they want my report to be like a fire blanket. I put it over the wet ashes and everything looks better, almost as if nothing bad had happened.'

'Ah!' said Ramírez. 'You are encouraging the dust!'

He made a rippling movement with the fingers of his right hand, and then used them to scratch his neck. He leaned back in his chair. 'But you're young. You're of an age to fight, aren't you?'

'Yes.'

Ramírez frowned. 'Were you wounded?'

'No. I was in a jeep accident.'

'Is that why you're not in the army now?'

'Well, no. I was seconded to the logistics department before D-Day, because I had some broken fingers that had to be reset. Then somebody saw that I had been born in South America and had some experience of organizing blankets and boots, and, well, it sort of led on from there. I found myself . . . '

'In a God Save Your Excellency world!' smiled Ramírez.

'A what?' blinked Cotton.

'That's what I have to put at the end of the reports I write,' said Ramírez. 'Actually, it's "God Save Your Excellency for Many Years". You were a captain,' he said.

'Yes, that's right.'

'But now you are paid as a major.'

Cotton nodded. Why was Ramírez insisting on demonstrating he had read his mail, even to Glyn Mills? Cotton already knew that, and knew just how claustrophobically close Ramírez's attention could be.

'That's not so small,' said Ramírez.

'How do you mean?'

'For us, a major is not so small.'

Cotton smiled. 'I was the best they could do in the circumstances,' he said.

Ramírez sighed. 'Thank you,' he said. He made the curious Spanish gesture of holding out an index and middle finger to signal closeness, even pointed at Cotton and at his own chest. He was telling Cotton that close attention was an act of friendship, an alliance. 'Now what would you say to a char-grilled mackerel and a game of chess afterwards?'

'Of course,' said Cotton, 'it's the only worthwhile board game, but unfortunately I'm rotten at it. And I really do have some work to do. And besides, I have to get spruced up later.'

'Why's that?' asked Ramírez.

'I had thought of visiting a lady then.'

'Oh, good boy!' said Ramírez. 'You never let me go disappointed.' He got up. 'I'll see myself out. *Suerte.*'

'*Oye,*' said Cotton.

'What?'

'Reading my mail is one thing . . .'

'*Faltaría más,*' said Ramírez. No need to say it. 'Your business with Antoñita is private.'

'If you say so,' said Cotton.

'*¡Hombre!* I do.'

Ramírez had not, however, gone towards the door, but to the window. 'You have an excellent view,' he said. 'The whole port. Ah, and most of Canalejas.'

He smiled and began towards the door, but then pulled up. 'Oh. One more question,' he said.

'More?' smiled Cotton.

'Yes. As an educated man – will the Americans roll their tanks into Spain?'

'I don't know,' said Cotton.

'Oh come on. Think.'

Cotton sighed. 'No,' he said, 'I don't think so.'

'Why not?'

'The Allies are going in the other direction, and you're a long way south of Berlin. There's the war with Japan. I know we're tired, and I imagine the Americans are not actually looking for more war. In any case, this is what they call a "democratic" war.'

Ramírez raised his eyebrows. 'What does that mean?' he said.

'An army of conscripts,' said Cotton. 'Fighting Hitler is one thing. This . . . would be something different. Spain hasn't invaded anyone, was a non-combatant, is now neutral.'

'Right,' said Ramírez, 'I see. So Franco is either very clever or very lucky.' He shook his head.

Cotton smiled. 'Possibly,' he said. 'And besides, the focus is changing. They're thinking beyond Germany now.'

'How do you mean?' asked Ramírez.

'Well,' said Cotton, 'before I came I was given a paper or two to read on Marx and Marxism.'

Ramírez nodded. 'Now that *is* interesting.'

'But remember who I am,' said Cotton.

'Even if you *are* a small fireman, as you say, your government's preoccupation with the Communists must run deep,' said Ramírez. He was looking positively cheered. 'I think you've just done my career some good. Enjoy yourself with Antoñita,' he said.

Cotton waited till he was sure that Ramírez had gone downstairs. Then, he took another piece of paper and wrote:

Estimado Señor Romero,

I was both touched by and impressed with your splendid gift. Unfortunately I am not allowed to accept gifts which might be seen to compromise my professional position. This may strike you as absurd, but I suspect not; anyone capable of providing such a gift will assuredly have the sensitivity and taste to appreciate that I must comply with the undertakings I signed when I agreed to serve in my present capacity.

Your thoughtfulness and generosity are, however, much appreciated.

My heartfelt respects,

Peter Cotton

Cotton rewrapped the riding lectern and called the porter. Would he see that the parcel and the note were delivered? He would. Then Cotton checked the coding machine. There was a message from Houghton:

Marie has several contacts in Spain on the lookout for information on Jewish refugees. The contact that brought Don José to her attention is in Ávila. No record of assistance or requests from Cadiz. B.

Cotton thought. According to his CV, May had been in Ávila ten years before and had stayed there for a year. There would have been a little human glue as well as the religious music. Ávila was not Oviedo, Toledo, Palencia or any other Spanish town or city. Houghton had just brought up Ávila again. 'People are just not that good, nor that complicated,' D had said. For the first time Cotton considered that May's boy and Don José might really be linked.

Cotton put the machine away, locked the safe, shut the office, and walked back to the hotel.

9

His hair still a little damp after washing it, Cotton strolled out of the hotel in the early evening. He went by way of the Plaza de España, and walked round the enormous monument to the Liberal Constitution in the middle. Cotton stopped for a moment to read the plaque. He saw that it had been put up long after the constitution had been overturned. He continued walking along by the pollarded trees, paused at the wooden dovecote, and briefly watched some small children throwing maize to the pigeons. To one side, a group of uniformed maids were chatting and watching the children. One of them came forward to separate two small boys who were fighting. Both of them turned on her, kicking her and calling *¡Puta!* – whore. She laughed and rubbed her ankles. The more aggressive child was no more than three. Cotton moved on.

He nodded drily as he passed the Simpsons' house, and kept going until he reached another square, the Plaza de Mina. Here, courting couples sat hand in hand on the stone benches under the trees, while their younger brothers and sisters, unwitting chaperones, played tag or hopscotch or complicated games with elastic skipping ropes. Along one whole side of the square was the Museum. It contained, the guidebook had said, paintings by Murillo and Zurbarán, neither of whom particularly interested him. He did not go into the square, but turned down a side road towards the sea. As he walked along, almost in the dark, his eye was caught by a plaque on a house. It commemorated Lord Byron's brief visit. That somehow cheered him.

At the end of that street, he came out on to a view of a garden, the Alameda, and beyond it the sea. He crossed the road and turned left. The gardens of the Alameda were different from any he had seen in Cadiz outside the British Cemetery. They lacked the layouts and ochre soil of the formal affairs. These were lush, and looked more tropical than subtropical – an impression created by the thick roots pushing up the paving stones, smells of resin as sweet as mango, and the nature of the shade, which was fleshier, deeper, more humid. Instinctively, he paused and looked around. Almost hidden was a small bust to a botanist from Cuba. And, just to make the point, the roots of a huge ficus tree had done for an octagonal Moorish-style fountain.

The air was oppressively still. When he walked towards the sea, however, he felt a mild breeze. He began to see something of what Ramírez had been talking about. At a rough guess, there was a drop of about fifteen to twenty feet, even at high tide, from the stone sea balustrade. Ahead there was a corner made blind by a fortress-like structure which would have added another fifteen feet to the drop. The thickness of the vegetation didn't help the view, but as he was estimating the height of the balustrade he saw a policeman lean over and look down.

Cotton turned away. He skirted the broken fountain. Across the road he could see several people hanging out of the windows. He looked to his right and saw what he had been looking for: the grandiose, colonial-style church of El Carmen. He crossed the road and turned left again. He was pleased to find that he had read the map correctly. Four houses along, he turned into a doorway and rang the bell.

A maid let him in and took him up the stone steps into a small salon, shuttered against the sunlight. It was so dark that Cotton had to use his hands to make sure of the chair he was invited to sit on. After two or three minutes his eyes became more accustomed to the gloom, and he suddenly realized that the painting on the wall opposite him was not a landscape but a portrait of a chubby angel; he had taken the wings for hills. Otherwise, the small room was rather like a china closet in a much grander house. The building was in total silence – something Cotton realized he hadn't experienced since his arrival in Cadiz. Then he heard a regular sound – a knife on a chopping board, he thought. It stopped.

After another ten minutes the maid returned and invited him to accompany her. He followed. She showed him through double doors into another small room, this one much lighter. In front of him, rather prissily curtained, was another set of double doors, these glazed. Again he was invited to sit, this time in one of two diminutive Isabelline chairs on either side of a round table.

He sat. The maid disappeared. At least he could see clearly in this room. The walls were hung in faded grey silk – a mildly moth-eaten moiré – and had over-framed paintings of all sizes and subjects hanging all over them. There was a cow under a tree in a very English landscape, in a frame that would not have been out of place in a rococo church; a naive portrait of a whiskered young man in a scarlet military coat; a print of a man in eighteenth-century dress who appeared to have his long hair in gold net. 'Smuggler of Cadiz' said the lettering. In another frame were some very Romantic mountains, and tucked away in a corner was a small chalk drawing of a girl. Cotton got up and went over to look closer. The name Antonia was written lightly in pencil above the head of a frizzy-haired child with a precocious air of gravity. Cotton had no artistic training and was not particularly interested, but even he suspected that the artist had kept to certain well-tried formulas – the eyes a little too large; a nose reduced to pretty nostrils – in an attempt to squeeze in the girl's nicest likeness to please whoever had paid him.

Cotton sat down again. As he did so, he noticed, on a bookshelf to his left, a photograph of a stallion preparing to mount a mare. The photographer had achieved an effect like an enormous sundial by using the shadow of the stallion's erection and by adding some Roman numerals. It was the only faintly improper thing he had seen there. The door rattled and the maid came in carrying a tray, which she set down on the table in front of him.

'Señorita Antonia will be with you presently,' she said.

'Thank you,' said Cotton.

He was beginning to feel amused by the slightly grubby gentility. The tray bore three small bowls of very ornate silver. One contained biscuits like plump, crunchy buttons – rather like those he had seen at the Germano-Spanish house – another salted almonds, and the third raisins. On a small plate were slices of skinned cucumber. There was a bowl of sugar and a tiny cup already filled with black coffee. But the article that most took his attention was a silver holder in which had been placed a glass of pale-brown warm milk.

'I knew the English took their tea with milk.'

Cotton turned round. Antonia's voice was pleasant – light and slightly fruity.

She was posed in front of the glazed double doors with her hands behind her still on the handles. She was diminutive. Cotton thought she had not grown vertically since the drawing. She was now a plump little woman with coarse hair, large eyes, and a nose that looked particularly snub under all the face powder. Her face was as powdered as a Turkish delight. She was wearing an ornate but cheap pink negligee, firmly tied. For a moment, Cotton had the impression of a prettyish woman without much vanity. Absurd. She was comfortable, vain and professionally kind. He stood and took her offered hand, and was pleased to find that it smelled distinctly of cucumber. She sat down, dropped two sugar lumps in her coffee, and sucked noisily. Then she took a clutch of button biscuits and began feeding them into her mouth one by one. Between biscuits she spoke in precise, well-pronounced Spanish.

'The English eat so sensibly,' she said. 'A good breakfast as a foundation, a light luncheon so as not to sleep away the afternoon, tea to refresh and unwind – did you see the cucumber? – and then a romantic supper. Is the tea to your liking?'

Cotton sipped dutifully. The tea was unspeakable. It tasted like Earl Grey in lukewarm, curdling milk. She smiled. Ignoring the napkins provided, she wiped her hands on her negligee. 'Are you interested in art, by any chance?'

'Well,' said Cotton, 'I'm always open to –'

'I'm just an amateur, of course. But it might amuse you? While you finish your tea?'

'Of course,' said Cotton.

Antonia rose and went to the lower shelves opposite Cotton. Her negligee – double layer at the front, single at the back – revealed, through cheap pink gauze, a view of her rear. She behaved as if she was quite unconscious of it, which couldn't be true, thought Cotton. He was, in spite of himself, a little taken aback by the oddly innocent, almost stolid, play of those plump cheeks as she bent to heave at a large portfolio. She turned and smiled. She undid the ribbon – pink again – and opened the grey, marbled folder.

'On your lap I think would be best,' she said with a simper.

Cotton hastily prepared himself to find animating illustrations of sexual tastes. Instead, he found himself turning over grossly incompetent drawings of female faces.

'My little friends,' said Antonia, before draining her coffee.

The drawings were exceptionally bad and all very similar. Did her friends exist in her mirror? Or was this some subtle test by a professional? If he said he preferred one, would that tell her something? The faces went on and on – all over-large eyes, noses reduced to nostrils, and considerable problems with the lips. Cotton felt nonplussed. He remembered '*Non plus ultra*'. No further. But here he had pages and pages of art to turn.

'Now you are getting to the chalk drawings,' said Antonia.

'Yes, of course,' said Cotton, raising his eyebrows, trying to look appreciative. They reminded him of cheaply coloured, rather worn porcelain.

'I have no talent whatsoever,' said Antonia. 'I expect I am embarrassing you. In the next one I tried green. Not altogether successfully.'

'Well,' said Cotton, studying the drawing, 'I'm not sure about that.'

'Someone told me once that it was the absinthe more than the French artists I admire.'

Cotton looked at her.

'More Toulouse-Lautrec than Boucher,' she explained.

Cotton smiled without separating his lips. He knew little of art, but recognized those disparate names. He thought for a moment. 'I should have said more Watteau.'

She seemed very pleased. Her breath whistled slightly, but she continued as relentlessly as before. They went through the entire portfolio until, at the very end, Cotton found a piece of blotting paper and a scrap of waxy stuff with a telephone number on it.

'There!' she said. She took the portfolio from him, closed it, and leaned it against the side of her chair.

'Oh,' she said, 'you haven't tried the cucumber!' She took a slice in her fingers and held it up to Cotton. 'Open,' she said.

Cotton opened his mouth.

'Put out your tongue.'

Cotton did so. She placed the slice of cucumber on his tongue. He brought it into his mouth and munched.

'I have always thought of cucumber as a naughty sort of communion wafer,' she said, bringing her palms together delightedly.

'Oh, let's get ready,' she said, and jumped up. She went over to the dressed double doors, opened them, and disappeared. Cotton could see a half-tester bed decorated with more gilt. He heard shutters clatter and rattle.

'Come,' she whispered. 'Come.'

Cotton got up and walked through. She slid past him and shut the double door.

'Now we're alone and in private,' she said.

More than ten years before, as schoolboys, Cotton and his class had received a talk by a chaplain on impure thoughts and troublesome physical reactions. The chaplain had suggested that they investigate 'modest religious experience and sport' instead. Amused but polite, Cotton waited patiently for the class to finish. But, at the end, one of his friends told him he was thinking of 'trying the religious suggestion'. It took Cotton a moment to understand that his friend was serious. The remark had induced in him a kind of disheartening tranquillity. Antoñita undid his tie. He made to help her.

'No. Let me,' she ordered.

She undressed him, taking care with his clothes, putting them on hangers, making sure his shirt did not rumple, brushing at the lapels of his jacket, getting the creases of his trousers just so, until Cotton stood white, naked and abashed.

With a cheerful smile and a theatrical shrug, Antoñita divested herself of her pink negligee and revealed a combination of cherub fat and fertility figure – and no body hair. Cotton blinked. The contrast between her white-powdered face and the colour of her body, rather like the tea she had provided for him, also impressed him. She then approached him with a delighted little rush – almost exactly the same, thought Cotton, as the way Spanish women enthused over babies. He shut his eyes and, while his mind wrestled with images of cooing and tickling and cheek-pinching, her fingers dealt with his flesh.

'That will do very well,' she said kindly, rubbing against him like a bald cat. Her breath whistled. Then she suddenly twisted like an acrobat and applied herself with such gobbling, muscular skill that Cotton almost didn't realize he was participating until his part was over. A combined throb and blink.

Antoñita turned and beamed. Her face was flushed under the powder. 'Such quantity!' she said complimentarily, reaching over and mopping herself with part of the top sheet. 'That technique is called the sea anemone. Did you like it?'

Lamely, Cotton nodded.

Antoñita took his head in her hands and looked into his eyes. 'Relax, my friend,' she said soothingly. She took his hand. 'Lie down. Make yourself comfortable.'

Cotton lay down on the bed.

'Would you like something to eat?'

'No, really, thank you,' said Cotton.

'Forgive me if I do,' said Antoñita. She hopped across to a chest of drawers and took two biscuits from a round tin. 'Oh, the metal's cold,' she said. She held up the biscuits. 'They're *Marías*, you know. Are you sure you won't?'

'Yes,' said Cotton, 'I'm sure.'

She clambered on to the bed, straddled his legs not much above the knee, and ate. 'I like to see the face,' she said. 'Close your eyes.'

Cotton did. Crumbs fell on to his thighs. She seemed unaware of them.

'You are very tense,' she said. 'Relax.' She moved forward and bent down, and began to rub her hair gently against his chest. She told him she had been born in Morocco. That her natural father had been a doctor from Santander. That he had put his money into houses. This had been one of them. She giggled. She caressed and stroked. In due course, she straightened up and announced, 'This is called the *convoy*.'

Cotton's eyes opened. Years before, he had been taken to the cinema to see a film called *Riders of the Purple Sage*. His South American *tata*, or nurse, had said the same thing: '*convoy*' to mean 'cowboy'. Antoñita raised an invisible Stetson in the air and dug her heels into his thighs.

After a decent interval, she curled up and whispered, 'That was much better. I think we have got along quite well, don't you? I'd be pleased to see you again.'

[*]

217

Cotton dressed. He looked round. Antoñita was covered by the bedclothes. He opened the double doors and found a small table barring his path. It had a small silver salver on it with an envelope. There was a card inside the envelope, written in French. Since HM Government was paying, Cotton was especially generous. Immediately he had put the cash in the envelope, the maid came to show him out.

She led him out of the house the same way they had come in. Cotton almost walked past the small, bald man sitting under the painting of the angel's wings he had taken for hilltops.

'What are you doing here?' he said, pulling up.

'Can't I enjoy myself too?'

'Very well,' said Cotton, and kept going.

'My friend,' said Ramírez shaking his head, 'I'm on duty.'

Cotton turned. That was not the first time he had used the word 'friend', but the tone sounded new. 'What's that supposed to mean?'

Ramírez got up and walked over. 'I'll accompany you,' he said.

'Why?' said Cotton.

'Because I want to. I understand, I do. You're annoyed I came. But you shouldn't be confused in your thinking. You shouldn't', said Ramírez, 'mix things up.'

'What are you talking about?'

'Private and public things,' said Ramírez. 'And you shouldn't be annoyed with me because you're embarrassed by your lust. Lust is natural. I'm the last person to intrude on intimacy without cause.'

'You are?' said Cotton.

'Yes. I hope you were generous with her. She's had a lot of trouble with the grocer,' said Ramírez.

'You're an extraordinary character!' said Cotton.

The maid opened the door to let them out into the street. 'Thank you very much,' said Cotton.

'*De nada, señor,*' said the maid, giving a little bob.

'This way,' said Ramírez. 'You know, you could get to your friends the Simpsons very easily from here.'

'I know,' said Cotton.

'Let me tell you about a film I saw,' said Ramírez.

'Why?'

'Because it will pass the time and let you calm yourself down. We are going to have to think clearly and with rigour. Clear your mind.' The little man put on his hat.

Cotton nodded. 'Very well,' he said.

'That's better. Yes,' said Ramírez, 'it's a wonderful film. It won the Oscar I think in 1935 – I can't really remember, because I saw it at a private viewing about four years ago. Of course the dubbing is terrible. Mexican. You cannot take Mexican voices seriously. Ah, I beg your pardon. I forgot your connection.'

'That's all right.'

'Well, Gable could never be a Mexican!' said Ramírez. 'But the quality of the production still shines through. It's very funny. The blanket scene is funny. The film's called *It Happened One Night*. Do you know it?'

'No, I didn't see it.'

Ramírez stopped. He put his hand on Cotton's forearm. 'Look, I waited for you and Antoñita to finish,' he said.

He seemed to think this was of importance. Cotton nodded. 'Yes,' he said.

'I waited,' repeated Ramírez. 'Now, have you a handkerchief, my friend?'

'Yes. I think it's clean.'

'No, no,' said Ramírez, 'it's not for me. You'll need it. I'm going to show you something very unpleasant. You may need to put the handkerchief over your face and breathe as little as you can. All right? It's just here.'

They went down a dank little alley of what appeared to have once been stables – some of the doors still had two sections – but were now storerooms or workshops. Cotton had to duck to get through the doorway Ramírez was indicating to him. They descended three or four stone stairs. Cotton could hear water dripping. A policeman was standing along the corridor.

'Now,' said Ramírez.

Cotton held the folded handkerchief over his mouth and nostrils. They turned into a bare, vaulted room lit by a blue bulb. The stench was appalling, even though the corpse lying on a scrubbed wooden table had been packed round with crushed ice. Worse, Cotton found the smell got through to his eyes. They were stinging.

Ramírez patted him on the shoulder. 'We had to send to a fish wholesaler for ice,' he said.

Cotton nodded.

'But you've seen dead men before, haven't you?'

'Not like this,' said Cotton.

'No? The subject was a tall young man of about twenty years of age,' said Ramírez, as if he was quoting.

Cotton squinted at the table. The throat had been opened back to the spine, but it was difficult to say much more because of the effect of the decomposition and the rats. Involuntarily, Cotton's hand came up. He managed to stop himself from retching.

'Yes?' said Ramírez just as Cotton made out the incisor marks on what flesh remained on the nose.

'Why . . . blue?' he asked, pointing to the light.

Ramírez nodded. 'It's what they had,' he said. 'Seen enough?'

They went out into the corridor.

'They're supposed to be moving him. But there's some stupid problem about masks,' said Ramírez.

'But this isn't where you found him?' said Cotton.

'No. He was found . . . near the Parque Genovés. It's one of the good things about the Levante. It certainly sniffs out corpses.'

'When was he found?' asked Cotton.

Ramírez looked at his watch. 'Four hours ago – a little less,' he said.

'Do you normally move corpses so quickly?'

Ramírez nodded. 'I admire the English,' he said, 'because they don't believe in systems. The Germans, for example, believe in systems. They work everything out, and they work it out thoroughly, until they are satisfied there are no flaws.'

'Yes?' said Cotton.

'But then when something goes wrong they can't believe it. So they lie to themselves. Saving the system means more than correcting the mistake. They ignore the mistake. Or they look for a scapegoat.'

'Do I follow you?' said Cotton, shaking his head. 'Why are you telling me all this?'

'Yes,' Ramírez insisted. 'Because all armies have Germanic tendencies. Our Spanish army has even copied their helmets and the goose-step! The English, on the other hand, always know that someone is going to be incompetent. They take that into account. Though I suspect you have scapegoats too.'

'Yes,' said Cotton.

'I suspect you have injustice too.'

'Yes,' said Cotton.

'So you don't allow the *shit-wit soldiers* to command everything, do you!'

Cotton managed a smile. Ramírez blinked and shook his head. 'The old antiquarian says it's his grandson,' he said.

'What?' said Cotton. 'He said that?'

'Well, he would, of course, wouldn't he?' said Ramírez.

Cotton shook his head. 'Does this tie in with what you told me before?'

Ramírez shrugged. 'Nothing ties in,' he said wearily. 'Come on. Let's get out of here.'

They went up the stairs into the alley.

'Do you feel like eating something?' said Ramírez.

'What?' said Cotton. He had to wipe his eyes. 'Do you?'

Ramírez put his hand on Cotton's forearm. 'I'm sorry. A drink, perhaps. I need company.'

The place was tiny – little more than a passage with a bar – and they had to squeeze past the two or three clients that were there in order to reach a door. Ramírez opened it. There was a small back room beside a minute kitchen. Ramírez looked relieved to be there. They sat down on rush chairs. A fat man wearing a dirty apron appeared carrying a bottle without a label and two tumblers.

'What have you got tonight?' asked Ramírez.

The man spoke as fast as an auctioneer, and it took Cotton some time to understand that he was reciting the menu. Ramírez nodded.

'I'm in your hands,' he said. He poured from the bottle. The liquid had the colour of dank straw. The fat man brought some bread and olives.

'Cheers,' said Ramírez.

'Yes,' said Cotton. '*Salud*.' He drank. 'Ah,' he said. 'What's this?'

Ramírez considered. 'Well, it's a type of *oloroso*. It's from Chiclana. That's along the road from here, about twenty-two kilometres. It's not what fine people drink, but I like it.'

'Yes,' said Cotton. He tasted it again. He did not like it. 'It's very good.'

In the kitchen the fat man was rattling pans. Cotton heard a hiss of very hot oil. He could hear strident voices and laughter from the bar and, quite near, children playing and shrieking. Yet he could see that Ramírez felt as comfortable as he would have done in silence.

'I'm going to tell you a little story,' said Ramírez.

Cotton turned his head, straining to hear.

Ramírez leaned across the table and spoke up. 'Three or four days before you arrived here, there was a trial – a military trial of a civilian.' Ramírez tapped his forehead. 'I have memorized what the prosecution said. Not the defence, oh no.' He jabbed his finger for emphasis. 'The prosecution!'

Cotton nodded to show he had heard.

'*¡Calláos!*' bellowed Ramírez. Shut up. There was a hush, then the noises started again. Ramírez smiled. ' "There is no basis" – this is what the prosecution said – "for a direct and specific accusation outside a rumour that can neither be traced nor verified. There is no indication whatsoever, no identity and no name, of the person the defendant is rumoured to have killed and robbed." The prosecution recommended clemency. Clear?'

'Yes.'

The fat man brought in the first little dish – grilled snippets of liver. Ramírez wolfed them down.

'Sure you won't eat anything?'

'I'm sure.'

'At least have some bread, *hombre*.'

Cotton dutifully took a piece. 'So what happened?'

Ramírez looked up. 'Condemned to death for murder and twenty years for robbery.'

'On what grounds?'

Ramírez smiled. 'The military judges considered rumour to be sufficient proof.'

Cotton frowned. 'Right. But what is the twenty years for, if the poor devil is to be executed?'

'He'll be executed all right. The twenty years is for the robbery. If he is being executed for murder on rumour, he is going to be imprisoned for robbery on rumour. It stands to reason. The army are very particular about consistency.'

'I understand consistency, but how do you serve a term of imprisonment if you are dead?'

'His family won't be able to bury him, may not even find out where the body is.' Ramírez sniffed. He spoke in somewhere between wonder and admiration. 'There are people out there too frightened even to grieve.' He turned towards the kitchen. 'Come on!' Then towards Cotton. 'Do you like it?' said Ramírez. 'I do. Of course I'm careful who I talk to.'

'Thank you,' said Cotton.

'I didn't mean it as a compliment,' said Ramírez. 'I'm just cautious.'

'Yes, of course,' said Cotton

Ramírez looked up. The fat man brought in a dish of tiny, fried squid and some sizzling prawns in garlic and oil.

'Are you sure you won't have anything? These prawns look good.' He tried one. 'Mm. Sure?'

'I'm sure,' said Cotton.

Ramírez rapidly ate what was left on the plates.

'I'm feeling better now,' he said. 'Shit, that corpse is *mine*!' He let himself sink back in his chair and shook his head.

Cotton raised his eyebrows.

Ramírez pushed up his sleeve and showed Cotton his wrist. There was a burn mark.

'That was the rope,' he said, and then laughed. 'I had to be lowered over the sea wall. It wasn't dignified. I don't have a stand-in. We got the body out by boat, wrapped it up in canvas, and then hoisted it up.'

'Right,' said Cotton. 'I'm sorry. You hadn't told me that. Where was it?'

'Well,' said Ramírez, 'you know that some of Cadiz has a foundation of sand, some is rock, and some is nothing.'

'What do you mean "nothing"?'

'Nothing!' said Ramírez. 'Hollow! Caves, holes, Arab sewers running into Roman drains. Hell, people sleep in some of them. They have nowhere else to go. The problem is that the sea keeps whittling things away. Below the Parque Genovés we found that the sixteenth-century fortifications had been worn away. There's a large hole that connects to a drain that connects to another . . . and so on.' He shook his head. 'It's a rats' paradise down there. There are thousands of them.' He shuddered.

'And the body was found there?' said Cotton.

'Yes,' said Ramírez. He leaned forward over the table. 'And if the military find out, they'll want it. I think I've done you a favour.'

'Why's that?' asked Cotton.

'Well, you don't want to have to deal with the Spanish military, believe me.'

'Right,' said Cotton. 'But why would I have to?'

'Well, it's near their patch for one thing. And the other is that the body is apparently that of a serving soldier.'

'But I had understood', said Cotton, 'that the antiquarian's grandson had deserted after May's death.'

'Mm,' said Ramírez. 'Even if he decided to commit suicide afterwards, it might have been because of May.'

Cotton shook his head. 'That's presumption,' he said. 'What else is there?'

Cotton smiled a little. 'May has been dead since the first of the month. How long has this corpse been dead?'

'I don't know,' said Ramírez. 'As soon as they've got their masks, they'll take the corpse to the forensic doctor.'

Cotton nodded. He was silent for a moment. 'Are you really suggesting', he said, 'that the grandson was here on the first of the month without the army knowing that he had deserted, and that this drain where he was found was some sort of meeting place with May?'

'I'm not suggesting anything. I'm thinking aloud with you,' said Ramírez.

'All right.'

'And if May murdered him?'

Cotton shook his head.

'Wait. Perhaps he knew the plan to get the boy out was not feasible . . . He knew you were coming . . . Perhaps he drank to get up courage, killed the boy, and jumped or fell into the water himself.'

'The boy could just as well have pushed May into the water and committed suicide,' said Cotton.

Ramírez nodded. 'Have you ever seen a suicide?' he asked.

'Not that I'm aware of.'

Ramírez belched and poured himself some more *oloroso*. 'Those who cut their throats are often tentative,' he said. He shrugged. 'Perhaps depression makes them feel they won't have to try very hard. They think of themselves as being very near death, and forget how tough a throat is.'

'So what happens?' asked Cotton.

'They need a few cuts before they're successful. That's why they sometimes hack at the end, and can open their throats to the spine.'

'Jesus!' said Cotton.

'Mm,' said Ramírez. 'Difficult to tell in this case how tentative this was.'

'What?'

'If it was a suicide, of course.'

Cotton nodded. 'Do you get tentative murders in Cadiz?'

Ramírez smiled. 'No, you're right, my foreign friend. We'll have to wait for the pathologist.' He nodded. 'I'll come and see you tomorrow,' he said, 'and tell you what he finds. But with a body in that state I'm not sure what he'll find.'

'Yes.' Cotton thought for a moment. 'You really are suggesting, aren't you, that the army didn't notice the boy had disappeared until days after he had done so?'

Ramírez raised his eyebrows and pushed out his lips. One eyelid came down. He nodded.

'All right,' said Cotton. 'Thanks for the *oloroso*. I'm going to go back to the hotel now.'

'Can you find your own way?'

'Yes.' Cotton got up from the table. 'If I get lost, I'll ask.'

Ramírez smiled. 'Thank you,' he said. 'I needed to talk to someone.'

'I'm not sure I've been very helpful. And of course, if I can keep May out of this, I will.'

'I understand,' said Ramírez. 'Ah, by the way, the clothes were separate from the body. And they contained the grandson's identity documents and tag. Not uniform. Clothes. It means we don't have to involve the military immediately.'

'Good,' said Cotton. 'All right.' He held out his hand.

Ramírez shook it briefly. 'Where's the food?' he called to the kitchen.

[*]

Cotton did get lost. Preoccupied by what Ramírez had said, preoccupied by the way Ramírez had fed him the information, he paid little attention to the street names. It was dark, and the street lighting was wretched. He found himself walking in the wrong direction. He needed to turn left. Immediately, he found himself among the slums. He could smell the poverty, the dank dirt and urine, the rotting timber in the crumbling, salt-eroded buildings. Some barefoot children latched on to him, begging. He had the impression that the begging was something of an amusement, something to do.

'Go away,' he said.

'Go away!' they repeated.

He decided to ignore them. He hurried; they ran or trotted behind him with no difficulty at all. They stopped pestering him only when he chose a right fork. He looked up and saw that he was in the Calle Cervantes. He saw some of the doors were curtained and had red lights above them. He walked quickly, ignoring the pimps, and turned left at a church. He was now in a large, prosperous square. San Antonio, said the sign on the corner. He recalled the street map and turned down the Calle Ancha – literally, Broad Street, but it was broad only in comparison with the others. Now he knew where he was. He took the left fork down the slope towards Columela. The street was cobbled, and the dew made it slippery. He was watching his feet when he heard someone speak.

'*Ésta calle es mía.*' This street is mine.

He looked up. In the middle of the road a drunken man had raised his arms. In one hand he held a knife.

'*Te pincho. Te pincho.*' I'll stab you.

Cotton paused momentarily. The drunk flopped round the other way and announced again that this street was his. Cotton walked on. 'Fuck you,' he muttered to himself, and kept going.

The drunk looked at him suspiciously, as if he might be a hallucination, and contrived to combine a stagger backwards with a sulk. Cotton got past him and walked smartly on, his back muscles tense, listening hard.

The drunk groaned. '*Yo no me meto. No. Pero al próximo – le pincho.*' I don't cause trouble. No. But the next one – I am stabbing. The drunk slipped; Cotton heard his shoe scrape, and then some put-upon muttering. It was the same man that Ramírez had slapped and told to go home.

Cotton turned left again, and within five minutes he was back at his hotel.

The old woman was waiting for him. 'This came for you,' she said, and handed him an envelope.

Cotton opened it. It was from the antiquarian.

Dear Mr Cotton,

Of course, I understand your reluctance to accept my small gift, but am glad you understood the spirit in which it was given.

Thank you again,

Agustín Romero

PS. You mentioned Lord Byron during our chat, and his visit here. I am indebted to you. When I returned, I looked up some of his work, wondering whether it really was as superficial and cynical as I had thought. Did you know that his plan for his womanizing hero was either marriage or hell? It is what I remembered. There are, however, some good things, and he tried, I think, to have a free heart in the right place. I was particularly struck by his references to the Spanish obsession with 'blood purity', a blot on our history that has more to do with religion than blood. Long before the Catholic Kings expelled Jews and Muslims from Spain – the same year Columbus discovered the Americas – many had been given the 'choice' to convert to Christianity. Jewish converts were called *marranos* – swine – but that was not identifying mark enough. Many ended up with surnames that are also the names of plants. Among these is Romero – I think the English is Rosemary: what gypsy women offer for good luck. An ancestor of mine around the time of the king called Alfonso the Wise chose to change religion and name. His name was Abraham.

Cotton closed his eyes and breathed out. He thanked the old woman and went up to his room. He took off his jacket and sat and reread the antiquarian's letter and its extraordinary postscript. He thought of the rat-chewed body in the blue light and the old antiquarian identifying the corpse as that of his grandson. What were the chances of a very old man writing a letter like that having seen his grandson dead? Against that, the Jewish element was hard to ignore. If Javier Romero *was* Don José and that wasn't his body, whose corpse was it? Why was someone worth murdering? To escape? Cotton thought of 'I am

Spain'. He knew he could not rely on the antiquarian being confused. There was too much risk.

Despite himself, Cotton sat where he was, brooding on the deep cut to the dead man's neck. Was that desperation? Or ruthlessness?

When the girl came in to turn down the bed, he told her distractedly to help herself to ten centavos on the chest of drawers, but after a few moments her lack of movement caught his attention. He looked up to see her fixed on something on the chest. Her mouth was open and then, very slowly, she stretched her neck, almost as if frightened to move her feet. Quietly, he got up. Her hand began to creep forward. He spoke quietly 'Mari-Ángeles.'

The girl gave no sign of hearing him.

'Mari-Ángeles.'

The girl started. He was quick to smile at her.

'Do you know what it is?'

She shook her head, but before she had finished her attention was being dragged back.

'It's five pesetas.'

That didn't appear to mean anything.

'*¡Es un duro!*'

That meant something – from the girl's point of view, a lot of money. Her eyes opened.

'*¿Pero quién es?*' Who is it?

'His name is Alfonso. He was King of Spain.'

'*Pero es un niño.*' But he's a child.

Cotton nodded, and picked up the coin between thumb and forefinger. 'Here. It weighs a lot.' He put it on the palm of her hand.

'Yes,' said the girl. '*Pesa.*' It's heavy.

He put a ten-centavo coin on her palm. 'A big difference.'

The girl nodded. He lifted the silver coin and held it for her to see the baby's profile.

'Do you think it is pretty?' And after she had nodded, 'Would you like to help me spend it?'

She looked up very smartly.

'I need to buy some things. Will you help me?'

The girl nodded.

'Good. Tomorrow I'll tell you the things I want you to buy with it. Do you think you can do that? It's very important. I'm relying on you.'

'*Sí, señor.*'

'Good. You take the ten centavos now, and tomorrow morning early I'll see you. Agreed?'

'*Sí.*'

After she had gone he wondered if the girl would have stolen the Alfonso XIII coin. He suspected that, if she had taken it, it would have been not for its value, but for the combination of size, worn silver and child's head.

10

COTTON WENT to the office before nine, opened *Don Juan*, and picked out his message, 'Please confirm Lambro visit.' By the time he had done this, checked it letter by letter, and sent it, he was slightly ashamed of the time it had taken – close to an hour. The reason was not so much his slowness with the code. It had more to do with a sensation he had that the thin thread connecting him to D had parted. He wondered if May had felt the same – a resentment or recalcitrance. More importantly, he had decided to keep news of another death to himself. He wasn't sure if this was possessiveness or caution. So at ten he went downstairs to see the vice-consul.

'Oh,' said Henderson, 'have you come about the funeral expenses?'

'I'm sorry, I haven't,' said Cotton. 'I'm actually here to tell you that yesterday afternoon a body was found that could possibly have some relation to May's case.'

'May's *case*?' said Henderson, blinking. 'I haven't heard anything about that. It's not in the morning paper.'

'No,' said Cotton. 'The Spanish authorities have decided to handle the matter with discretion.'

'Would that require a material response?' said Henderson.

'I don't know,' said Cotton. 'I should think not.'

Cotton waited. Henderson said nothing.

'That would depend, of course,' said Cotton, 'on what has happened.'

Henderson tapped his desk a while. 'Are we talking of a British subject?' he asked.

'Not as far as is known,' said Cotton.

'I see,' said Henderson. He nodded.

'I am keeping you informed, vice-consul, in case the matter becomes embarrassing.'

'Why should it do that?' said Henderson.

'There is the possibility that May had something to do with this death.'

'You said that. But May is dead, isn't he?' said Henderson.

'Yes, of course. But this body has been dead for some days as well. There seems little doubt that it was a murder.'

'Oh good heavens!' said Henderson, sounding as much exasperated by the vulgarity of murder as shocked or disgusted. He sniffed. 'Yes. Well, you can take it that I have understood what you say.'

'You do appreciate that the Spanish authorities are carrying out a full and thorough investigation?'

'Yes, of course, I do. That's their job!' said Henderson. 'But the matter does not concern this vice-consulate, does it?'

'No. It's certainly not a direct concern,' said Cotton.

Henderson considered this. 'Nor indirect,' he said.

Cotton nodded. 'Do you wish me to keep you informed, vice-consul?'

Henderson thought. He wrinkled his nose. 'Well, perhaps in an informal way,' he suggested.

Cotton smiled politely. 'Very well,' he said. 'Thank you for your time and attention.'

'Yes,' said Henderson. 'Look . . . I hate to be a stickler, you know, but . . .'

'The funeral expenses are in hand,' said Cotton. 'I've done the paperwork. But you know how it is. The wheels of authorization have been a bit slow.'

'Ah,' said the vice-consul. 'Good. Yes, yes. In that case, thank you, Mr Cotton. I'll look forward to hearing from you in due course.'

'Exactly,' said Cotton. 'Good day, vice-consul.'

Cotton ordered coffee to be sent up to his office and, while waiting, used May's binoculars. There was one tramp steamer out of Bilbao docked at the quay, a tugboat, and a pair of trawler fishing boats. His office was not well placed to see out into the Atlantic, but he could see across the Bay of Cadiz towards Rota and, by turning right, towards Puerto de Santa María. The light was very bright, and the water in the bay looked extraordinarily calm, almost false, as if it were of blue-painted material.

When the waiter arrived, Cotton drank down the coffee in one, gave him the cup and saucer back, and added a tip. 'What would you recommend for lunch?' he asked.

'There's octopus,' said the waiter, 'and *garbanzos* and *rodaballo*.' *Garbanzos* are chickpeas.

'Is *rodaballo* a flat fish?'

'And round,' said the waiter.

'Which of those would you recommend?'

'Oh, the octopus,' said the waiter.

Cotton smiled. In the port, an engine started up. 'I'll think about it and tell you later,' he said.

When the waiter had left, he crossed again to the window. Belching smoke, the tugboat was preparing to cast off. Cotton looked towards the Atlantic, but there was nothing to be seen. He went back to the chair and sat down to wait for Ramírez. He came at eleven thirty, poking his head round the door.

'I'm going to a funeral,' he said. 'Will you come?'

'Yes, of course,' said Cotton. He got up and put on his jacket. 'I didn't know it was going to be this quick.'

Ramírez shrugged. 'Lock up,' he said.

Cotton did so.

'Going down I prefer the stairs,' said Ramírez.

So they trotted down.

'It's good to see you,' said Ramírez. 'You're as tall as an actor.'

Cotton smiled. 'Are actors tall?'

'Maybe you're not quite good-looking enough to be a film star.'

'They can help with that,' said Cotton. 'I think they pull teeth to give actresses more cheekbone. They also use false teeth – white, regular teeth. For all I know, Clark Gable has false teeth.'

Ramírez shrugged and smoothed his moustache. 'That's all right,' he said. 'So do I.'

They stepped out into the street.

'This way,' said Ramírez, pointing towards the car waiting for them.

'Who are we going to bury?' asked Cotton.

'You saw the body for yourself last night,' said Ramírez.

'Yes,' said Cotton, 'of course.'

Ramírez nodded wryly, but said nothing until they were in the car and moving. 'I've been thinking,' he said. 'Do you British have a system of identity cards?'

'Not normally. Not in peacetime,' said Cotton.

'So, in a murder case, how do you identify the body?'

'People usually know, I suppose. The police ask around.'

'That's inefficient,' said Ramírez.

'Perhaps,' said Cotton.

'Of course, it's usually husband kills wife,' said Ramírez.

'That's the English argument, surely? What happens when the body has been half eaten by rats?'

'Well, matches become difficult. We have a system, but we need all the parts to make it work,' said Ramírez.

'So what did the pathologist say?' asked Cotton.

Ramírez shrugged. 'What you'd expect. Male, age about twenty, and so on.'

'Didn't you say the antiquarian had identified the body? He said it was his grandson?'

'Well, it fits, it fits,' said Ramírez. He pulled a face. 'But distress and rats are not good for identification.'

'No,' said Cotton. 'Indeed.'

They passed through the gate in the city wall.

'There's always cross-identification,' said Cotton. 'Other family members. Friends.'

Ramírez shook his head. 'No. The grandfather is the head of the family. He speaks for them all. That includes the servants.'

'You've spoken to them?' asked Cotton.

'No point. They haven't seen the body.'

'What about the mother?' said Cotton.

'What?' said Ramírez. 'Oh, yes. You can see her every blessed day twice a blessed day on the way to and from church, with a maid carrying her prayer stool. She wears black. She's a black sack of piety. But for God's sake! We're not barbarians. We don't make mothers smell possible sons.'

'No, I see,' said Cotton. 'I'm sorry.'

Ramírez waved his apology away. 'No, no. I feel uncomfortable too. I don't like funerals – whoever it is that's being buried.' He looked up. 'Ah, we'd be buried in different cemeteries, you and I. Yours is over there.'

'I know,' said Cotton.

'You have to turn left. We have to go right,' said Ramírez.

They did, and then turned left again parallel to the beach. They bounced slowly along a much more rutted road than the one to the British Cemetery. More use, thought Cotton. The cemetery was a large rectangle surrounded by a high, limewashed wall. At the entrance there was a double gateway of dressed stone, and a studded door. There was a small group of men, smoking and chatting, and a couple of beggars.

'Park over there,' Ramírez told the driver. To Cotton he said, 'They're late. They'll be coming from the church. I didn't sleep much last night. Do you mind?'

He tilted his hat over his eyes and lay back.

'We'll wait till they open the gates,' he said. 'In the meantime . . .'

'Yes,' said Cotton – 'rest.'

It was already hot, and there was nothing in the way of breeze. The cigarette smoke from the murmuring men at the gate rose, but otherwise barely moved until it reached the height of the cemetery wall. The murmuring sounded good-natured and unconcerned. The car creaked. Cotton could smell engine oil. Ramírez made a sighing sound, but Cotton did not think he was asleep. For a time, Cotton watched one of the beggars adjusting the grubby covering on what was left of his leg. A little later, in a wing mirror, he saw a black horse's head. The men at the gate stubbed out their cigarettes and straightened up.

'They're here,' said Cotton.

'I know,' said Ramírez. He put a hand under his hat and rubbed at his eyes. Then he sat up, adjusted his hat, and smoothed the glossy, dyed hair above his ears.

'All right?' he said.

'Yes,' said Cotton.

They got out of the car and waited for the cortège to arrive. Behind the hearse walked more than a hundred people, all men. The hearse was somewhere between a fairy-tale coach and a cabinet for flower display. The men at the gate lined up behind to take out the coffin. Then a motor car drew up, and the old antiquarian was helped out.

With the help of a black, silver-topped cane, the old man walked behind the coffin. Cotton and Ramírez tagged along at the rear of all the people. They went through the cemetery gate, across a paved area that had a well in it, and through an archway into the cemetery itself.

Tombs in Cadiz were above ground, in rendered brick-built blocks. It was, thought Cotton, like being buried in apartment blocks, each compartment just enough to take a coffin. Each one was thirty tombs long by seven high, and was back to back with another like it.

The cortège walked down the central path, but had to take detours where rich families had special arrangements and relative splendour in the form of mausoleums in the middle of the path. The blocks loomed on either side. Cotton calculated two hundred and ten tombs a side, making a total of four hundred and twenty in each stack. He saw a ladder to enable people to climb up and change flowers. He noticed that some of the flower-holders were black jam jars fixed in rings like those he had seen in bathrooms for a glass. He saw two men in overalls waiting respectfully for the mourners to pass. Beside them, on a wooden pallet, was a bundle of bones tied with string. The skull was the size of an orange, and both hair and bone were the colour of rust.

'It's the iron,' murmured Ramírez. And then he pointed at a gnarled little tree. It looked like something between a vine and a yew.

'See that? Cypress doesn't grow well here. It's the sea salt, I think.'

Cotton nodded.

They stopped. The mourners crowded in between two blocks.

'Look up there,' said Ramírez, pointing.

On top of the blocks was a colony of cats, all scruffy, some asleep or basking, some looking down at the disturbance.

'Clever animals.' Ramírez spoke with admiration. 'Look around. There are no rats here.'

'They look thin,' said Cotton.

'But they're alive! They're safe here. Do you see? They hunt at night. More difficult to get caught.'

He smiled without showing his teeth. Cotton raised his eyebrows. Ramírez leaned a little closer.

'Do you know the expression *gato por liebre*?' A cat for a hare.

'Yes,' said Cotton. He paused. 'That's when you are sold something that isn't what it's claimed to be.'

Ramírez nodded, then smiled, showing his teeth this time. 'That's it. Very good. That's it exactly!'

Cotton glanced at Ramírez. He was staring straight ahead at the funeral group. A priest murmured Latin. Another swung incense. They heard rather than watched the coffin being slid into a niche, and then everyone turned away.

'You'll pay your respects?' said Ramírez.

'Yes.'

'Good. Just line up like the others.'

Cotton walked back with him along the path, looking behind him to see how far the line of mourners would stretch. When they were almost back at the first arch, Ramírez wished him well.

'I'll be waiting in the car,' he said, and went off.

The antiquarian came down the path shaking hands, receiving condolences, talking a little, nodding, thanking people over and over again. When he reached Cotton, he held out a hand.

'Hold me up,' he said, without ceremony.

Cotton took his arm.

'Yes,' said the old man, 'walk with me.' He sighed, raised his head a little, and breathed in. 'I remember', he said, 'how *exotic* England appeared to me as a young man. Do you know Newcastle upon Tyne?'

'No,' said Cotton.

'It absolutely belched with power. Soot everywhere. I went to a funeral when a worker got mangled. I was so surprised to find grass and enormous soot-covered monuments. Some of them were the size of cottages, but very ornate. And there were blackened angels everywhere, with huge wings.' The old man jabbed his cane behind him. 'We wall up our dead above ground,' he said. 'They say it is so as to be nearer salvation, but the real reason is much more prosaic. It's to do with drainage. But they still remind me of Roman aqueducts. A rather nice image, don't you think? Will you come and see me this afternoon?'

'Of course,' said Cotton.

'About seven. Most of these people will have gone by then. You think I'm doing well?'

'Yes, I do,' said Cotton.

'I'm not,' said the old man. 'I am such a coward. I think it was one of your explorers . . . Mungo Park, perhaps . . . ?'

'Ah, perhaps.' The old man was certainly accomplished.

'Yes. He said there is a kind of calm when the absolute worst does happen. I don't know. I feel more stunned than calm. Bless you for coming.'

Cotton was about to reply, but saw the old man wasn't listening. 'They had to get my son out to make room for him. They were his bones – did you see that? – bundled together with string. It's so that they take up less room. And they'll have to get him out when I die.'

Cotton felt him shudder as he shook his head. He stopped walking and looked up at the Englishman.

'Do you know *why* I am an antiquarian?' he pleaded, his chin crimping and trembling.

'Yes, I think so,' said Cotton.

The old man nodded. 'We'll have a look at some of my things. Shall we do that? See how the past is standing up?'

'Yes,' said Cotton. 'I should like that.'

The old man began walking again. They were now in the courtyard. He made a sound rather like a stifled laugh. 'You know, I really have been trying to think of something worse. Do you see over there?' he said, pointing. 'That's the bone well. They toss bones in there, and sometimes, I believe, they let our medical students poke about. Not at all like Hamlet. Of course the bones belong to the poor. Those whose families can't afford to keep up the rental for a tomb. Till seven, then?'

They shook hands formally.

'Till seven,' said Cotton.

'What did he say?' asked Ramírez when Cotton got back in the car.

Cotton told him.

'Aqueducts?' said Ramírez. 'They remind me of God's barracks. You'll go?'

'I said I would. He wants to show me some of his things.'

'Good,' said Ramírez. He paused. 'They say he has some valuable pieces.'

Cotton looked at Ramírez. 'Am I missing something here?' he asked.

'What do you mean?'

'Will we go together?'

'No, I'm not invited.' Ramírez raised his eyebrows. 'Do the English invite the investigating officer to the wake and then to visit an antique shop?'

'I don't know. They might do.'

Ramírez laughed and touched Cotton's elbow. 'I have other things to do,' he said, and then, almost coyly, 'This is not my only business, you know.'

'No,' said Cotton. 'Not more deaths, I hope.'

Ramírez smiled. 'It's all public health. Oh, look,' he said pointing at a worker putting up a poster. '*Mutiny on the Bounty* is on at the open-air cinema.'

'Isn't it odd to show that when *Gone with the Wind* is banned?'

'No, no,' said Ramírez. 'Some mutinies are justifiable.'

'You'll have to explain that to me some time,' said Cotton.

'What's to explain? Gable mutinies against the English.'

'And *Gone with the Wind*?'

'Obvious,' said Ramírez. 'That's banned because it's about a civil war. Ours is still too close for comfort.'

'Ah,' said Cotton. 'I see.'

'They didn't give him an Oscar for it, you know,' said Ramírez.

'Gable?'

'Yes. They say he was furious.'

Cotton looked around. Ramírez had told him something about Gable and Oscars before. Ramírez shook his head ruefully.

'Rank injustice,' he said.

'I don't know,' said Cotton. 'I haven't seen *Gone with the Wind*. Someone told me it was very long. Have you seen it?'

'No,' said Ramírez. 'How could I? It's banned. But I've read about it.'

The car pulled up at Cotton's office.

'We're here,' said Ramírez. 'I'll be seeing you. OK?'

Cotton nodded and got out. 'Thanks for the lift.'

'My pleasure,' said Ramírez.

Cotton watched the car go off and looked around. Along the avenue men were rigging up lines of bunting. In front of the palace, a dais was going up. It was a military project. Some soldiers were slopping paint on peeling walls; others were scrubbing cobbles. Cotton walked down to the corner and bought a newspaper. It was a special edition, very thin, on very poor quality paper, and full of that extraordinarily pompous language that dictators' hacks use. *El Caudillo, El Generalísimo,* Saviour of Spain and Defender of the Faith, Francisco Franco Bahamonde and his wife, Doña Carmen Polo, would favour Cadiz with a formal visit the very next Saturday.

Cotton stuffed the newspaper into his pocket and went immediately upstairs to his office. There was a message waiting for him from D. He barely needed to get out his codebook to decode it.

Lambro visit confirmed for Saturday morning, 16th September. Portuguese President Salazar due that afternoon.

Cotton nodded. He thought of writing back, 'Saw it in local newspaper first.' But there was no point at all in that. He paused and breathed in. He now had the information he required.

'It takes about ten seconds to sum up a situation or a person,' D had said. 'We try to deny it, but it's usually an excuse. It's the same with most actions. We may not like it, but the information is there to be acted on. We just have to recognize it. Betrayal is usually particularly quick. One likes to get it over with. At least I always have. It's the waiting, worrying if anything will go wrong, that's tedious. Incidentally, betrayal is not rare. What is rare is when you are not betrayed.'

Cotton got up and took May's binoculars and looked out at the port. The solitary ship, the tramp steamer from Bilbao, had been joined by a bigger, even rustier affair out of Havana, Cuba. It was called *Flor de Canela*. Was that Cinnamon Flower? He shrugged. He didn't even know if cinnamon had a flower. Still, though a little later than announced, the ship had arrived. A moment later he saw El Palo, the man he had dismissed, scuttling away from the Cuban ship with something tucked under his arm, and he couldn't help smiling. How many people were watching the poor devil try to make a living?

Cotton went and sat down. He took a deep breath and drummed his fingers on the edge of the desk. It was time to get on. First he typed letters, formally ending the lease May had signed on the office, and giving instructions to close the bank account he had opened. He included details of the account in Madrid where all monies should be remitted as soon as the cheques issued and listed were cleared. Small things slowed him as he cleared up. He looked again at May's manuscript on the spirit of Spain, turned over the pages, hesitated for a brief moment, but then decided it should join all the rest of the stuff he was going to throw out. He fiddled with the elastic bands May had left. There were two kinds: quite thick and brown, and thin and blue. He took off his jacket and hung it over his chair. He loosened his tie and collar. For a few minutes he simply whiled away the time, separating the elastic bands. He tried the thin ones first, but they barely got round his wrist and tugged unpleasantly at the hairs. The brown ones had something like talc on them, but were still too small. He glanced at his watch, and finally wrote out the cheque to the vice-consulate for May's funeral expenses and did the necessary paperwork for his own department. He wondered if he really ought to make another visit to Henderson, but decided against it. Instead, he wrote him a post-dated note thanking him for his help 'in this delicate matter'. He would deliver it the next morning.

Around two thirty he called Eugenio, the porter, and ordered a steak from the bar downstairs. Eugenio made a face and scratched at his head.

'No, I'd like some meat for a change,' said Cotton.

'It'll be tough,' said Eugenio. 'I wouldn't want to mislead you.'

'Then make sure they give me a serrated knife.'

Eugenio rocked a little from side to side to show the difficulty of his position. 'How would you like it done?'

'Rare,' said Cotton.

'Well, just as you wish,' said Eugenio. 'What do you want to drink?'

'A beer, I think,' said Cotton. 'Another thing. Could you give me some help around five? To get rid of some of this stuff?'

Eugenio looked up, and Cotton nodded.

'Of course, yes, it'll be worth your while,' he said. He saw Eugenio was looking at May's clothes.

When the porter had left, Cotton looked at the elastic bands again. He fiddled with two, then one, pulling it until it snapped. It was quite an effort. It made him sweat. He went to the window and looked out. The tug was bringing in a ship, modern and well painted, from Argentina.

'Is that meat on that ship?' he said when Eugenio came up with his lunch.

'Not today. Not here,' said the porter, looking down dubiously at the plate. 'Hope you enjoy it.'

Cotton took the tray and sat down at his desk. Before eating, he opened a drawer and took out the tin that contained May's wine-cork collection. He opened it, selected a cork, and, using the serrated edge of the knife, cut it into discs. He picked another and simply cut it in half. That cork was too dry, and squeaked when he cut it. He found one with more give, and cut that. He listened.

Better. It made almost no sound at all. He put the discs and halves of cork into a side jacket pocket. He wiped the knife and tried the steak. The porter had been right. The meat rasped under the blade and bled, but was fabulously tough. He drank some beer and ate some tomato and a piece of bread for lunch.

During the siesta time, Cotton sat back and looked at *Don Juan* again, as a narrative poem. He skipped over the shipwreck scene and read again through the episode that the notes described as illustrative of Byron's idea of freedom. Washed up on an island, Juan is rescued by the lovely Haidée. Conveniently, the free-spirited girl has a kind of nanny to keep house or cave for her and provide meals. Juan does not know that the girl's father, Lambro, is a pirate on another part of the island.

Cotton half closed the book. He was anxious not to sleep. He remembered the question he had been asked about Byron's command of English. He toyed for a while with a message he might send. Something like 'Have met accomplished foreigner. He agrees with Eliot.' After a while, he reopened the book and skipped on to read, rather more closely, the scene in which Juan is sold as a slave. He noted with some pleasure that this struck him as sharper, less indulgent and quicker. He decided he should stop there. Then he prepared for the porter's visit.

In the end, he decided to throw almost everything out, including May's mother's letters, the guidebook and its street map. Eugenio was keen to get May's clothes, '*Sisisisí,*' he said. Eugenio also said he 'had a use' for the ink and the pens, so he took them off to his cubbyhole.

By the time they had finished clearing up, all that was left in the office apart from the furniture provided was the typewriter, May's binoculars, the coding machine, Cotton's attaché case with the autopsy report, May's papers and *Don Juan*. It was nearly six. Eugenio declined a tip. He said Cotton had done quite enough for him already.

Cotton put on his jacket and retied his tie. He checked the pieces of cork in his side jacket pocket. He looked out at the port once more. The Cuban ship, *Flor de Canela*, was taking on supplies. He checked the coding machine, book and binoculars, though he knew there was no need, and again made sure that all the drawers were empty. He locked up and took the lift down. He told Eugenio that he would return at nine the next morning. He stepped outside.

The light was still very bright, and it was very hot. Automatically, he squinted and kept to the shadows on his way back to the hotel. He was glad to get inside. He walked upstairs to his room. The shutters were closed, and he did not turn on the light. Instead, he breathed in and rang for service.

Almost at once, as if she had been waiting outside, Mari-Ángeles, the little servant girl, came in. She was carrying a brown packet and a twist of paper.

Cotton smiled. 'Did you get everything?' he asked.

'*Sí, señor*,' she said. Despite his smile, she remained wide-eyed and nervous. She handed him the parcel. The twist of paper was the receipt wrapped round the change. She turned to go.

'Wait,' said Cotton.

He opened the parcel. It contained a dress bow tie and a hatpin. He picked up the pin, walked to the window, and opened the shutter a little. It was hardly a shock, but it took him as an unpleasant surprise to see that the pin was not machine made. It had been beaten out, and was slightly rusty. At the decorated end was something between a spring and a bobble in the shape of a pine cone. He had wanted something smoother, more solid and with more handle. But it would do.

'No tortoiseshell?'

'No,' said the girl.

He nodded and turned back. 'When did you buy these?'

'This afternoon, *señor*. Just as you told me.'

'Good,' said Cotton. 'Our secret, isn't that right? You haven't talked to anyone about this, have you?'

'*No, señor.*'

He looked down at the little girl and bent to look into her eyes. To one side of her lips there was a grain of sugar. Cotton almost put out a finger to touch it, but straightened and smiled instead. 'Good,' he said. 'He had a moustache. Am I right? Quite old? Dyed hair? You've seen me with him?'

The girl's lip started to wobble and her face to girn.

'No, no. It's all right,' said Cotton. 'It's all right. Let me tell you a secret. You've done well. Very well.' He picked up a peseta from the change. 'Here. This is for you,' he said.

The girl did not know what to do.

'Take it, go on,' he said. 'Our secret.'

The girl took the coin and, rather slowly, retreated.

'It's all right,' said Cotton. 'You've been very helpful.'

When she had gone, Cotton measured the pin against his right forearm. He took the discs of cork out of his pocket and was for a moment struck by how fatuous, cruel and crude some things were. He swallowed. It was not something to be dwelt on. 'Concentrate on the next task.' He laid the discs of cork out on the bed next to the bow tie and hatpin, then washed, combed his hair, prepared himself, and, a little after seven, walked along to the antiquarian's house. Cadiz was stirring again. He could smell coffee, cologne and tobacco. Women and children were out shopping, walking or playing. The trees in the squares were thick with small birds.

11

THE OLD antiquarian was sitting with a shawl around his shoulders and a hat on inside his own house, quite alone in a small darkened room well away from the noise of the wake for his grandson. He looked up as Cotton was shown in.

'I could never understand', he said, 'how someone could be an atheist.'

Cotton pulled up.

'Oh, do come in. I was just thinking aloud. Won't you take a seat? They'll bring some refreshment in a moment. It's teatime, I suppose. But I am Spanish. I have coffee.'

Cotton nodded and sat. The room was airless and hot. He could feel his skin prickle, before sweating.

'Do you know now why they shot my son?'

'No.'

The old man sighed. 'I just thought Ramírez might have told you.'

'Nothing new,' said Cotton.

'Ramírez is a good sort, I suppose, within his limits. He's not a very cultured man. But then, I don't know, do you need culture for his kind of work?'

Cotton did not take this as a question to be answered.

The old antiquarian nodded. 'It's strange, isn't it?' he said. 'My son was killed and I'm always wondering *why*.

As if there might be a *reason* that would explain his death. I'm not going to get an answer, and it wouldn't take away the *fact* of it, would it?' He shook his head at his own lack of understanding. 'It's rather like when you were young. You liked a girl, but she didn't like you. Her choice, of course, and one couldn't be churlish and ask for an explanation, so one couldn't learn whether it was a matter of taste – she preferred someone else – or something you had actually done to offend her.'

It seemed to Cotton a curious comparison, but he nodded.

The old man looked up. 'It's awfully good of you to come,' he said.

'No,' said Cotton. 'I'm sorry it has to be like this.'

'Yes,' said the antiquarian. 'Are you a believer, Mr Cotton?'

'Well,' said Cotton, 'I can't say I – '

'No, no, I shouldn't have asked,' said the antiquarian. 'Life has always had its cruel side, hasn't it?'

'Yes, it has,' said Cotton.

The old man shook his head again. 'I'm altogether too old, you know. I should have been glad to take my son's place, but at the time I was too distressed and shaky to think of it. Now it's too late.'

To Cotton's surprise, the old man laughed sheepishly. 'I don't know,' the old man said. 'I get lost in myself. Must think of other things. Well, I don't even know if you really like antiques!'

'I hardly know either,' said Cotton.

'Why should you? You've had other things to do.' The antiquarian looked at him. 'I don't know,' he said.

'I don't know whether it's age or cowardice, but I just don't know.'

'Don't know what exactly?' said Cotton.

'Anything much. That's why', said the old man, 'I'm putting everything in your hands.'

Cotton squinted a little at him.

'I'll abide by what you do, Mr Cotton,' he said quietly.

'Ah.'

'It's pure shirking,' said the old man.

A maid brought in coffee on a heavy silver tray.

'Ah, good,' said the old man. 'I'm very fond of cats' tongues.'

'What?' said Cotton.

'These little biscuits. We'll eat some and have some coffee and stroll along to the shop. Would you like that?'

'Yes,' said Cotton. 'That would be . . . interesting.'

The coffee was thick, Turkish style, served in tiny porcelain cups, which didn't stop the old man dunking his little biscuits. The contents of the cup were barely a mouthful, but very strong – a mix of bitter coffee and too much sugar.

'It gets my heart working,' said the old man. 'Some water, perhaps?'

'Yes, thank you,' said Cotton.

'And do have one of these little biscuits.'

Cotton was struck that the old gentleman was offering him the biscuit almost like a reward for having taken medicine. The biscuit was also very sweet, and tasted of vanilla. A maid brought some water, and Cotton drank to dilute the stuff in his stomach.

'Now,' said the antiquarian, 'can I offer you some excellent Scotch whisky?'

'No, thank you. Really,' said Cotton. 'The coffee was enough.'

The old man almost laughed. 'Really? You know, I've always needed a little . . . What do you call it . . . Dutch courage? Are you sure you won't join me?'

'Quite sure.'

'It's genuine Scotch,' said the old man. 'Single malt. The Glenlivet. I believe that's one of the best. Is that true?'

'Yes, I think it is,' said Cotton. 'But it's not as if I'm an expert.'

'Ah,' said the old man. 'Well, it's not as if I'm a drinker, either, you see. I don't like drinking alone. It should be a sociable thing, don't you think?'

'Ah. Then a little. Very little,' said Cotton.

'Just a taste, then. To keep me company. Good.'

The old man smiled and called for the maid. Cotton considered him.

'*Güisqui,*' said the antiquarian, 'for my guest and for me. Bring some more water. Ice?'

'No, thank you.'

'Go,' said the old man to the maid. 'Do you take water with whisky?'

'I'm really not much of a drinker,' said Cotton. 'I'll see.'

'I tend to drink it neat or with lots of water – make a long drink of it. They call that a canary whisky. From the colour, I suppose. It becomes pale, more straw-coloured than yellow really. And they drink it in the Canary Islands, of course. Flavoured water really.' He looked round. 'I believe whisky colour really comes from the oak barrels. It leaks out into the clear liquid. Oh, but you knew that, of course. The sherry-makers ship their old barrels to Scotland. So, in a sense, this whisky is coming home.'

'Yes, I see,' said Cotton obligingly. He was quite relieved when the maid came back. The old man's mix of distraction and anxiety was difficult to follow.

'A little shot,' said the antiquarian when the tray had been put down. 'Isn't that what they say?'

'A very little shot,' said Cotton.

'One finger? It's odd, but we Spanish measure whisky and foreheads by fingers.'

'I'm sorry?'

'Haven't you heard the expression, let's see . . . "anyone with more than two fingers' worth of forehead"? It means anyone not totally stupid.' The old man poured far more than two fingers into the tumblers. Then he stood up, gave Cotton his glass, and picked up his own.

'Your health, Mr Cotton.'

'*Salud*,' said Cotton.

The old man, still trembling, downed his drink. He dribbled a little, and wiped his chin. 'Mm. Well, I *hope* that's better,' he said. He tried a smile. 'I'm on my feet, Mr Cotton.'

'What?'

'Well, now that I'm up I thought we might . . . '

'Of course.'

'Drink up.'

Cotton picked up his glass and stood. He swallowed a mouthful. No, he was definitely not a whisky man. He breathed down his nose and made a rueful face, but the old man simply waited. He drank the rest and put the glass down on the tray.

'Good,' said the antiquarian. 'It's not far really, but I'll need the key.' He rang the bell. The maid came prepared, carrying his coat, leather gloves, a walking stick and a huge old key.

'Looks like a castle key, doesn't it?' said the old man. 'It's only a shop.'

They went downstairs. Some people were in the hall, waiting to pay their respects. The antiquarian ignored them. He ushered Cotton out into the street.

'It's not far really – no more than a step.'

They turned left at the first corner, walked along a narrow little alley, crossed a small square full of playing children, and went into another alley on the other side. The alley was dark and smelled dank. The antiquarian stopped by a battered old door.

'The lock is sometimes a problem,' said the antiquarian. But the key worked, and they went into a cavernous, damp, fusty room. The old man shut the door and turned on a solitary bare light bulb hanging from the high rafters.

'I usually open the shutters,' he said, 'but I don't want any confusion today about whether we are open or not. Bad form, I think. After a funeral.'

Almost the first thing that Cotton saw was his returned present, still in its wrapping paper, on a dusty console table. He looked around. There were a couple of suits of armour, a life-sized blackamoor with a candelabra, a faded, fragile-looking leather trunk on a walnut table, a huge gilt mirror frame containing only a corner of spotted looking glass, and any number of holy-looking paintings propped against the walls – virgins with their eyes raised, a martyrdom or two, some stiff neoclassical stuff with pillars and soldiers.

'Well,' said the old man wearily, 'only remnants of the past. None of these paintings are up to much. Mm? Oh, Goya was here. And there are some paintings by Zurbarán and Murillo in Cadiz. But these are more "school of", if you know what I mean. The trunk is good, though. And I have something over here you might like to see.'

He pushed at some chairs and revealed another trunk, covered with faded snake or lizard skin. 'In here', he said, passing his trembling hand over the surface, 'is a lady's dress from the sixteenth century. It's a marvellous thing, but so fragile now.'

Cotton waited, expecting him to open the trunk, but he did not.

The antiquarian turned. 'And over there', he said, 'I have a complete set of surgeon's instruments from about the same time. You know Cadiz has had a medical school for centuries?'

'Yes,' said Cotton.

'There are things there that look like instruments for torture, and a syringe for the baptism of unborn children.' He looked up. 'I have some nice Roman things,' he said, 'and even some Carthaginian pieces.'

'Antiquities,' said Cotton.

'Oh, yes. I have some nice little statues. A winged horse, for example. And a figurine of Hercules – or Melkart as the Phoenicians called him. He has his legs apart and is holding up not a club but a torch. It might be a copy of the statue mentioned by the ancients, some sort of wonder, perhaps a lighthouse, now under the sea, of course.' The old man paused and put his gloved hand to his forehead.

'Are you all right?' said Cotton.

'I don't know,' replied the antiquarian. 'Oh, perhaps the whisky wasn't such a good idea after all.'

'Would you like to sit down? Can I get you anything?'

'No, no. At my age you get waves of . . . How are *you* feeling?' asked the old antiquarian.

'I'm all right, thank you,' said Cotton.

'Yes,' said the old man, and sighed. 'It's something to do with blood sugar,' he said. 'I thought the malt might help.'

He looked up, and then round at the contents of his shop. He made a face. 'Oh, it's not looking very good today. The things look old: they don't look valuable. They're not speaking, are they?' Shakily, he breathed out. 'Um, there is another room, you know. It's just there, at the back. You may find something more interesting there.'

Cotton nodded. 'Yes, I suppose I might,' he said.

'Yes,' said the old man. 'I am so sorry to have been such a bore.' He bit his lip and blew out. Cotton waited. 'Why don't I just sit down for a moment and let you wander about and explore?'

'Are you quite sure?'

'Absolutely. You go ahead. Don't worry your head about me.'

'As you wish,' said Cotton. He turned away.

'Yes. Mr Cotton?'

'Yes?'

'My thanks to you.'

'There's no need,' said Cotton.

'*Son de corazón,*' said the old man. They are heart-felt.

Cotton nodded. He swallowed. He threaded through the furniture and gently opened the next door.

'Light's to your left,' whispered the old man.

'Thank you.'

Cotton felt with his hand and found the switch. Another single bulb flickered and settled.

This room was even more of a warehouse. There were bedheads stacked against the limewashed walls, stacks of mirror frames, chests of drawers, and piles of things he thought of as sturdy hampers or bakers' baskets stuffed with old books. Against one wall there was an eighteenth-century half-tester bed – to Cotton's taste a ghastly thing of soiled green silk and chipped gilt.

Cotton moved slowly forward and feigned interest in the ornate bed. He heard wicker creak, the hinges of a door, and then a voice murmured, '*Abuelito*' – Grandpa. He turned.

Cotton was not sure what he had expected – certainly someone who looked at least haggard and unkempt.

Javier Romero, the antiquarian's grandson, was tall and very slender, with a flop of dark hair parted in the centre. The hair came down on either side at eye level. He wasn't as good-looking as in Ramírez's photograph. His chin was a little long, his nose short, but the eyes were large and dark. He was wearing a greatcoat from some other war over an open-necked shirt, a pair of jodhpurs and riding boots. Cotton's eyebrows went up. He was surprised not so much by the clothes as by the boy's clear skin and pleasure in seeing him.

'Forgive the get-up,' said the antiquarian's grandson. 'It's what I could find.' His English accent was not nearly as good as his grandfather's. It was a little hoarse, with too much drawl; the Spanish vowels were overcompensated, and the consonants too soft. The penultimate word of his sentences dipped and clipped too much, and the last was far too emphatic. He had said 'git-ahp' for 'get-up'.

Cotton allowed himself a moment to check he had understood. 'That's not a real problem,' he said.

Javier Romero smiled. He moved forward, and looked as if he were about to offer his hand. 'No, you're right. Well? What have you brought me?'

Almost to his own surprise, Cotton parodied a Spaniard looking about himself in disbelief. He was very anxious not to shake hands. 'I came to Cadiz to tidy up – and then close up,' he said.

The slender boy shrugged. 'I know that.'

'Originally I was to be sent to Cadiz to relieve May, without ceremony.'

'Yes, I know that.'

'When I was in Madrid I found out he was dead.'

'Yes, yes,' said the boy. 'I know that too.'

Cotton nodded. He was half intrigued to find himself weighing up the boy while watching his own reaction to him. He felt a strong desire to annoy him. He immediately quashed it, and found himself speaking again.

'Look,' he said, 'I have . . . a certain leeway, and I haven't spent much money yet. I have reason to believe that you could be got on a boat for Portugal.' He paused. 'I could probably make arrangements for that.'

The boy blinked.

'Think,' said Cotton. 'Your grandfather has just pretended to bury you.'

The boy shook his head and looked away.

'Write to him from Portugal,' urged Cotton.

Javier Romero turned away. 'This is not what I had expected,' he said.

'No?' said Cotton. 'Didn't you know that May was exceeding his authority?'

'"Leeway"! "Exceeding his authority"! What are you talking about? What kind of language is this? This is clerks' language!'

For a moment Cotton thought he had said 'clerics'.

The boy wrinkled his nose. 'I knew May was a fool,' he said. 'Of course I did!'

'There you have it.'

But the boy had not finished. 'He was sentimental,' he said.

'Yes.'

'Lost. He stuttered, you know. Oh, but not when he was drinking. Not then. Ah, and he couldn't say no. He would get overexcited.'

'All right. Do you know how he died?' asked Cotton.

'What? No. How could I? I wasn't here.'

'Surmise,' said Cotton.

'Why?'

'Because I don't know who else might be involved.'

The boy snorted. Cotton narrowed his eyes. To his surprise, he almost laughed at the poor job he was making of handling the antiquarian's grandson. He could feel himself sweating. Fear at what he was going to have to do? There was something snobbish in the young man that went with the shyness and the bitterness. But then he surprised Cotton.

'I am not a coward,' said Javier Romero.

'Whoever said you were?'

The young man waved a finger in the Spanish *nononó* gesture. 'I am not', he said, prodding himself in the chest, 'going to swell the number of embittered exiles out there.'

Cotton said nothing. He felt a kind of dread. It was general rather than specific, and mixed with more boredom than pity.

'Why should *I* go?' said the young man.

'Oh,' said Cotton. 'Well, you've deserted. That's just one thing.'

The boy blinked. 'You don't understand,' he said.

'Then tell me,' said Cotton.

The boy snorted again, and shook his head.

'Tell me,' said Cotton. 'Remember, I'm a foreigner. You can talk.'

The boy looked up sharply, swallowed, and looked away. Then he shrugged. 'You can't shame me,' he said. 'You can't trivialize what I'm doing.'

'Oh, I'm not doing that,' said Cotton. 'In no way am I doing that, I assure you.'

The boy nodded a while, and then shrugged again. Cotton held out the palm of his hand before leaning back against a table. Instinctively he checked it, and saw it was mahogany – what the Spanish call English style, meaning Georgian. In this case Chippendale. He rubbed dust from his fingers.

'Tell me what you're thinking,' he said, as if making an offer.

The boy considered him and then nodded. Cotton could not resist bringing his left hand over to his right forearm, brushing his jacket sleeve and the little disc of cork under it. He could see that the boy felt better when there was theory behind possible actions.

'Very well,' said the boy. 'One. The Allies will not come into Spain unless they are pushed.'

'That's possible,' said Cotton. 'But I don't know.'

'I do. Two. Spain has a dictator. Remove that dictator and the whole situation changes.'

Cotton shrugged. 'There are other generals, other ambitious men,' he said.

The boy shook his head and smiled. 'These people have cronies,' he said; 'they don't have successors. Do you think the Nazis will survive Hitler's death?'

'They're not neutral,' said Cotton. 'They are in a war with the Allies. Spain is not.'

Once again, almost good-humouredly, the boy shook his head. 'Franco's death will mean nothing? Is that what you are saying?'

'No, I didn't say that,' said Cotton.

'Well, what are you saying?'

'That I am here in order to avoid any implication of my government in an attempt to assassinate General Franco.'

This amused the young man. He shook his head. 'We had been working, you know, on the idea that I would have to look for the *Generalísimo*, travel hundreds of kilometres to get at him. Hunt him out.'

'Yes,' said Cotton.

'So can you imagine what it was like when I heard he was coming here?' The boy shook his head in wonder. 'General Franco is going to drive down the avenue here in his black Rolls-Royce, flanked by his Moroccan cavalry! And he's going to harangue the people gathered together specially for him to harangue. They will cheer, of course, until . . . ffft! . . . I shoot him.'

'What if you fail?'

'Is that what you're worried about? You can't be serious. How can your government be frightened of Franco?'

'My government does not believe in assassination.'

'What? Oh, please! What happened in Oran?'

'I don't know,' said Cotton.

The boy frowned. 'In Czechoslovakia a German general was killed with British help.'

'Ah. That I have heard of. There were terrible reprisals.'

'But there have been thousands of reprisals here already!' said the boy. 'At this stage a few more wouldn't matter if I can get the Allies to act.'

Cotton sighed. 'You don't know how they are going to react,' he said. 'Whatever happens, Spain is not a threat to the Allies. I suspect it's what you would call realpolitik. Nobody minds Spain being weak. Franco? He's bearable for now. People want to go home. They've had enough war.'

'His death will cause a vacuum of power,' insisted the young man.

'Enough to suck in occupying forces?' said Cotton. 'Is that what you have in mind?'

'Money and support would do.'

'Then you should be talking to an American. Not to me.'

The boy smiled. 'You're all I've got,' he said.

'I have my orders.'

'Orders can be changed.'

'In retrospect.'

'Absolutely.'

Cotton nodded. He stopped leaning and stood up. 'Look at it from my superiors' point of view. An eighteen-year-old – '

'Nineteen.'

Cotton began walking up and down, largely to calm himself down. 'All right. A nineteen-year-old offers himself to assassinate the carefully guarded head of a state that, in strictly legal terms, is neutral in the war my country is waging. The young man's contact is with a British operative. Let's say that their relationship, or a version of it, is already known to the British and the Spanish authorities even before the British national is found dead. In addition, a young Spanish soldier is found murdered.'

'They think it's me.'

'Do they? Do you really think that it's all been filed and forgotten?'

'They only have to be confused.'

'You think?' said Cotton. 'Who was the boy they buried today?'

The antiquarian's grandson shrugged. 'It could have been me.'

'No,' insisted Cotton. 'Tell me who it was.'

'He was from Burgos, sent to do his military service here. He had flat feet and bad eyes. He worked in the office, for heaven's sake.' The boy shrugged. 'I have his permission.'

'His what?' said Cotton.

'I have his . . . pass.'

'What happened?'

'It was easy enough.'

'Just tell me.'

The boy shrugged again. 'I chose him because he was about my height and build. We had to plan it quite carefully. Then May picked him up.'

'And?'

'He was an obliging sort. There's a companionship, you know, especially when you have to be secretive to survive.'

'Meaning?'

'May told him about me, and he forged a permission . . . a . . . '

'I understand,' said Cotton. 'It's called leave.'

'Yes, in his name. And he sent it to me by post. Don't overestimate the controls and censorship here. The professionals delegate all the time.'

'And then what? May killed him?'

'Ah, he had to,' said the boy. 'The boy wasn't strong, and we couldn't take the risk he'd work something out and panic.'

'Why didn't he pay him?'

'That would have made him suspicious.'

'Right. So what did May do with the money?'

The boy sniggered. 'That was for me to hunt Franco. Travel; pay bribes.'

'And when you learned that no travel was involved?'

'Oh, a new life. A fresh start abroad.'

'So where's the money now?'

'I have it.'

'I see.'

'I don't need it!'

'No?'

'What? Do you want it back?' demanded the young man.

Cotton nodded. 'Oh yes.'

'*Por Dios,*' for God's sake, said the boy disgustedly. He put his hand in his greatcoat pocket and brought out a wad of notes. He tossed them at Cotton.

'Thank you,' said Cotton. He put the money in his own pocket. 'And do you know how May died?'

'I imagine he had to drink so much to do it.'

Cotton shook his head.

'He couldn't swim!' said the boy. 'He could only flounder.'

'When did you get here?'

'Oh, the night I deserted. I got off duty at 2 p.m. I was here by midnight. Not bad going. I had the pass. Well, enough of one to be another national serviceman hitching home. You think the authorities move quickly here? They don't. I had hours' start, and had arranged for someone to fill in for me at the next roll call. People do it all the time.'

'So where have you been?'

'Here, of course,' said the boy. 'You have to do the obvious. And now I'm dead, you see.'

'Splendid,' said Cotton wearily.

The boy raised an eyebrow. 'May told me you were coming.'

'And?'

'I was rather hoping they'd send someone more competent than him.'

'Ah.'

'It's not so difficult really,' said the boy. 'You were going to be a cooler customer in any case. What's the matter with your arm?'

'What?' Cotton saw he had gripped his own right forearm. 'Oh, I got bitten by something,' he said, and scratched.

The boy smiled and made another sniggering sound. 'There's malaria here,' he said. 'You should be careful.'

Cotton realized that almost everything the boy said infuriated him. He smiled back, telling himself not to get distracted. 'What does your grandfather think?' he asked.

He watched for the boy to glance back at the door to the main shop, but he did not. They were alone then.

'He thinks you're helping me to find a way out.'

'To Portugal?'

'No. That was a *farol*, a bluff that May set up. My grandfather thinks I'm going to get out through Gibraltar as a Sephardi. He may think there's a romantic kind of justice in that.'

'Ah,' said Cotton, 'I take it you're a Jewish refugee, code name Don José.'

The boy shook his head and laughed. 'Take it.'

'How did you become Jewish?'

The boy shrugged. 'Oh, that was May. He said he knew a woman slightly in Madrid. He had her fed a few snippets. She was trusting and clever, he said.'

Marie. Cotton nodded. He wondered if Houghton and Marie had once put up May as they had him.

'How did he feed her?'

'Oh, May had some contact in the Post Office, some man with private initiative,' said the boy.

Cotton almost grunted in irritation at himself. The man they called The Goat, *La Cabra*. 'We might still be able to do that,' he said – 'get you into the Jewish run.'

'No,' said the boy, shaking his head in case Cotton should misunderstand. 'I'm not moving from here.'

'You have nowhere else to go,' said Cotton.

The boy opened his hands. 'So?' But then he answered himself. 'Either way I'm dead. If I fail they'll kill me. If I succeed I'll be executed. I accepted that a long time ago. I hardly thought May would be up for the part that had me escaping.'

'And me?'

The boy shook his head again. 'You could have helped, but that's a detail. Now I don't need your assistance.'

'You have a weapon?'

'Naturally,' said the boy. He held up two fingers and pointed them at Cotton. 'I'm not a bad shot,' he said. 'And I've improved since I've been in the military. Quite a bit. They've helped my aim.' The boy smiled. 'Franco for me? I'm happy to pay the price.'

For a moment, Cotton searched for another question. Then he realized that he had already started sliding the long pin down his forearm, that he had all the information he required. There was a moment when he almost began re-examining the whys again, but he stilled that.

Clumsily, even to himself, he made his left hand remove the cork tip from the pin and pushed the metal further along the palm of his hand. He could see the boy peering at him. He tried nodding, but then moved towards him.

'I'm telling you,' said the boy, 'if I fail, I'll shoot myself. You don't have to worry that I'll talk.'

Cotton felt as if he were moving very slowly. He saw that the boy was trying to turn away. 'No!' said Cotton.

The boy half turned back. Cotton slid the pin out beyond his hand, gripped, and pushed hard at a point a couple of fingers below the top of the boy's sternum. He struck something solid. The boy struggled with a whip-lash reflex far stronger than he had anticipated, but that may have dislodged the obstruction. The metal pin slid forward and Cotton felt his knuckles drive against the boy's skinny ribs. The boy let out a gasp – almost as if he was trying to hold in his breath – and then another. The boy's knees gave first, and then his eyes dulled.

What shocked Cotton next was the lack of blood. He stared through blinks at the boy, then at his own hands. He had skinned his left knuckles, possibly on the boy's teeth, when he had forced the boy's head back, and he had a raw line and a wound on the palm of his right hand where he had grasped the decorative cone of the hatpin. The boy lay quite still. If he had pierced the heart the boy would be dead, but surely there would be blood? Wouldn't there? That was the nearest Cotton came to panic. Where was the damned blood?

Later, when he remembered this, he would remember kicking the boy's shoe, first timidly, then quite forcefully, and then slowly accepting that he really was dead. And then that he could not decide whether to leave the body where it was or to drag it and cover it.

12

YEARS BEFORE, when he had been at school, playing cricket and not paying much attention in the slips, Cotton had been caught high up on his forehead by a ball flying off the edge of someone's bat. He had barely felt a thing, and was not in any way aware of losing consciousness except for one clue: he could definitely feel something like a shadow creeping down his forehead towards one eye. Apart from that, he was looking around and assuring everyone he was quite well.

In fact he had been poleaxed. He came round flat on his back with one side of his face spectacularly bloodied. The seam of the cricket ball had opened his skin in a tight zigzag pattern. He had needed a couple of stitches, but what puzzled him most was the illusion that he had not lost consciousness at all.

'Oh, that's the brain for you,' the bluff school medical officer had said. 'It can run a kind of film for you in the time you're out of it. It's surprisingly common.'

Cotton had looked askance at him then. Now, in the storeroom, his brain appeared to be bobbling in dream like a devil's apple in water. But at another, lower, level he behaved briskly and practically. He picked up signs of the dead boy's living there – a squashed cushion, a folded blanket and, tucked behind a lamp, a plate with a glass on it – as he searched for a rifle. It was just behind the bedhead: an old .303, to which someone inexpert had fixed a telescopic lens. A screw had splintered the wood on one side of the barrel. He laid the rifle by the boy's body and moved on.

When he recalled this later, he remembered a sensation of panic at being closed in, of running through to the front of the shop and finding the door locked from the outside, and then he could also remember, in vivid and convincing detail, flailing to find the back door behind the half-tester bed, ripping at old, green silk as he heaved it aside.

But again that was wrong. In fact he had found the door simply by looking along the wall. It was only half blocked, by a stack of those large, wheeled hamper-like things with old books in them. All he had to do was push them aside and unbolt the door. He paused. He pushed. He stepped outside and blinked.

Cotton didn't know where he was. He did not recognize the cobbled little street. He remembered glancing to his right, possibly seeing someone waiting in the shadows, but then he closed the door behind him, turned briskly left, and started walking. At the first crossroads he turned right, and knew where he was.

It was evening-walk time again in Cadiz, with so many people dressed up and out for a stroll that there was barely room to move. Someone's perfume acted on him like smelling salts. Cotton almost stopped dead. He glanced down. His left hand hurt, and he had a blood blister on the knuckles of his third and fourth fingers. Then someone called to him.

'Cotton! I say, is that you?'

'Peter, isn't it?' added a female voice.

Cotton spun round. It was those ghastly people, the Simpsons. He rejected raising his throbbing left hand, but when he started to raise his right he saw, dangling from his sleeve, one full end of the dress bow tie he had used to secure the hatpin to his arm. He yanked it down and stuffed it in his side pocket.

'Mr and Mrs Simpson! How nice!' His voice sounded unsteady.

'Been up to something?' said Nora Simpson.

'I just slipped on a cobble,' said Cotton more firmly, 'but otherwise I'm about done for Cadiz.'

'Well!' said Mrs Simpson. 'Us too, you know!' She beamed.

For a moment, Cotton didn't know what she was talking about. But then – this was familiar and easy – he slipped into the required mode. 'Oh,' he said, 'are congratulations in order?'

'I'll say!' said Mrs Simpson. 'William's got his promotion!'

'Well done!' said Cotton. 'You must be very pleased!'

He didn't really mean to offer his hand, but William Simpson took it anyway and looked modest.

'Kiss for me, I think!' said Mrs Simpson, turning her head. 'I get some credit too, you know!'

Dutifully, Cotton kissed her powdered cheek. He could smell Chanel No. 5 and whisky.

'Who you marry is very important, you know,' she pronounced. 'You can't have a career if you marry the wrong wife.'

'Yes,' said Cotton. 'I imagine so.'

'Of course, we have to wait for this damned war to be over,' said Nora Simpson, 'but it can't really have that much more to go, can it?'

Cotton became aware that they were causing a bottle-neck in the street. He attempted to move aside to let people past.

'Oh, don't mind them!' said Nora Simpson. 'How about a drink to celebrate?'

'Yes,' said her husband. 'What do you say, Cotton?'

'Oh,' said Cotton, 'you must let me. Where will you be going?'

'Buenos Aires,' said Nora Simpson. 'One of the best postings in the world! It's quite the New York of South America.'

'We'll go down here,' said her husband. 'We don't go to the casino any more,' he said pointedly. 'Well, you've got to show some support, haven't you?'

Cotton gave in. He was also aware that they were helping him in ways they didn't know, and that helped him go along with them. Of course, everywhere they knew was special, a secret find to let him in on. They led him upstairs to a kind of lounge bar. There was one other person there, a fat old man, smoking a cigar and drinking brandy. Cotton got the Simpsons their whiskies, chose wine himself, and rested. Nora Simpson was describing herself as a free spirit, and was saying how much more invigorated Bill was now that he had heard the news. Cotton nodded. It wasn't quite like lying in a warm bath, but as long as he paid some attention to the Simpsons and didn't think of the body, or whether or not Ramírez was being as competent as he thought he would be, it did almost as well for a while.

At around nine fifteen Cotton said he had to go because he really did have to make an early start next day, but it was well after ten before they all went downstairs, and another half-hour of drunken pleasantries and good wishes before he got away.

Cotton walked directly but very slowly back to his hotel. It was still warm, but there was moisture in the air and his shoes echoed. He pushed through the revolving door, went over to the hotel desk, and rang the bell. Puri, the old lady, shuffled out.

'I shall be leaving tomorrow,' he said. 'Would you have everything ready before nine, please?'

The old lady behaved as if she didn't understand. 'Is everything all right?' she said.

Cotton heard the revolving door behind him begin to turn. 'Yes, yes. My visit is over.'

'You're not going to another hotel?' Puri looked worried.

'What? No, no,' said Cotton. He even managed a smile. 'I'm going home.'

He could hear the little shoes with their lifts clicking in the bare patches of the carpet. He realized he was shaking.

'I'm leaving Cadiz. My work here is finished,' he said to the old woman.

He turned. The diminutive, elderly version of Clark Gable, Ramírez, was in dress uniform – an extravagant blue and white outfit with gold epaulettes, gold lanyard, and a peaked cap with gold leaves on the brim.

He held up a hand to stop Cotton speaking. 'Let's have a drink,' he said, putting his hand on Cotton's arm.

They went through to the bar. Ramírez sat down heavily. 'A dress rehearsal for Saturday,' he said, indicating his uniform. 'I've put on some weight since I last wore this. My feet have got too fat for these shoes. Look, I don't need laces. They hurt a bit. What would you like?'

For a moment, Cotton was unable to think. He found himself twitching his fingers as if recalling what drinks there might be. Ramírez blinked at him.

'Yes, beer. Let's have two cold beers,' called Ramírez. 'You're sweating. It's hot tonight, close. They say this year is the hottest since 1917 or something. The heat slows things – and minds – doesn't it?'

'Yes,' said Cotton.

Old Puri brought the beers.

'Where are the olives?' said Ramírez. 'Bring some olives. I don't want my friend to leave thinking Cadiz is mean. And some salted almonds. You're sad,' he said to Cotton.

'What?'

'You're sad to be leaving our hospitality. Going somewhere else always makes me feel vulnerable, disconnected. So I stay here if I can.'

Cotton nodded. 'Yes, I see.' He looked down into his glass.

Ramírez looked very patient. His lips twitched. 'Do you play cards?' he asked.

'No, I don't.' Cotton made an effort. 'But I had a grandmother who played.'

Ramírez smiled. 'You think cards are for old people?'

'No. I think she put me off. She . . . took a long time to get ready.'

'What do you mean?'

'Oh, you know, she had to have her shawl on the back of her chair, her spectacles just so . . . '

Ramírez nodded. 'Everything laid out. A ritual?'

Cotton nodded.

'What did she play? ¡Ah, por fin!' he said, when the old lady finally brought the olives and almonds. At last! He took an olive and pushed the almonds towards Cotton. Cotton took one and licked the salt.

'She played bridge,' he said. 'And patience when she was talking.'

Ramírez smiled. 'Did she cheat?' he asked.

'I don't know. I don't think so. But she'd get irritated at the cards. It made conversation with her . . . jumpy.'

Ramírez smiled. 'Good,' he said, nodding. 'You've given me a clear idea of her. I play *mus* sometimes.'

'I don't know what that is.'

'Oh, just a local card game. If we're actually talking games, I think I prefer dominoes.'

'I've never played that either,' said Cotton.

Ramírez smiled. 'No,' he said. He paused, and then spoke very quietly. 'You've done well.'

'What?' Cotton looked up.

'Admirably.'

Cotton shook his head.

'Oh, forget Judas,' said Ramírez.

Cotton stared at him. Whatever his state, it had not included biblical references and guilt.

'We were always on Pontius Pilate's staff. We're part of the finger-bowl brigade. And we bring towels to dry the fingers.'

Cotton did not find it hard to look doubtful.

'You took responsibility!' said Ramírez. 'You cleaned up a horrible mess! ¡*Joder!*' Fuck! 'How many do that? How many step up?'

Cotton winced, squeezed his eyes shut, then opened them again. 'Is the President of Portugal coming too?' he asked, though he already knew the answer.

'Salazar?' said Ramírez. He shrugged. 'Yes. It's an Iberian summit,' he said without sounding impressed. He drank some beer. 'Portugal has always been a British ally, hasn't it?'

Cotton shook his head. 'I think so. But I'm not sure at the moment.'

Ramírez nodded obligingly. 'He'll say Cadiz reminds him of Lisbon. The Portuguese always do.'

'Are you in charge of that?' said Cotton.

'No, no. I'm purely local and domestic.' Ramírez took a drink of his beer. 'I'll get Doña Carmen – the *Caudillo*'s wife – and her ladies-in-waiting. Salazar is an ascetic. He's not married. So she'll kick around. Doña Carmen is very fond of antique shops. But I understand that anti-quarians are not so fond of her.' He shrugged. 'She believes cash is only one form of payment.'

'How does she pay, then?' asked Cotton.

Ramírez smiled. 'By choosing things from their shops.'

Cotton nodded, but Ramírez didn't let him speak. He placed his hand on Cotton's arm.

'I have no interest in fame or public praise. I don't even like rumour. Making things public here can bring disadvantages. It can encourage envy and resentment.'

'I understand. You have my word.'

'Good. I am in favour of symmetry and economy,' he said.

'What do you mean?'

Ramírez nodded. 'A sealed coffin can go to Burgos. Accidental death. No one likes to hear that their boy was murdered. That is if the military pay for the transport, of course. They'll probably just bury him here. In which case his parents, if they can afford it, can come to Cadiz and see his closed grave.'

'And the antiquarian?'

Ramírez shrugged. 'Burgos? Portugal? *¿Qué más da?*' What's the difference?

'He thought he could get the boy away,' said Cotton.

'Did he?'

'What do you mean?'

Ramírez took an olive, chewed and swallowed. 'Fear and old age,' he said. 'Horrible combination.' He wiped his hands on a paper napkin. 'You can't remember things. All you feel is the fear, and you can't remember how you ever dealt with it. All you know is that you need help and that you're tired out. At that age, death is simply the next thing.'

'What?'

'At that age you think everybody dies badly and it can't be helped.'

'I don't follow,' said Cotton.

'That's because you're young. He knows people die ignorant, misled and unprepared. He's lived too long even to pretend to understand anything any more. But he has also got to think of the rest of his family. He has got to look after the women, provide for them when he's not there. The boy had forgotten his own family.' He looked up. 'You've heard the expression "a broken man"?'

'Yes, yes.' Cotton squeezed his eyes and briefly shook his head.

Ramírez raised his eyebrows. 'It's all right,' he said. 'It's not always a passive state. You can have had enough of life.'

'Maybe, yes.' Cotton looked up. 'What now?'

'You'll have to write a report for your superiors,' said Ramírez.

'Yes.'

'So will I. They don't have to match, but it would be safer if they concurred on the salient points.'

Cotton examined that elderly version of Clark Gable's face for something beyond that way of speaking.

'Pass me the almonds, will you?' said Ramírez.

Cotton pushed the dish across.

'Bad for me, and not so easy with dentures,' said Ramírez.

'No,' said Cotton. He nodded. 'All right. I think I understand.'

'Good,' said Ramírez. 'I knew you would.' Ramírez sighed. 'How do I put this?' He paused, then nodded. 'We have one spare body that needs a home. May is yours and done. An accident. If we accept that the antiquarian's grandson has already been buried, what we have left is a boy from Burgos.'

'Right.'

'So,' said Ramírez, 'if the army is asleep . . . '

'I see. Symmetry. In this case that means . . . ?'

'Death by natural causes. A heart defect. It happens.'

There was a second in which Cotton remembered the death certificate that Marie had sent him. He decided against. 'Can you manage that?'

Ramírez shrugged. 'Probably. The pathologist . . . Well, we get on. But if the army is awake and cantankerous . . .'

'What?'

'I have a candidate.'

'Who?'

'*La Cabra!* He is going to go down anyway. I don't mind what for.'

Cotton made a face.

'*No, no, no,*' said Ramírez. '*A mí nadie me torea ni me toma por pelele.*' Nobody makes me the bull or takes me for the dummy.

Cotton considered, and even tried to muster some sympathy for *La Cabra*. He shrugged. 'What about the boy?'

'Wasn't found in any uniform I recognized.'

'But with an identity card issued in Burgos?'

'Naturally. They do have their advantages.'

Ramírez smiled. '*Estamos en paz, ¿no?*' We're quits, or, literally, we are at peace.

'Yes.'

Ramírez got up. '*No te quedes ahí parao,*' he said. Don't stay still.

'No?'

'No. Remember, there's Antoñita, you know.'

Cotton tried to smile. 'Too tired,' he said.

'*Pena*,' said Ramírez. Pity.

'I think I'll write the report,' said Cotton.

'All right.'

Ramírez held out his hand. It struck Cotton as touchingly small but impressively hairy. He held out his own, but leaned back. They shook almost at arm's length.

'A privilege,' said Ramírez. 'Don't say any more.'

'An honour,' said Cotton.

Ramírez smiled and touched his shoulder as he left. Cotton listened to his shoes as they clicked away. He thought Antoñita might sound like that in her mules. He sat back and closed his eyes.

'Have you finished?' demanded the old woman. 'I have things to do.'

Cotton finished the beer and walked upstairs to his room. He took off his jacket, undid his tie, and stripped off his shirt. He had made a mess of the inside of his forearm. He should watch for infection, he thought. And he must remember in future not to rely on that stuff he'd been given about making use of household goods 'so as not to arouse notice or suspicion'. He considered the boy again – in the past – and felt something he thought of as odd: a kind of serene gall and a very quiet, nearly catatonic, determination not to ask certain questions. He went back to his jacket, took out the dress bow tie, and tried to flush it away. It didn't go, of course. It spun, looking soggy and black. He'd flush at intervals then.

He washed his arm and put on his pyjama jacket. First he opened *Don Juan*, and suddenly knew his answer to the stupid question about Byron's prose. 'Foreigner has accomplished, schoolboy is dead.' He wouldn't be sending that. He took a pencil and wrote out the message he would send: 'Matter resolved. Money recovered. Office closed. Report follows. P.'

He went to the bathroom and flushed at the dress tie again. It circled and stayed. He did try to write the report, but was too tired for it not to seem pointless. How could he drain it all down to something brief and dry? On that thought, he fell asleep in his chair.

He woke abruptly. At first he couldn't even see his watch. He stumbled through to the bathroom and flushed again. He peered down into the bowl. This time, he thought, one end of the tie had dipped. He looked at his watch. It was three o'clock in the morning. He blinked, thought of the report again, but this time went and lay down on the bed.

When he next woke it was just past six. For a moment he didn't know where he was – almost a habit now. Then he remembered. Cadiz. He just wanted to get out of the place. He got up and went through to the bathroom. He flushed. This time the tie curled and vanished, like black tape. He took off his clothes and stood under the shower. The water came out in a bare splatter, very cold. His arm hurt. He scrape-shaved. He was beginning to feel skinned and raw.

He dressed and packed. Then he opened the shutters and the windows, and sat down to watch the sky take on light. Outside he could hear sounds of people watering the gardens and pavements. He smelled bread. He was quite anxious to remember the particular shade of blue in the sky over Cadiz, and the way the sun added colours. But not much more. He felt hungry.

At eight he went downstairs, ordered breakfast, and gave instructions to call the hotel porter to carry his luggage. A little before nine he delivered the note and cheque to Henderson's office and let himself into his own office for the last time. He sent his coded message. He wrote a note to Marie:

Dear Marie,
    I am returning the documents you sent me. Despite my best efforts no genuine candidate for Don José appeared. Now, as instructed, I am closing the office and leaving Cadiz.
    Very best wishes,
    Peter

He wrapped up May's binoculars. Then, after locking up, he took the machine and his attaché case down with him in R. A. May's pigskin suitcase, gave the keys back to Eugenio, shook hands with him, and went back to the hotel. The Buenavista's porter was waiting for him. Cotton put May's suitcase beside his own.

'You've got more this time,' said the porter.

'What?'

'You're making me carry more.'

'Yes, that's right. I am.'

Cotton settled the hotel bill. To his surprise, he was given a basket containing food and drink. There was water, beer, bread, chorizo, ham and peaches. The old woman, Puri, and the two old men, Evaristo and Hipólito, came to the door to see him off. Cotton shook hands with them and thanked them.

'*Y la niña. Me ha tratado bien.*' And thank the girl. She treated me well.

'Come again,' they said.

'*Ni en sueños,*' muttered the porter, picking up Cotton's luggage. Not even in dreams. Or perhaps, fat chance.

Cotton and the porter walked out. The dais for Franco was being decorated with foliage and Spanish and Portuguese flags.

'That's for the *Generalísimo,*' said the porter.

'Mm,' said Cotton. 'I'll be missing that.'

'So are you going to give me a tip?' said the porter.

'If I don't miss the train,' said Cotton.

The porter laughed. They walked down the avenue to the station. Cotton turned his eyes towards the port. Men were loading boxes on board *Flor de Canela*. He looked out for someone who might be Italian, but saw no one that convinced him.

'As a matter of interest,' he said, 'does cinnamon have a flower?'

'*¡Y yo qué sé!*' said the man carrying his luggage. How would I know! 'I'm a hotel porter in Cadiz, not a professor in Salamanca.'

Cotton smiled. 'All right,' he said.

He looked around once more at the glistening surround of sea. He smelled a whiff of freshly landed fish from the quay, *caballa* – mackerel – and then, almost at once, the smell of burning sugar as a stall started making sweets.

He thought, as they walked on towards the station, that memory might just be that blunt and contrasting.

'¿*Te vas?*' called a beggar. You're going?

Cotton nodded.

'*Allá tú*,' said the beggar. That's your problem.

They crossed the Plaza de Sevilla and turned into the railway station. Standing demurely by the doorway to the platforms was a very pretty, pert-bodied, red-haired girl with two suitcases.

'¡*Qué cabrón!*' thought Cotton. What a bastard!

And then he realized he no longer had to play that part. While training, someone had told him that there was a Frenchman whose job was blowing up sections of railway track, who always began and ended his reports with the sentence '*J'ai joué le jeu*.' I have played the game. It had struck him then as an absurdly brave misunderstanding. Now he saw it differently, as an acknowledgement of protracted, stumbling luck.

'Miss Carroll,' he said.

'I just don't know how to thank you, Mr Cotton, really I don't,' said Miss Deirdre Carroll.

'Don't then,' said Cotton. 'Did you have any trouble with your employers?'

Miss Carroll blushed and blinked. 'They were very cool, Mr Cotton, but they gave me a reference.'

'And your moral status?'

'There was this policeman . . . '

'Of course.'

'And I do have a stamp from the bishopric, you know.'

Cotton nodded. Her reputation and references were intact.

'That's good,' he said. 'Now, do you have a ticket?'

'I do.' She produced it. There was a second in which Cotton did not mind that they would be in separate carriages.

'We'll upgrade you,' he said.

'Oh, I couldn't possibly let you do that,' said Miss Carroll.

'Yes you could,' said Cotton. 'Otherwise you'll be a young woman in a carriage on her own.'

Ticket upgraded, Cotton had the hotel porter wheel their cases along the platform to their compartment and tipped him.

'*Caballero*,' acknowledged the porter. You're a gentleman. 'Good trip.'

'*Ojalá*,' said Cotton. I hope so.

Cotton clambered up and joined Miss Carroll in the compartment.

'Oh, Mr Cotton,' said Miss Carroll apologetically, 'I think you've done something to your hand.'

Cotton looked down. He had opened the blood blister on his knuckles caused by the boy's teeth.

'I have a first aid kit,' said Miss Carroll. She jumped up and fetched a small box out of a case. 'We have to make sure that cut is quite clean,' she said, and dabbed iodine on it. The iodine stung, and Miss Carroll was rather clumsy.

'Are you all right?' she asked.

'Thank you,' said Cotton, between his teeth. 'May I?' He took the swab from her and pressed it against the wound made by the hatpin on the palm of his other hand. He saw he had dislodged a fleck of rust. Somehow he knew it was not from the hatpin but from the bolt on the door out of the antiquarian's shop. And then it suddenly occurred to him that the iodine stain on his skin matched the colour of the cathedral cupola, although in the station he had mercifully no means of checking it.

'My! You're going to look as if you have been in the wars.'

Cotton shook his head. 'Spain is a neutral country,' he said.

For some reason Miss Deirdre Carroll laughed and smiled. The train whistle sounded. Wooden bits of the train creaked and groaned. The ancient boiler threw off steam, and the metal links between the carriages clanked.

At 11 a.m., on Thursday 14 September 1944, two days before Generalísimo Francisco Franco and Doña Carmen Polo's official visit, Cotton leaned back in his seat, shut his eyes, and felt the express train bound for Atocha station in Madrid pull him away from Cadiz.

Acknowledgements

Enormous thanks to my editor Kate Parkin – perceptive, to the point, and extraordinarily patient – to my agent, Maggie McKernan, for all her encouragement and advice; to my family for their good humour; and especially to many people in Cadiz. Though this is a work of fiction, their real generosity in talking to me of a particularly grim time in their city's long and varied history was remarkable, and is very much appreciated in providing a setting that is my responsibility, not theirs.

Read more . . .

Michael Cox

THE MEANING OF NIGHT: A CONFESSION

The bestselling mystery of murder, love and obsession

After killing the red-haired man, I took myself off to Quinn's for an oyster supper . . .

Edward Glyver, book lover, scholar and murderer, is determined to overcome his deadly rival, Phoebus Daunt, and reclaim his rightful destiny as heir to a fortune. His path takes him from Victorian London's foggy streets, brothels and opium dens to England's most enchanting country house, home to his arch-enemy Daunt and the ravishing Emily Carteret, who steals his heart. But for each step Glyver takes towards entrapping his rival, the further he seems to slip from his grasp.

'A tale of obsession, love and revenge, played out amid London's swirling smog' *Daily Mail*

'An unadulterated pleasure' *Independent on Sunday*

'The atmosphere crackles' *Evening Standard*

'A spellbinding mystery . . . Dark, atmospheric storytelling with wicked twists and turns' *Good Housekeeping*

Order your copy now by calling Bookpoint on 01235 827716 or visit your local bookshop quoting ISBN 978-0-7195-6837-4
www.johnmurray.co.uk

Read more ...

Julia Navarro

THE BIBLE OF CLAY: AN EPIC QUEST FOR THE ULTIMATE RELIC

From the international bestselling author of *The Brotherhood of the Holy Shroud*

Two thousand years before Christ, a man named Abraham tells his tribe stories of the creation of the world. A young boy, in awe of him, writes down his account on simple tablets of clay.

Today, a young archaeologist searches for a treasure that will rewrite history – an explosive account of the world's creation, recorded millennia ago on to the legendary Bible of Clay. But when she begins excavations in war-torn Iraq she realises her enemies will stop at nothing to have her killed.

Order your copy now by calling Bookpoint on 01235 827716 or visit your local bookshop quoting ISBN 978-0-7195-6249-5 www.johnmurray.co.uk

Read more . . .

Emilo Calderón

THE CREATOR'S MAP

**A mysterious map, espionage and a love story set against a
continent devastated by war**

Rome, 1952. José Maria Hurtado and his wife Montserrat discover
that their friend, Prince Vivarini, Fascist and Nazi-sympathizer, has
been brutally murdered. In the event of his death, they were told they
would receive a mysterious package containing secrets he could not
reveal while living.

Who was the Prince? And why were Hurtado and his wife chosen as
the repository of these documents? The answers lie in Rome, during
the tumultuous period of the 1930s and 1940s. For there an exiled
Spanish architect, a passionate and beautiful young librarian and an
elegant and influential Fascist prince became enmeshed in a web of
political intrigue, love and deceit involving a fateful map which has
the power to destroy them all.

'Admirable' *Daily Mail*

'Subtle touches of humour follow this unlikely spy, and evocative
descriptive passages afford the reader satisfying moments of
reflection' *Financial Times*

'A powerful mix of romance, spy story and thriller, this fascinating
novel captures life in the Eternal City under Nazi rule. It's a real
page-turner' *Choice*

*Order your copy now by calling Bookpoint on 01235 827716 or
visit your local bookshop quoting ISBN 978-0-7195-9650-6*
www.johnmurray.co.uk

Read more . . .

Andrew Williams

THE INTERROGATOR

A war is fought on many fronts . . .

Spring, 1941. The armies of the Reich are masters of Europe. Britain stands alone while Hitler's submarines prey on the Atlantic convoys that are the country's only lifeline.

As the Blitz reduces Britain's cities to rubble and losses at sea mount, interrogator Lieutenant Douglas Lindsay becomes convinced Germany has broken British naval codes. But he's a lone voice, and his superiors don't trust him. In one last desperate throw of the dice, he sets a trap for his prize captive – the U-boat commander who sent his ship to its doom.

'A flair, grasp of detail and strong characterisation that reminds me of *Enigma* . . . This is a terrific first novel. Harris had better watch out' *Daily Mail*

'One of the most gripping books I have read for some time' *The Times*

'A terrific, mostly untold story' *Independent*

Order your copy now by calling Bookpoint on 01235 827716 or visit your local bookshop quoting ISBN 978-0-7195-2381-6 www.johnmurray.co.uk